Advance praise for
Maybe Marilyn

"A novel about a sweet and sad story: What if Marilyn Monroe ran away from Hollywood and lived a long life by the ocean among books and flowers?"

—**Jacquelyn Mitchard,** author of
The Bird Watcher & The Deep End of the Ocean

"Lois Cahall turns the mystery of Marilyn Monroe's death into a thrilling page-turner that challenges all we believe about Hollywood's most glamorous star and the power of glamour itself."

—**Jan Tuckwood,** *AARP* contributing writer and
author of the forthcoming *Dressing Jackie*

"*Maybe Marilyn* does for the 'what-if' genre what Marilyn Monroe did for movie starlets: she defines it. Before the #Metoo movement had a name, Marilyn embodied strength and sensuality. She paid a terrible price, but what if her suicide was faked? With a host of supporting characters, Cahall illustrates the stark differences between Hollywood and a quiet New England town, and asks the question: *what must a woman do to rewrite the script she was given?*"

—**Christopher Shaw Myers,** author of Robert
Shaw: An Actor's Life on The Set of JAWS

Also by the Author

The Many Lives & Loves of Hazel Lavery

Court of the Myrtles

Plan C: Just in Case

MAYBE MARILYN

A NOVEL

LOIS CAHALL

A POST HILL PRESS BOOK
ISBN: 979-8-89565-638-9
ISBN (eBook): 979-8-89565-639-6

Cover design by Cody Corcoran

Post Hill Press
New York • Nashville
posthillpress.com

Published in the United States of America
1 2 3 4 5 6 7 8 9 10

For Marie, always
&
for Mark Oristano, FADE IN…

PROLOGUE

Cape Cod—1999

"Closed for the Season" signs *slam* against weathered clapboard. Clam rakes, secured to metal baskets, jiggle against sea shanties awaiting quahog season. A winter sun struggles to stay alive past 4 p.m., and the beach is so deserted you feel marooned.

A lone swooping seagull gives us a bird's eye view of someone...

A woman.

It seems everything about this place was designed to draw us to her.

Down at the shoreline, she tiptoes barefoot as if bitter January was made for someone else. You might guess her age is a playful late sixties. Could be early seventies.

She lowers her heels now, crisscrossing her feet like the wet sand is a catwalk. Her relaxed rhythm almost seduces nature, as if everything bends to her. The wind tickles the seagrass. The sea salt licks at the frozen beach plums. She locks her arms in her white fleece jacket, running her fingertips through her windblown platinum-white bangs, tucking them under her hood.

Isolated, sure, but she seems content in being alone—it's not the same as being lonely. With hands on hips, she faces the tide, inhaling its mightiness like some raw energy force that feeds her.

There's certainly one good thing about a fishing village compared to Hollywood. No agenda. The locals aren't looking to track her down or expose her. She doesn't need to run anymore because there's no one left to run from. They're pretty much all dead.

The sun cracks through a cloud, a ray of light on her face, weathered with age, but somehow stunningly gorgeous. The woman bends to scoop an empty razor clam into her palm before skimming it across the waves.

Contentment.

After all these years, she did it! *She got away!* The world *thinks* they took her image, her body and her heart, but they *could* never, *would* never, take her soul.

She moves up the dunes now, clapping her flipflops together to brush away the sand. Sliding them on her feet, she heads up the beach path lined with frozen rosa rugosa. Yet, you'd think she was walking a red carpet, her sexy sway still apparent.

She's no longer Marilyn Monroe. Now she's just Marie Morton, mom to Grace and grandmother to Nell. *Oh, Nell! Pure joy!* The light of her life and a carbon copy of the innocent woman that Marilyn once was when youth and beauty were at her fingertips. Now as Marie, her only hope is that the world will be kinder to her granddaughter than it ever was to her.

She glances at her wristwatch. *It's getting late!* Time to get home to pop that seafood pie into the oven—the one with her super-secret bisque sauce ladled over its shrimp, lobster, and potato base. The one that her man loves. She'll grab a bottle of Sauvignon Blanc from the liquor store too. It's her husband's birthday, after all. And I know what you're thinking…

No, her husband is not JFK or even RFK. Sadly, they didn't get a second chance. And besides, that would be some crazy conspiracy theory.

No, she's married to her sweet James. The love of her life…

Until death, really *until death, do they part.*

CHAPTER ONE

Cape Cod—2019

Nell runs her fingers across the book spines on her grandmother Marie's shelves.

Fiction, nonfiction, all alphabetized by author. She lands on Erica Jong's *Fear of Flying*. Nell pauses, hesitates, twists her lips in a pucker before plucking it from its spot. The shelves are in need of a proper dusting. She spreads the book's fifty-year-old pages, marked with once-visible yellow highlights now looking anemic. Nell plops on the overstuffed armchair, longing to learn about controversy in the second wave of feminism.

A Polaroid slips from the pages, cracked and oxidized with age. Nell's brow crinkles. She reads the ten-digit date on the back with the year: 1979. Flipping it back over, a gradual smile crosses her lips. It's a photo of her grandparents. Her grandmother would've been about fifty in the picture based on the year, her mischievous bangs slipping from a red gingham kerchief.

If pictures tell a story, then this one suggests that Nell's grandmother always seemed so carefree, smiling her big toothy smile with a *bursting* satisfaction while gazing at James. His long, sturdy fingers grasped her shoulder, but not in a possessive way…more protective. Mocha skin and gentle features, James could have put John Legend to shame if only John were alive back in the day.

The snapshot captures their expression…one that practically screams to Nell that her grandmother, "Nan" as she calls her, didn't know that type of love existed. That *that* was the version of herself that was utterly *whole* when she and James were together—the version of themselves that always prompted her grandmother to declare years later, "James is the love of my life."

In the background of the worn photograph is a band performing at The Beachcomber, a shack where perspiration practically rises off the plank floor.

How many times as a young girl had Nell frequented the famous hot spot in Wellfleet for an early supper? Nell remembers those afternoons—the baking sun carving through the walls like a crystalline abstract; sharing hotdogs, clam rolls, and coca colas with Nan; and wearing thick sunglasses. Her grandmother recited historical facts that she'd repeat again and again, almost like a mantra, in that familiar breathless voice: "*You know, my Nelly, back in August 1961, President Kennedy created this national seashore. Right here, honey bunny, in Wellfleet.*" And then she'd spread her arm across its 43,500 acres of ponds and woods and beachfront. "*In that nature was a mere twelve-square-mile town. But some 'grandfather' clause allowed this Beachcomber to remain a commercial property. It's the only oceanfront restaurant on the entire Atlantic side!*" She'd exhale, like she was looking at heaven. "*Aren't we lucky? We get to eat here with this delicious view!*" Then she'd dab the ketchup from her lips. "*And we have President Kennedy to thank for that, my sweet pea.*"

Nell seems to remember that her grandmother, Nan, had that dead president to thank for a lot of things…

Nell rises from the easy chair, placing the photograph in front of a crystal-cut vase of Nikko Blue hydrangeas. The kind only found on Cape Cod in July. The kind of fluffy blue beauty deserving of a beach wedding…like the makeshift one Grandmother had with James. Nell was all but five, walking with perfect posture on the sand. She tip-toed with caution through the dunes, balancing that white satin pillow that held their silver bands of eternity.

Nell's tiny feet had landed in front of Grandmother's unpainted summer toes on the shore.

Nell was happy for her grandmother. She had always liked James, who taught her to ride "a big-girl bicycle without training wheels," as her grandmother said.

Nell's grandmother had been afraid of men before that.

For decades, Grandmother's fridge door had a magnet securing a handwritten note. It read: "There is a road that leads upward and a road that leads downward. If only *they* understood that they are one in the same." Nell realized that the *they* were men. Mean men. *Hurtful* men…

Just then, Nell's cell phone startles her back to reality with a text from Frederick, Nell's gallery assistant. "WTF? Are we going over financials?"

Oh, no! Shit! Nell scrambles to find her purse and her keys. She's late. *Exhale. Onward…*

CHAPTER TWO

Los Angeles—2019

Tom Hogan attempts to fit in at a Hollywood auction, though his rented tux doesn't. The jacket is large and loose in the shoulders, but the pants are too snug, bulging in the crotch. His tie is a clip-on. The rental agreement was $89 for the weekend—pick it up Thursday night and return it Sunday, dry cleaning negotiable. But Tom hopes he can drop it off early and get a credit, because he had to hire an Uber after paying the tow guy when his Hyundai didn't start. *At 196,000 miles on the odometer, what did you expect?*

Tom's eyes scan the joint, coming to terms with the fact that this is nothing like *Antiques Roadshow* in a New Hampshire barn—the type of auction his grandfather used to *drag* him to with tchotchkes and sea captain collectibles. No, not at all. This is a big Beverly Hills affair. A formal ballroom where Bentleys, billionaires, and Botox abound. There's Hollywood royalty too. De Niro, Pacino, Beatty, and Bening in glamorous attire; men in Armani and women wearing pearls, Bulgari and Harry Winston flash at every turn. Baccarat crystal and twenty pieces of fine cutlery at every place setting. The waitstaff has cleared a first course of foie gras torchon with vanilla roasted pineapple. Guests are now dining on the main course of Dover sole meunière.

Tom taps a paddle on his knee as the guests hang on the auctioneer's next bid. A supermodel assistant holds a white satin pillow which offsets a very familiar pair of red shoes. Behind her a banner reads *City of Hope Hospital: The Hollywood Auction.*

"And now, ladies and gentlemen, one of the evening's main attractions. We present easily the most famous pair of shoes in Hollywood history. With apologies to Fred Astaire," the auctioneer proclaims. The crowd chuckles in delight. The supermodel gently places Dorothy's ruby reds on a revolving platform.

Tom's photographer colleague, Becca Busa, leans in. "It's better than the last bid," she whispers. "Who the heck wants Tony Danza's baseball uniform from *Angels in the Outfield?*"

"At least its laundered," says Tom.

"Yeah, obviously…but who *was* Tony Danza?"

"*Is*," Tom clarifies. "He's still alive. An old dude from sitcoms."

"Gotcha," Becca giggles with an infallible burst of energy, her youth transparent.

"Zach Galifianakis's man-bag satchel from *The Hangover* was amusing," says Tom, glancing at the auction list. "And James Cameron's fusion camera from *Avatar* was a worthy bid."

"C'mon! This is far from headline stuff." Becca yawns. "However, Leo's pants from *Titanic*? I'd have bid on those if only I didn't have so many school loans."

"Yes, indeed, ladies and gentlemen," says the auctioneer, admiring the red slippers. "From *The Wizard of Oz*. And tonight, some lucky little munchkin will take these beauties home. Assuming no wicked witches fly in to upset the proceedings." The crowd chuckles some more. "We'll start the bidding for this *astounding* chunk of Hollywood history at a mere five hundred thousand dollars."

A woman at Tom and Becca's table nonchalantly raises her paddle. Her uber-carat diamond is so large, she could hide a drug cartel and their cocaine stash in her ring finger.

"I'd rather have brains than money," whispers Becca to Tom while observing the woman. "I mean…these women think just because they married money that it automatically elevates them to smart."

Tom hisses in agreement, studying the room. A lot of older men with younger women. "This might be a stupid assignment, but there *is* a bright side."

"There is?" she asks.

"Yeah, I mean, it's refreshing to see so many fathers taking out their daughters."

"Oh, Tommy. You're funny," says Becca. "They're not *daughters*. They're *dates*!"

"Really?" says Tom, the look on his face horrified. "All of them?"

She shrugs. "You're such a sweet boy from New Hampshire," she says, admiring his innocence.

"Technically Orlando, but yeah, originally New Hampshire."

Becca nudges him to pay attention…

"I have ten million!" says the auctioneer. "Do I hear eleven to go to Kansas?" And suddenly the room is abuzz. The price is climbing, *soaring* upward to twenty million.

"This is incredible!" says Tom. "Twenty million is a lifetime. It's a hundred lifetimes!"

"Omg, it's up to twenty-*five* million! For a pair of shoes!" adds Becca.

Tom eyes the front table, where an incredibly beautiful redhead bounces up and down in her seat. She sits next to a man who looks familiar—like that lawyer Tom has seen on MSNBC. The one who likes his women tall, thin, and mute. He even represented that hooker from a big political scandal. The redhead squeezes the attorney's bicep. *Wait a second! That* is *the hooker. She's sleeping with her lawyer!*

Tom leans into Becca. "You see those two in the front?"

"Sort of," says Becca, craning her neck to glimpse between tables. "Is that who you think it is?" She starts fiddling with her camera.

"Go get some shots."

"I can't right now," she says, glancing down at her camera, "it will be too obvious." She looks to Tom. "Oh, what's wrong, you big baby? I said I'll go, but give it five..."

"God, this is so cliché," whines Tom, slumping in his seat. "Another pathetic political scandal."

"Yeah, I know, but sleeping with her lawyer gives it a twist," she asserts. "So, what's wrong with that?"

"Everything," says Tom. "I should have listened to my grandfather. I'd be a combat journalist in Syria right now instead of... this...this..."

"Snobs, snubs, and pretenses?" Becca teases. "Tabloid shit?"

"Sold!" says the auctioneer, slamming his gavel. "For a record twenty-eight million dollars!" The auctioneer wipes his brow. "Dorothy's ruby slippers! History in the making, good people! History in the making."

"Wow," says Tom. "That's gotta shatter all previous auction records for movie memorabilia, no?"

"Yah think?"

Becca discreetly edges her way to the front of the room where the staff stands behind a wall. In this moment of history-making chaos, the crowd's shattering applause, Becca has the perfect opportunity to very efficiently poke a long lens through a tropical plant to get a tight shot of the hooker with her hands close to the lawyer's cummerbund.

"So whatcha thinking now?" asks Becca when she returns to the table.

"I'm thinking big story," says Tom. Going viral, big." Tom sits back, gaining some unexpected confidence, and sipping his Kluge Estate sparkling rosé. *He's the shit!* At least in this moment. Maybe his dad would have been proud of him. Maybe not. His dad who died fighting in the Gulf War. Code name: Desert Shield. And here is Tom playing paparazzi. Code name: Desert Disgusting.

But hey, this will pay the Hyundai loan and land him one set of tickets to the Lakers.

"Before we wrap up the evening," says the auctioneer, "one last curiosity, which we are pleased to present as a matter of small interest..." The assistant uncovers a painting. It's a landscape. Could almost be an Andrew Wyeth if it had tawny and gray tones. It has a similarly haunting appeal, but with vivid colors of stark red, white, and blue. Tom stares at it intently. It's talking to him. Telling him it might be an elevated addition to his Ikea-furnished living room. It's all-American. Like Tom's father was.

"This painting was reputed to have hung in Marilyn Monroe's trailer during the filming of her last movie, *The Misfits*," says the auctioneer. "That is all we know about the provenance of this particular piece." The room is quiet...on the verge of uninterested. "And we offer it to you tonight, with the caveat that we cannot really prove much, if anything about it. We'll start the bidding at four hundred and fifty dollars."

Dead silence from the audience. Nobody moves a muscle, let alone a paddle. Even the gilded high ceiling reverberates utter silence. Tom's mind wanders to something his grandfather once challenged him to answer about integrity. "*What is a true philanthropist? Is it someone who genuinely wants to give back to the community or somebody who attends fundraisers for their own reasons...to wear sequin gowns and have photo ops in next week's society pages?*" Tom's grandfather taught him that old money is still better than loud and new money. This coming from a grandfather who didn't have *any* money but was a hard-working American at a hardware store before he bought a small farm. Spent his off-hours volunteering with veterans. Of course, Tom's not sure what the balance is in this room—old versus new money—but there's certainly a lot of it. And, his grandfather *worshipped* Marilyn Monroe, so...maybe, just maybe, he should bid.

"Come now, ladies and gents," says the auctioneer. "In the spirit of the evening, four hundred and fifty dollars…it's no Thomas Cole or even an Edwin Church, but it's only a measly four hundred and fifty dollars." Silence still. Tom stares at the painting. "Ladies and gentlemen," says the auctioneer. "I don't think I can overstate the fact that if this painting did indeed hang in Marilyn's dressing room, surely it's a bargain at under five hundred dollars."

"Six hundred dollars!" shouts Tom, with no idea he was going speak until the words left his mouth.

The entire crowd turns to stare at him…the lone man waving a paddle. The auctioneer sighs in relief. "I think it's safe to say 'sold' to the gentleman for six hundred dollars! And thank you, sir, on behalf of the City of Hope."

"Really, Tommy?" says Becca, tight-lipped to conceal a giggle. She rolls her eyes.

Tom falls back into his chair and unclips his tie. The look on his face says he'll have to cut back on Netflix and cancel his subscription to *Field & Stream* for the next year, but hey, the painting is for a good cause. Grandpa would be proud.

CHAPTER THREE

Los Angeles

A dilapidated and abandoned warehouse has been home to *The Hollywood Record* for five decades. Once a flagship to a bustling block, now the letter *H* is missing from the illuminated letters that only read *ollywood.* Lush landscaping and ample parking have since fallen to the wayside. A For Sale sign highlights the dandelions that pop through the asphalt's cracks.

This is journalism circa 2019. In one word: Dead.

Inside, the once-robust newsroom teeming with storyboard ideas and typewriters ablaze has dwindled to a handful of employees. Oxidized from time, a row of black acrylic framed yellowed articles remain in the hallway. "MAGIC HIV POSITIVE!" "O.J. VERDICT: The Juice Found Innocent." "FATAL VOYAGE: Natalie Wood Found Dead."

The editor in chief, Glenn Ritter, has been employed at *The Hollywood Record* for over two decades, and certainly long before #FakeNews destroyed the press's integrity. Ritter, on the older end of the baby boomers, holds onto his job as if it's his only identity. *It is.* He's lucky to be one of the last men standing…and have a pension.

With multiple layoffs, that leaves Editor Ritter constantly complaining about how he's stuck with these fresh-out-of-college "Chippies," as he calls them. According to Ritter, they spend all their time with noses buried in their iPhones instead of doing research.

Prime example: Sid Spooner III, a rich kid appropriately named for being born with a silver spoon up his ass. He's late for his third editorial meeting this week. When Spooner's around, there's no air to breathe. He occupies it all. Strolling through the office with a sense of entitlement—albeit charm—Spooner stops at every cubicle as if he's running for Congress. "You look *great!* You losing weight? Keep up the good work." Next, Spooner bypasses Becca and winks. "Hi Betsy."

"It's Becca," she corrects him. Not that he's listening.

It's hard for Tom to not feel bitter. He's always at his desk on time. He landed the scholarship to UCLA by working his ass off. He stayed out west after graduating to work for the *Record.* And Tom has never been late for an editorial meeting, nor has he ever so much as *glanced* at his phone while Ritter is speaking.

Spooner finally enters the meeting room, sporting remnants of a black eye and a swollen nose. Tom shares a look with Ritter, which Spooner catches and comments. "You should've seen the other guy..."

Ritter shakes his head. "Christ, Spooner! The assignment was to infiltrate the salacious doings of the Asian Dragon Spa...not sleep with the masseuses!"

"It was research." Spooner flops, defeated, into a chair next to Tom. Acts like he might cry.

Tom and Spooner *stare* a look, rather than share one. One that begs, *Why is it that Tom slaves away at long working hours and Spooner can just stroll in part time?*

The answer might be that Spooner's billionaire daddy was Ritter's Cornell roommate. Sidney Spooner Sr. studied economics. Glenn Ritter studied journalism. Spooner Sr. made a *fortune* on Wall Street. Ritter ended up a reporter turned dinosaur editor.

Young Spooner doesn't need to work, but his father demanded that his son experience urgency or at the very least...integrity.

Evidently, journalism seemed ideal. All those deadlines for the sake of true news.

Ritter looks around at the group gathered for the editorial meeting. "In our day, we reported news. We didn't finesse it. And we used these." He glances around, patting the desk. "Why can't I find any steno pads in the supply room?" Ritter shakes his head. "The institution of investigative journalism is close to dead."

"It *is* dead," says Spooner, cocky, never looking up from his iPhone.

"Why is that?" asks Ritter, looking instead to Tom Hogan. "Why is journalism dead?"

Tom shrugs, knowing he's next in line for job cuts.

"Google, boss. We all google," chirps Spooner, now scrolling his Tinder feed.

"Then you should've googled *this*," says Ritter, sarcastically slapping some pages on the table and leaning into Tom's face now. "See this Hogan…" Ritter's fingerprint crushes the lawyer's photo face on one of the pictures he'd printed out. "That's the twin brother of the lawyer who sent that guy to prison for embezzlement. And this…" he points to the supposed hooker's photo, "this is the twin brother's redheaded *wife* from the Hollywood auction." Ritter smudges his finger back and forth on the two photos.

"But I thought…" says Tom.

Ritter turns into Tom's breathing space. "Get me a *fucking* retraction, fuckwit!"

"With all due respect, Mr. Ritter," says Tom, "We don't issue retractions. We're online. We just take it down."

"Then take it down!" screams Ritter. "This nonsense is why we're going under!!"

"That's not why we're going under, sir," chirps Tom.

"Your old business model—advertising and numbers—stopped working," explains Spooner, feeling compelled to speak up. "News is free now. Free and manipulated by the Russians."

"*BuzzFeed* and *HuffPost*," adds Tom.

Ritter leans forward. "It's like you two little *shits* speak another language. You and all your twitface!"

"Twitter," Tom corrects.

"Next you'll tell me you each have your own peapod!" blasts Ritter.

"Podcast," says Spooner.

"You sassin' me?" asks Ritter.

"No, boss," says Tom, leaning in. "Getting back to my lawyer story…I thought I checked everything, sir. I guess—well, I guess I made a mistake. I'm truly sorry."

"I *know* you made a mistake. That's what I'm worried about," says Ritter. "Well, here's what I think…I think you don't know the first thing about reporting. I think hiring you was the biggest mistake I made since Spooner's father tried to tout me on this little stock called Microsoft, but I saw a picture of the guy who started the company and I thought, 'Nah, this guy's too much of a geek to ever amount to anything.' So, call it karma. I hired you because I wanted to make good on the Microsoft geek. So actually, no, you didn't make a mistake. *I* made the mistake, Hogan! I'm the one who's *sorry!*"

Tom stares out the window like an indoor cat. Sad. Punished. "I tried, sir."

The group is rivetted by what Ritter might say next. Instead, Ritter glances out of the conference room to his glass office just a few carpeted feet away. "Hogan?" he asks. "What does that sign say out there on *that* office door?"

Tom glances up and looks out to read it. "Um, it says, 'Glenn Ritter. Editor.'"

"And what does your office door say?"

"I don't have an office door."

"Ah-huh!"

Tom wants to die. Right here on the spot in front of all his colleagues.

Ritter glances outside the conference room, knitting a brow. A couple of burly men carry boxes into his office.

"What the?" asks Ritter, leaning forward.

"I meant to tell you, Mr. Ritter," says a quiet boy from accounting sitting at the other end of the conference room table. "The real estate company from up the street is renting from us. They're taking over your office space."

Now the look on Ritter's face is one of total defeat. It's as if he's witnessing locusts coming through and clearing out everything he's ever believed in. Ritter looks down to his lap, trying not to sulk. The conference table of reporters sulk for him. Except Spooner. He could care less. He's comparing prices on Expedia for plane tickets to Amsterdam.

After a few moments of rearranging his dignity, Ritter speaks again. This time softening. "All right Hogan. I'm giving you one more chance."

Tom sits up, hopeful. "Yes, sir. Anything!"

"And stop calling me 'sir.' This isn't boot camp, though God knows it feels like it."

"Yes, sir, I mean, Mr. Ritter."

Ritter points under Tom's nose. "I'm only doing this because I didn't believe you when your school resume said that you got that tip on Bruce Jenner becoming Caitlyn…so now we're even."

"I'm happy to do whatever you—"

"I want you to shut up. Totally. Super glue shut up! And understand that the only reason I'm not firing you is that I'm three reporters short. You're back on general assignment. Forest Bend Nursing Home in Brentwood. Tomorrow. I want a piece on all the has-been and never-were movie actors living out there."

Tom nods with delight. "For the Weekend Arts section?"

"You do well," says Ritter, "and maybe you'll still have a bright future in journalism."

"There is no future in journalism," says Spooner, chuckling at something on his iPhone.

"Meeting adjourned," says Ritter, who's clearly had enough. The group clears out.

Becca approaches Tom to give him a hug of reassurance. "I'm partly responsible too, you know."

"Thanks, Bec. Care to discuss it over an early dinner?" asks Tom, hopeful.

"I can't," says Becca. "I'm kind of spoken for." She looks over the conference table to where Spooner is chuckling, his eyes glued to a Korean soap opera he's downloaded onto his phone. "Sorry, Tom," she says, "maybe another time…"

"Him? Really?" says Tom. "But he calls you 'Betsy…'"

"I know, but it's not too far off from 'Becca.'"

"You deserve better than that."

"I'm right here, numbnuts," says Spooner. "I can hear you."

A knock at the conference room door startles them. A courier is carrying a large, flat package wrapped in bubble wrap with brown paper. He glances to the invoice. "They said I could find Mister Thomas Hogan here?" says the Courier.

"I'm Tom Hogan," he says, excited to get a gift before realizing it's that stupid painting he bid on. *Could the day get any worse?*

"I'll need your autograph," says the courier, tapping on his electronic device to the signature box as he drops the painting haphazardly to the floor.

CHAPTER FOUR

Cape Cod

The gallery is up in Wellfleet, Massachusetts—in the outer Cape between Eastham and Truro, just short of Provincetown and best known for its Wellfleet oysters. A winding sand-shouldered road leads to a charming town with a thrift store, a pizza shop, a news dealer (a.k.a. Wellfleet Marketplace because let's face it, there's not much news this time of year), and a package store—or "packie" in New England, slang for a liquor store—because one really needs alcohol in the off season.

Nell scurries past the church just down from Winslow's Tavern, towards Bank Steet, her arms overloaded with art catalogs and a power shake.

"Morning!" She calls out while pushing her backside against the door to enter the gallery.

"Don't you mean, afternoon?" asks Frederick, standing at the counter. Nell's assistant is a hipster dressed more Manhattan Lululemon than Cape Cod khaki. "So glad you could finally join us."

"Sorry, so very sorry," says Nell, panting, and making her way to him. "Can you help me with these?" He doesn't.

She slams down the pile of catalogues onto her desk, dropping her cell phone on top.

Frederick rolls his eyes, imitating her with a sing-song tone, "Sorry I'm late! Sorry I'm late!"

"You know I am," she says, offering Frederick a sip of her shake.

He pushes it away. "Honey, as the saying goes..."

"Oh, you just behave. I will *not* be late for my own funeral. You won't let me be."

"Well, whatever. But change of subject," says Frederick, "you just missed a very interesting woman. Claimed to be the distant cousin of Edward Hopper. Said she had some of his work that she wanted to offer for a retrospect and blah, blah, blah." He flits his hands.

"What do you mean, 'and blah, blah, blah'? That's huge!"

"I know," he adds, "but you weren't here."

"Omg," says Nell, her crystal-blue eyes practically popping out of the socket. "Hopper's 'Cape Cod Morning' is one of my favorite paintings! The one with the woman gazing out the window? Love it!" Nell moves about the gallery, her hands forming theatrical moves. "And my gosh, what of the classic? 'Nighthawks'!"

"The famous diner scene with three people sitting at the counter?"

"Yes," she says, moving to the counter and getting in Frederick's face. "Please tell me you got her contact info?"

"Yes," he says. He dangles a business card, unable to resist Nell's bohemian beauty.

Nell snaps it from his hand, studying the gray embossed lettering before narrowing her eyes. "Wait a second, this isn't Edward Hopper, it's *Edwin Hooper*."

Frederick plucks the card back. "Oh dear, my bad. I thought she said "Hopper." Frederick moves to the computer monitor, firing it up. "Well, whatever, but we have to come up with a new financial plan. If we don't, by next year, this gallery," he circles his pointer finger in the air, "is going to be a jewelry accessory shop. Because here's what I know..." Frederick enlarges an Excel spreadsheet, spinning the screen around to Nell. "Numbers are down from this season, hon." Nell pouts. "Nellie, you really must reconsider doing a retrospect of your grandmother's paintings. People love that touristy stuff..."

"I know, and we will. I really want to show Nan's paintings," says Nell, moving to a backroom wall and fingering through some of Nan's canvases with red, white, and blue flags. "I just think the showing has to be in the summer. They're so all-American. But the patrons always want to meet the artist and I'm not sure if—"

A phone rings. "I'm not here," says Frederick, panicked.

"You're not?" asks Nell.

"No. If it's the *stalker* from The Vault, I'm not here."

"You were up in Provincetown last night?" she asks. "Ooh la la. What's his name?"

"Just answer the phone!"

Moving to the receiver, she adds, "Um, shouldn't *you* be picking up the phone. It's what I pay you to do." She winks.

"Just answer already!" he says, ducking behind the desk.

Nell giggles and then changes her voice to work mode, her voice sing-songy: "Good afternoon, *Gallery*!"

Frederick rises from the desk and saunters to the paintings against the wall. He begins analyzing and then separating them to various spots.

Nell hangs up. "It wasn't the stalker guy from The Vault. It was Mayor Bisbee. Though you do owe me juicy details."

"What does he want?"

"Just asking if I figured out my costume for the party. But we have loads of time." Nell moves to the docking station to download some music. "Okay, I think we really must convince Edith Vonnegut to do a retrospect of *all* her paintings. She lives near me in Barnstable. It would be amazing!"

"Kurt Vonnegut's daughter?" he asks, scrolling Instagram. "Sure. Maybe."

"Are you kidding?" says Nell, hands on hips. "Whose gallery is this anyway?"

"Yours," he says with a bored tone.

"Frederick, are you listening to me? Edie would be the most incredible show!" Nell moves about with a natural sway in her hips, even though she's somehow completely oblivious to her stunning beauty. She'd much prefer to be thought of as cerebral. "Seriously, Edie exhibited in galleries all over the country, and her book *Domestic Goddesses* is everything I believe in!" Nell moves to center of the room as if it were center stage. Again. Her arms move overhead with excitement. "She portrays women in these heroic terms because if you think back through history and even Biblical times—and if you think of say, a Rubens-esque painting of a woman—they're always just naked showpieces sprawled out helpless on a canvas. But Edie well, c'mon, she captures them in daily situations...the way essential workers or even housewives should be recognized."

"Okay, I'm convinced," says Frederick, craning his neck to the window at the postman. "Nice biceps! Is he new in town?"

CHAPTER FIVE

Los Angeles

With a quiet push of the glass door, Tom enters Forest Bend Nursing Home.

Heavenly sunbeams stream across the polished tile floor of a long hallway, giving him pause. Like that saying, "at death's door…" This is most certainly it. A strange custodial scent pierces Tom's nose. If this were a movie set, the scene would be called "Lysol." Tom takes in the wallpaper. Multiple shades of greige. He shakes his head. He can't believe the boss gave him *this* assignment.

Just ahead, "*Wheeeel. Of. Fortuuuuune!*" can be heard echoing white noise to old folks gathered around the television. Some of the younger at heart are hopeful, dressed in their best attire, waiting to attend the Academy Awards of their minds. Gazing out the window to the parking lot, a woman longs for a limousine that will never arrive.

At each turn of the corridor, it's like a cast of characters. And in the corner, a couple dances an arthritic tango.

Tom's chest forms an automatic clutch…reminded of his grandmother. One of the last things she said on her deathbed was that it was hard to watch all her other friends die. She was the last to go. Technically, Tom's grandfather will be the last to go, for now still hanging in there up on Lake Winnipesaukee, New Hampshire. Grandpa's still active in the rotary club, with the veterans, and tending to Grandma's prize-winning rose garden. On Sunday, he still prepares her traditional pot roast dinner, just like she did…

with parsnips and all the fixings. As far as Grandpa's concerned, his wife might be in heaven, but they'll *always* be married.

Tom moves inconspicuously through a second set of automatic doors, poking his head around the room to spy inside a small library. Classic MGM videos line the shelves. A cat puzzle sits unfinished on a card table next to a chess game with knights and kings to strategize.

A displaced frail woman with a yesteryear-elegance approaches. She's dressed in blue pastel with a vintage cloche hat, an heirloom diamond brooch on its band. Her look is vague, haunted. Tom attempts to intervene. "Hi there," he says, but she says nothing, instead staring right through him as if *he's* the ghost. "I bet you're an actress," he adds.

"Of course, I am!" she snaps, coming out of her trance. "Don't you recognize me? All the boys wanted me. I used to be *very* beautiful. Did you see my pictures?"

"All of them," says Tom, a white lie and an earnest grin. "Every single one."

Pleased, she smiles stretched wrinkles, batting her lashes—well, what's left of them. A note of recognition crosses her face. "Why don't you come to see me more often?" she flirts.

"This is the first time I could get away," he says.

"I understand," she sighs, clasping both of his hands in hers, transparent skin with delicate veins. Her lips tremble, "The war is over. Paris has been liberated." She pouts. "Have you forgotten Paris like you forgot about me?"

"I remember every detail," says Tom, searching his tenth grade history class memory for an answer. "The Germans wore gray. You wore blue, right? There was a café?"

She gently places her hand on his cheek, then rubs it with remorse. Tom allows her the privilege. Their eyes gently lock. He feels sad for her. Aging isn't a fun thing. Not at all.

"It's nice seeing you again..." he says softly, very sincerely. "You haven't changed a bit." She continues stroking his cheek. Her mind gone elsewhere—Paris, probably—to that café and afternoons lingering over a noisette and croque monsieur. "But...I just have to leave you for a moment," explains Tom. Ever so cautiously, he places her hand back to her side. Like a dutiful boy, he gives her a gentle peck on the cheek.

She watches him go, but he doesn't turn back. Instead, Tom's suddenly drawn to the voice of a hearty male, the first sign of someone in this place that's actually having a lucid conversation with another person. Five steps from the voice's door, Tom hears him say, "What do you think...I don't know medicine? Thirty years in the coroner's office, for Christ's sake!" Tom peeks in the doorway to find a technician adjusting the IV in a man's arm.

"It was infiltrated, Lolly," says the tech, shaking his head before turning to go. He bypasses Tom in the doorway with a warning. "Don't let him bite."

"I heard that, you putz!" Lolly shakes his head before his eyes scan Tom's. "And who the hell are you, little *piss*-ant?"

Tom smiles, stepping forward with caution, extending a hand. "Hello, sir, I'm Tom.

Tom of *The Hollywood Record*."

Lolly ignores the handshake. "I don't speak to reporters."

"I'm guessing there's lots coming around."

"More than you might think, wise guy."

"I'm doing a story on movie people who reside here."

"You mean fading stars and starlets who come here to die, don't you?" says Lolly. "So, say so." Tom's eyes lower to the floor. Lolly now extends a hand. "Wagner Lutz. Only call me Lolly."

Tom shakes his hand. "Why Lolly?"

"Because I told you so."

Tom thinks of his editor. Maybe the idea of a pen and paper for an interview isn't so dead after all. He flips the cardstock cover to the first page, clicking the back of his pen to the pad. "So, tell me...how many films were you in? I heard you say you played a coroner—"

Lolly hisses. "I didn't *play* a coroner. I *was* a coroner. Assistant coroner of Los Angeles County. Autopsied Janis Joplin, RFK, Natalie Wood...all the big ones!"

"When?"

"Fifty-nine to eighty-nine," says Lolly.

"Oh, so you worked for that famous coroner...?"

"Noguchi?" says Lolly. "Yeah...I worked. Noguchi did TV shows. I worked. Noguchi did book tours. That bastard didn't want to do autopsies unless it was somebody famous. 'Coroner to the Stars,' they called him. Which made me Assistant Coroner to the Stars."

"Was that a bad thing?"

"The difference is I never got fired for sensationalizing celebrity deaths. Like the deaths in this town need sensationalizing." Lolly huffs, attempting to get out of bed and juggling his IV pole. Tom goes to steady him by the arm. Lolly pulls back. "Whadya think? I'm a frail old man?" says Lolly.

There's something about Lolly. Reminds him of his grandfather's moral complexity, his persistence to be heard, his longing for the respect once conquered and now dismissed. Today, sadly, his life's work and contributions mean absolutely nothing.

"So," says Tom, "how come you get to come to a motion picture old age home?"

"Please!" says Lolly. "Cinematic Senior Center. Jesus, kid, try not to make my life sound so terminal." Lolly grasps the arms of his wheelchair and plops in like he's done this a few times. "I was the technical advisor on *Quincy*," says Lolly. "You're probably too young to know that the actor, Jack Klugman, played a medical examiner. It was before your time."

"I know the show. I've watched reruns on Amazon with my grandfather."

"Amazon?" asks Lolly. "The shipping company?"

"They do TV now too. Streaming," says Tom. "So...you were the one who taught Klugman to be so ornery." Tom's eyes land on a framed black-and-white picture on Lolly's nightstand. A small group of people, all in black, at a wall of crypts in a cemetery. "That's a cheery photo to look at every night," says Tom, pointing at one of the people. "Who's that guy?"

"Joe DiMaggio."

"The ballplayer? Why do you have *this?*"

"I could tell you, but I'd have to kill you."

Just like *Quincy* might do, Tom darts his eyes up, down, and all around. There's an empty cigar box on a desk.

"You like cigars, Mr. Lolly?" asks Tom.

"Love 'em. But can't have 'em in here. Bad for my emphysema."

Tom turns to look up at the wall by the door, and his eyes snag on a painting. A landscape. Red, white, and blue. If it could jump off the wall, it would be an earthquake. It's easily a nearly identical sister painting to the one Tom bought at the auction.

"Whoa," says Tom. "Where did you get that?"

"It's not what you think."

"What was I thinking?" asks Tom.

"Why are you interested?"

"Who's interviewing who?"

"For a dozen Havanas, I'll tell you." Tom raises a brow. "Fine," says Lolly. "If you must know, Marilyn Monroe gave it to me in '64 after she 'died.'" Lolly makes quotation marks in the air with his fingers for *died*.

"Huh?" Tom is taken aback. "What? Was she reincarnated?"

"No." Lolly picks up the photo on his bedside table. "This is her funeral. Like I told ya, that's DiMaggio, her second husband. The kid in the marine uniform is his son. That there's Lee

Strasberg, the acting coach. Gave one hell of a fake eulogy for Marilyn." Lolly spins his wheelchair toward the painting. "Keeps me company. She painted it for me. For keeping her secret safe. For helping her escape."

"Wait a second," says Tom. "So, you're saying Marilyn Monroe *didn't* die?"

"Yup, that's what I'm saying," says Lolly, staring intently at Tom, seemingly joyful for his line of questions. This might be the best fun Lolly's had in *years.*

"C'mon… This is some sort of joke. How could you keep something like this a secret?" Tom can tell that Lolly sees him as an ambitious opportunist, and that Tom sees *him* as some lonely old guy looking for a little attention. "You realize if what you're saying is the truth, then it's the biggest story of your life! And probably mine, too!"

"Sure is," confirms Lolly. "Defies everything the world *thinks* they know."

Tom guffaws, drops his notepad to his thigh. His narrative energy increases. "You're telling me that the coroners, the morgue guys, the cops, her friends…*somebody* would have blown the lid off this casket by now to some tabloid piece of crap!"

"Like *The Hollywood Record?*" asks Lolly, almost unapologetically.

"Well, yeah, I mean, *heck* yeah! Somebody would have paid you guys big bucks to leak to *our* newspaper!"

"There was only a few of us to pay off," says Lolly, his tone changing from untamable to serious. Lolly stares into the distance as if it's all coming back to him like a movie reel moving in a picture show. A tear forms in the corner of his eye.

"May I?" asks Tom, sitting on the edge of his bed.

Lolly nods. "Sure, kid, sit." Silence for a moment before Lolly exhales like a lifelong burden has been lifted. "God, this feels good. It's time…" Lolly's voice lowers, almost crackles now. "It wasn't the tabloids that would have slipped us some money. Sure, somebody slipped us a couple hundred G's but to keep quiet, not to talk…"

"Who?"

"I can't say. I told you I was paid," says Lolly, deadpan. "But let's just say we were petrified of the mob, if you catch my drift. Hoffa, Giancana's people…even Monroe's ex-husband, DiMaggio, hung out at Toots Shor's, a joint financed by the mafia. They were all interlaced." He sighs. "I'm an old man now. Look at me—I'm dying. The mobsters are probably *already* dead. And you're the first person who's ever walked in here and asked me about that painting after all these years."

"Okay, but two hundred thousand? That's not very much."

"In 1962," explains Lolly, "that was a lifetime. Inflation. Who knew?"

Tom stares at the painting. Like his painting from the auction, it's talking to him. "This is just crazy!" he says.

Lolly wheels to the top side of his mattress. Pulls out a flask from underneath it. "Only two people ever saw her 'dead.'" Lolly forms air-quotations again. "Eunice Murray, the housekeeper who found her…she was the first. She protected Marilyn. The second one was Dr. Ralph Greenson, who loved her like a daughter. When Marilyn was depressed, which was a lot of the time, she used to stay at the Greenson home for slumber parties…as if she was Doctor and Mrs. Greenson's daughter. They were the only two to really love and protect her…Murray and Greenson…" Lolly shakes his head. "That Greenson. He was another one. Never mind Noguchi being hailed 'Coroner to the Stars,' Greenson was the crackpot *shrink* to the stars. Vivien Leigh, Tony Curtis…"

"Before my time…"

"Frank Sinatra!" shouts Lolly.

"Okay, okay, I've heard of him, and I can certainly *hear* you." says Tom, nervously shaking his ankle on the edge of the bed frame. *This can't be. Can it?*

"I've been dying to tell the truth." Lolly nurses from the flask, wiping his lips. "I remember around November of '82…twenty years after her death…the district attorney was still harping on us about Marilyn's murder. They focused on the overdose, the acute barbiturate poisoning, the murder that wasn't, the suicide that was, what she ate, what she didn't eat, and why the FBI files on Monroe had been so heavily censored. But the most important fact is that from the time Marilyn's body was found by Eunice to the time the police were called, hours went by. What was Marilyn doing all those hours? I'll tell you what she was doing…she was planning her escape."

"But to where? This is *fricking* incredible!" Tom looks over his shoulder wondering if anybody else is entering the room to overhear. Maybe that technician is going to return.

"Yeah, well, you heard it here first, off the record…" says Lolly. "She was a phenomenon," Lolly sighs with a shit-eating grin. "You know Adlai Stevenson?" Tom shakes his head. Lolly chuckles. "Well, Stevenson said that the dress she wore the night she sang 'Happy Birthday' to Kennedy was just skin and beads." He smirks. "Those torpedo breasts and silk stockings. Marilyn was one hot dish to be had."

"So where did she go?" asks Tom, as if he can feel Marilyn calling him from her grave.

"Where did she go?" asks Lolly. "Good question. That's for you to figure out, Clouseau."

Tom nods, moves closer to inspect the painting corner to corner.

"How come it's not signed?" asks Tom.

Lolly wheels over and looks up to inspect the piece of art. "What was she supposed to do? Sign it 'Love and kisses, come find me sometime, xo Marilyn Monroe'?"

CHAPTER SIX

Los Angeles

His computer's blue light illuminates the newsroom cubicle where Tom sits, burning with newly tapped ambition. Sleeves rolled up and jacket off, his eyes are locked on three internet pages, but he repeatedly clicks back to a copy of the County of Los Angeles's Coroner Case Report for Marilyn's postmortem. Name: Marilyn Monroe. Post Mortem at: Coroner. Crypt #33. Date and Time of Death: 8-5-62, 3:40 a.m. Place of Death: 12305 Fifth Helena Dr. - Brentwood. Weight: 117 pounds. Height: 65 ½ inches.

To the right, down toward the bottom, the form asks "Door Sealed" and it's checked "Yes." In Noguchi's handwriting directly above, it states, "per mortuary." *Did they not allow anyone into the morgue because it supposedly contained the body of Marilyn Monroe? Or because it didn't?*

On the left of the front page is a question mark next to "Suicide" and "Homicide." The words "Natural" and "Accident" are not checked or questioned.

On another page, he zooms in on the image of the front outline of a body on one page with hand-drawn lines showing scars from appendix and gallbladder surgeries.

Tom suddenly feels inexplicably connected to this story. He's even humming '60s sentimentality…Frank Sinatra's "I've Got the World on a String."

Wearing a straw fedora, a Cuban souvenir that Lolly gifted Tom, this kid's feeling confident. Striking his keyboard with rapturous fingers, Lolly's words reverberate: "Monroe overdosed on Nembutal and chloral hydrate pills found on her bedside table. It's a 'knockout' pill as famous as the ingredients in Mickey Finns. Yet, there were *zero* pills found in her digestive tract. The yellow dye on Nembutal should have stained her stomach. It didn't. Because it wasn't her body in the morgue. The bodies were swapped. But it doesn't matter, kid. It was all a cover-up. I can't believe she got away with it. I can't believe *we* got away with it!"

Tom glances over his shoulder, making sure Spooner and Ritter are nowhere in sight. Instead, Jim Burke approaches. Burke is old-school and admired. He's in his late seventies, refusing to retire despite a cut in pay. A real fact checker. He crosses his t's and dots his i's, though he hasn't cleaned the mounds of papers from his desk in twenty years. Nevertheless, Burke's a lovable bear… overweight, sloppy, a cliché cigarette dangling from his lips.

Burke enters Tom's cubicle with a tilted paper plate. "Hey, Tom, want the last bagel? Fresh from this mornin'. You gotta eat something."

"Thanks, Jim, but no," Tom says without turning around. He clicks his various screens to close them all out. All but one.

"A few carbs never killed anyone." Burke shrugs and bites the bagel, tossing the plate into the trash. "You workin' on that Weekend Edition for the boss?" Tom looks up at him like a little lost puppy caught red-handed shredding the sofa. Burke moves closer to Tom's screen. "Come on, Tom," says Burke, patting Tom's back. "Don't let Ritter get you down. We all make mistakes. You gotta try harder. Get back up on that horse and ride."

"Okay, Jim, why don't you ride with me," says Tom, wearing a politician's smile and pulling up one particular article about Marilyn's suicide. Burke's article. Tom spins around. "You covered the death of Marilyn Monroe. That's your byline."

The headline screams "MARILYN DEAD."

"One of my first assignments. Sure. I was a kid then. Like you," says Burke. "Listen, Tom, I don't think the boss wants you covering *dead* celebrities that our paper's already written about... just the *new* dying ones at the senior center, remember?"

"I know," says Tom. "But did you ever get anything, I don't know, odd off the story?"

"Odd how?" asks Burke, about to drop his cigarette onto the newsroom floor and stomp it, but Tom's quick to catch the butt in a dirty coffee cup.

"You think there was any kind of cover-up. By the press, maybe?"

"I *was* the press," says Burke, shrugging his shoulders. "There were tons of conspiracies...but it's old news...been done to death."

"You sure something's not missing?" asks Tom pushing with intent.

"Jeez," says Burke, "Every decade's gotta have a villain. In the sixties, it was communists. Nineties brought us the evil stockbrokers. In the 2000s...evil terrorists and the stockbrokers *together*. Now, it's most certainly you millennial journalists..."

"I think of myself as more Gen Z," says Tom.

"Is that like Generation X?" Burke asks, but with genuine affection in his tone.

"Gen Z...the digital kids," says Tom smiling. "Not old enough to remember 9/11 and Columbine, but old enough to know about ISIS, Sandy Hook, and the banking crisis in '08."

"Now there's some *fond* memories," says Burke, running a hand through his thinning gray hair. "And I'm a boomer." Burke smiles back to the hippie days. "Vietnam, Woodstock, the Kennedy assassination, and Joplin. Love Joplin."

"Yeah, but the good news is we're all sort of the same."

"How so?" asks Burke, sitting on the edge of Tom's desk.

"Curiosity. Open to anything." Tom turns his computer screen to Burke. "So...please...just hear me out," says Tom, segueing back to Marilyn now that he's won Burke over. Sort of. "There's a lot of inconsistencies in this report. You know they never did any in-depth toxicology on the drugs she took that night? I mean, they did, but it didn't pay off. There was nothing in Monroe's system. Apparently, some cop came in—or so it was rumored—and cleaned the place up before she was pronounced dead by her psychiatrist, Doctor Greenson. I find that a little strange."

"No, that's not accurate," says Burke. "She was pronounced dead by her internist. A guy named Engelberg…"

"Then how does her shrink fit in?"

Burke makes designs with the dust on the top of Tom's cubicle wall, like he's ticking through the dust of his mind. "If memory serves me, her housekeeper tried to get in the house and couldn't. She looked in the bedroom window and saw Monroe on the bed. She called Marilyn's shrink, Greenson. But before he could get there, somehow Engleberg did, I guess. Broke into the bedroom with a fireplace poker."

"How come none of that is in these stories?"

"Those were the old days. We didn't pry so much into people's lives like we do now."

"What do you make of coroners?" asks Tom.

"I see dead people?" jokes Burke. "Your point?" Burke places his hands in his pockets and jiggles his change. "Tom, look, take some advice from an old and tired but very wise guy. You got one chance to cover the nursing room story for Ritter. Don't blow it on some old autopsy report that doesn't add up." Tom's face is eager but respectful. He gazes straight ahead at the cubicle wall. Burke picks up on his stubbornness. "Okay, Tom, here's a tidbit to shut you up."

Tom lights up. "I'm listening…"

"*Nobody* saw Monroe's body," says Burke. "It was wrapped up when they brought her corpse out."

"Really?" says Tom, sitting straight up, his mind short-circuiting with too much information but no place to put it. "So how do you know it was *her* body? Maybe they switched it in the morgue? Some Jane Doe in a drawer or something, I don't know..." Tom's hoping to bait him.

Burke shrugs. "Wanna know something even crazier?" Burke seems to relish the idea of laying out even *more* legendary information to a novice. "There was a rumor that came to me a few years later. Someone said Marilyn was supposedly having sex with one of her bodyguards. He was there the day she died." Burke goes to Tom, pats his shoulders again. "I guess we all guard bodies in different ways, huh?"

"Who was he?" asks Tom spinning his desk chair around and standing up, finding himself practically nose to nose with Burke.

"A would-be actor," says Burke, folding his arms. He goes back to cubicle-leaning. "Let's see. Did a couple of B pics. Used to escort Marilyn to Vegas on weekends. Hung out with the Rat Pack." Tom says nothing, leaving space for Burke to spill more. "His name was something 'Powers.' Can't remember it, but it sounded like some kind of jewelry. I don't know. I do remember his film though. He dropped out of sight after *Jump Rope Jungle.* Yeah, that was it."

Tom goes to his desk and scribbles the name of the film on a sticky note.

"Look," sighs Burke, "I gotta go. Having a drink with my chiropractor." Burke moseys over to the light and flicks off the switch in the coffee room. "See you tomorrow, Tom," Burke calls from down the hall. "And at least get a sandwich. You gotta eat."

Tom turns back to his computer screen. *Where to begin?* It's all too much to process. If it's all true, the magnitude of this is career-making, world-changing, life-altering. *It's fucking* Pulitzer *material! Grandpa will be so proud!*

Tom stands up, stretches, yawns, and heads to the men's room, where he notices a light on in the real estate office that was once his editor's space. The sign that read Glenn Ritter, Editor has been removed. Tom opens the door to see Spooner in a desk chair leaning into a gorgeous brunette's cleavage while topping off her champagne. She's breathing heavy. The woman and Spooner glance up startled to see Tom. "Sorry, guys," whispers Tom, closing the door and heading to the bathroom.

But Spooner doesn't find "sorry" good enough. When Tom returns to his cubicle moments later, he's stunned to see Spooner snooping around. A screenshot of Jimmy Burke's article is pulled up on Tom's computer. And Spooner's eyes are transfixed on the sticky note with the movie title *Jump Rope Jungle*, sitting next to Noguchi's *Coroner* book.

"Look, I'm sorry I interrupted…" says Tom.

Now Spooner's in Tom's face. "What's the Monroe angle you're working on?"

"Ah, nursing homes?" says Tom, more a question than an answer, with a tone that practically stamps the word *liar* on his forehead.

"Marilyn Monroe isn't *in* a nursing home, you shit-for-brains. She's dead! Suicide. So, what's your angle?"

"You stealing my story ideas now?" asks Tom. "Why don't you just file your own stuff and leave me alone."

"Fine. I'm out the door to an assignment as we speak," says Spooner, deliberately knocking Tom's backpack to the floor as he turns in a huff.

"You're actually working?" asks Tom sarcastically, calling after him as he picks up the spilled goods of his backpack from the stained carpeting. He glances up in time to see Spooner give him a middle finger from a distance.

The clock reads 7:45 p.m. Tom hits the power button on his computer to hibernate the image on his screensaver. It's one of Marilyn in the back of a limo, wearing a black dress, sitting on her mink stole, and blowing out a single candle on a coconut birthday cake.

CHAPTER SEVEN

Cape Cod

A heavy downpour pools ankle-deep puddles at every street corner. The dense air bends the light of the streetlamps, creating a shimmering effect. The only sign of life, aside from the dancing of the lamppost, comes from the gallery. Wind pounds against the door, whipping the "open" bell against its glass.

Inside it's cozy and lit up. Nora Jones plays on the speakers, but we don't see Nell. We do see Frederick, slouched on a barstool at the register.

"C'mon, get moving! This isn't a Paris runway!" says Frederick. He leans on the desk, filing his nails.

"I'm almost ready," she calls out.

"That's what you said six costumes ago!"

Suddenly from the backroom, the curtain opens, and there's Nell dressed as Joan of Arc. "Whadya think?"

Frederick sits upright and conceals a laugh.

"What? Too much?" she asks.

"Yes! Off with her head! Next!"

"Joan was burned at the stake, not beheaded," says Nell, giggling. "Okay, give me five..."

"I've already given you twenty-five!"

"Oh, hush," she says, back behind the curtain, feeling a bit insecure. It's not about the costumes. They're ridiculous. She knows that. But she's never been sure about her looks. Never studied herself in mirrors as her Nan never really allowed them except one in the bathroom. Nell would often study Nan studying herself when they by passed the marketplace, Nan watching her reflection in the mirror as though she wanted to be sure she was slouching just right, looking just meek enough, trying to fit into a certain local's role.

Nell used to tell Nan, "Take off those big glasses!" But Nan said they protected her eyes from the sun.

Nell would put on her grandmother's sunglasses, study herself in the mirror, twisting her head left and right and left again. Big aviator-style frames with tinted lenses. Everyone wore black Hollywood sunglasses, but not Nan. Instead, it was always some style that was out of style, something that made her quirkier than everyone else.

Nell knew she got her looks from her mother, Grace, and of course, her Nan, who tried so hard to conceal them. She knew men always glanced back or did a double take. But while she was supposedly pretty on the outside—a face that could light up a Fourth of July sky, Nan claimed—deep inside her soul, she always knew something was ugly. Something was amiss. *But what was it?* She couldn't be certain.

Sometimes, without hurting Nan's feelings, she'd like to talk more about her beautiful mother, Grace. The mother she never really knew. She was too young when her mother died accidentally. Not old enough to appreciate the mother she wished she had now. And with Nan losing her only daughter, Nell felt it was her destiny to stay on Cape and care for her grandmother. She needed her. And Nell knew that she needed her grandmother in return. Sure, Manhattan would have been great. Nell always thought she'd make it in New York, be an actress, destined for Broadway. But tell God you have a plan…and well, she stayed here in her seaport town.

Funny because Nan always talked of how she would have liked to be a "serious" actress. The type who performed Shakespeare.

Lady MacBeth maybe, now that she was too old for Juliet. Instead, she focused on her other passion, painting. And one day, she took out a loan to open her very first gallery. The gallery Nell now stands in.

"Hello," says Frederick. "Is there anyone behind curtain number one? Or is this charade over?"

"Okay, okay, I'm coming!" she says, wiping tears from her eyes and pasting on a smile. Finally, she's there again. "What about..." She emerges dressed in a drab black dress with a white apron. On top of her head is an odd white bonnet.

"I'm confused. Are you a maid from *Downton Abbey*?" asks Frederick, squishing his face in disdain.

"No, silly," says Nell, twirling about the store. "I'm the Salem Witch. Sarah Good."

"Well *good* for you! But, honey, you're never going to meet a man dressed in that nun thingy."

"Oh, fine," she says, drooping back defeated to the backroom.

She leans against the wall behind the curtain. Let's face it, if she hasn't met a man by now, there's never going to be one. Most guys here are all blue collar and she wants the artsy ones, but like Frederick, they're gay. The businessmen—the town lawyers and doctors—are already married. And the old timers, the retired big-bucks sugar daddies with their speed boats, will never be her thing. They hit on her, the cute twenty-something blonde, when she pops into Baxter's for a lobster roll, but there's no way she's hooking up with someone her grandmother's age. So that leaves her to be married to this gallery. What else is there to do when Nan paid for all of this, believed in her granddaughter's passion. And besides, if you could have seen the look on Nan's face the day she'd handed Nell the key, well...

"In this century, please!" hollers Frederick.

There's a lot of commotion coming from under the curtain. We see blonde wigs, black wigs, stilettos, platform shoes, and even a tutu being pushed aside from under the curtain.

"Ta da!" she says, entering. "Well?"

"Ohhhh, Nellie," says Frederick, his hand to his heart. "Perfection! Twirl around." She does. "Love the square smokey sunglasses. And the long legs! Are you Twiggy?"

"Gloria, silly!"

"Gaynor?" he asks.

"Steinem!" she declares. Though the singer who belted out "I Will Survive" might be the better bet just about now.

CHAPTER EIGHT

Los Angeles

The address on Spooner's cell phone matches the location he's standing in front of, though technically it doesn't compute. By all standards, today's Sunset Boulevard is one of PR firms, film distributors, nightclubs, tattoo parlors, piercing joints, and clothing boutiques. *But this?* A yellow stucco building with a gaudy gold awning? A sign with '50s-style lettering blinks bright red at the front door. *Frankie's Place.*

Pulling open the heavy brass door, Spooner steps in, his eyes adjusting in the dark. Scanning the dimly lit steak joint of red leather banquettes, Spooner's eyes fall on a worn baby grand sitting in a corner untouched. A lone bartender polishes glasses with a dish towel. A total time warp. In its day, this place may have rated…not Zagat rated, but perhaps "Best local Italian." There's a very ring-a-ding-ding feel here, like Tony Soprano might belly up to the bar at any moment.

From an old speaker system, Tony Bennett's "Anything Goes" crackles as Spooner slides into a small booth replete with the remnants of a large eggplant parmesan dinner and an untouched salad…the kind with iceberg lettuce, overkill garlic dressing, topped with croutons and raw purple onions. Across from him sits Angelo "Tony Spits" Spittone, a tough, flat-nosed, gray-haired guy practically cuffed to his glass of Chianti. Stoop-shouldered, Tony Spits is savoring every sip. Dabbing his lips with a red cloth napkin, he's as stylish as one can be for his age. Impeccable pinstripe suit and perfectly-knotted black satin tie. He hasn't spoken a word, but his vibe is one of muted impatience.

Tony Spits sits back against the leather banquette extending his arms in front of him to massage his fingers on the table edge. He wears a lot of loud gold and diamond rings, and he glances over to a large no-nonsense man sitting alone at a nearby table. Spooner's gaze meets the eyes of the large man at the table. The man is staring Spooner down. Clearly, Tony Spits has "people."

"Tell me, Spits," asks Spooner. "What was it that made you come to me to do this little job for you?"

"I always liked the way you write, kid. You got style. Not many people have style no more. In the fifties, we all had style. Ties, hats, cufflinks, shine on your shoes…women wore furs…"

"Well, thank you," says Spooner, grateful for the compliment but trying to remember the last time he actually wrote a story anyone might have read. Could have been that piece on "Dames & Dogs" for the Animal Rescue League Ball in Santa Monica. Just an excuse for Spooner to get lucky with that breakout actress who adopted that annoying Shih Tzu. *What was her name? The dog's name, not hers…*

"What I want is to give you something," says Tony Spits, his voice strong with conviction. "The biggest story you'll ever get."

"Okay," says Spooner, bracing himself.

"I want you to find my kid."

Spooner is hesitant but has to ask. "What makes you think finding your kid would be the story of my life?"

"When you find her, you'll find out. Besides, I never seen her, and I want to. At least once before I die. It'll be big. Really big."

"How do you know she wants to see you?" To this question, Tony Spits gives a look that says he could kill Spooner for asking that. "Never mind," Spooner retracts. "I'm sure she'll be delighted." Tony Spits nods so slowly its almost sadistic. A cue for Spooner to soften. "So, what's your kid's name?"

"I don't know," says Spits.

"I love a challenge," says Spooner. "How about the mother's name?"

Tony Spits picks at his tooth with his pinky before answering. "Goes by Marie Morton."

"What do you mean 'goes by.' Was she your wife?"

"If she was my wife, would I need you to find her?" asks Tony Spits.

"So what did she do…this Marie Morton? How did you come to know her?"

Tony Spits leans back in his chair. "I can't say," says Spits, taking a long sip of his wine. He savors it before signaling the waiter to bring a second glass for Spooner. The waiter immediately appears with a goblet. He pours a glass of red for Spooner, who's more a Vodka martini kind of guy but doesn't dare to offend Tony Spits. The two men raise their glasses.

"Salut!" says Tony Spits, sipping and then gently placing the goblet on the table. The look on Tony Spits's face…one of deep and painful longing. Finally, he speaks. "Someone once said, Grace Kelly was safe, Doris Day was undesirable, Liz Taylor was unobtainable…and Audrey Hepburn, she was democratic…"

"That's great," says Spooner. "You could say the same about the Kardashians. What's your point?"

"My Marie. She was everything and more than all those women put together."

"I'm sure she was." Spooner discreetly checks the screen on his cell phone under the table. It's past nine. He's late for his dinner date. "So, what's the going rate on this?"

"My usual deal times three."

"Can I ask the usual deal?"

"No. Too late. You're in it now, kid." Tony Spits cracks his knuckles while circling his neck until it cracks too. He leans into Spooner. "One more thing. You find her, you call me. You don't talk to her. You don't write anything." His tone snitch-friendly but serious. "You got it?" Spooner nods, trying to suppress a laugh because in his way of seeing things, who the fuck cares about some sentimental dying mobster's ex named Marie Morton? "And don't you double-cross me, kid," says Spits, "because you know, I sincerely do not like to be double-crossed." Tony Spits signals over to the guy at the next table, who nods with a ferocity that says he can draw blood. With his teeth.

"Now get outta here," says Spits. "We never had this meeting."

"What meeting?" asks Spooner, rising to go and not looking back.

CHAPTER NINE

Cape Cod

Nell pulls her Subaru into the parking lot of the historical Sturgis Library, Barnstable village, where they're having a book drive. The parking lot is full of tables, boxes, and loads of books from every genre.

"Nellie!" says Alice, the library's director, almost relieved. "Always such a pleasure to see you, sweetheart." They come in for a big hug. No air kissing here. After holding tight, Alice backs away first, grabbing Nell's elbows in her hands, looks sincerely into her eyes, and runs a hand under Nell's chin. "Your mother would have been so proud of you. You know that? Caring about literacy the way you do."

"Thank you, Alice. You're always so kind. I miss her."

"We all do," says Alice, with a sentimentality of years gone by. She glances in the trunk. "So whatcha got?"

Nell goes to grab a box. "Not sure any of these are helpful," she says, beginning to unload the boxes of fiction and biographies. "They're Nan's old books."

"Here, let me get someone to help you with those," says Alice, grabbing a second box.

The woman from Youth Services is there now. "Any kids' books?"

"Sadly no. I don't have children. And I'm not planning on having them."

Oh God, why did she just say that? Who's she kidding? She'd love to have children. But first, she'd need a meet-cute with a man, fall madly in love, and then, well, live happily ever after. Funny, she just wasn't raised believing in such things. Her grandmother never believed in happily ever after. She believed in self-reliance.

No, the only thing Nell can do is keep giving. When the chips are down and you're still helping others, you're supposed to feel a satisfaction that money can't buy. Nell only wishes that satisfaction would kick in already. Because let's face it: She's scared, though she doesn't let on to Frederick. Tourism *was* way down last season, he's right, and the foot traffic into the gallery was at an all-time low.

Nell scans the advertisements on the peg board. She reads an ad:

> GOOD PEOPLE NEEDED
>
> If you are interested in running for the Town Council, the School Committee, or the Housing Authority, nomination papers will be available starting October 18th, at 6 p.m.
>
> 367 Main Street, Hyannis.

They may need good people, but what she really needs is a good nap.

She pulls out her cell phone from her the pocket of her overalls. Rings the gallery. "Hey Freddie, can you handle the showroom? I'm way down in Barnstable headed over to Cotuit. There's a fundraiser for the Arts Center, and I'm dropping off some gently used furniture from the attic." A pause as Frederick inquires. Nell explains, "It's for their furniture painting drive or something." She heads back to her car, waving to the ladies in the library lot. Then continues to Frederick, "And while I'm already there, they have a big brush painting series. I'm wondering if maybe my grandmother's work might be better served at their place. I'm meeting with David, the man who runs it, so I'm also suggesting some of the locals for their upcoming production of *Charlotte's Web*."

We can now hear Frederick's reply. "Geez Louise. Library drives, furniture donations, Lower Cape, Upper Cape, Mid Cape. You're like God. Everywhere."

"Very funny. Okay, I'll see you later! Maybe dinner?" Good ole dependable Frederick. At least she'll have someone to share a table with.

Nell moves to the driver's side of her Subaru. The one covered in bumper stickers. Audubon society. Maritime stickers. Save the Whales. Save the Harbor. Save the Turtles. The truth is, she's the one who needs to be saved. She's exhausted. She's yawning at the wheel. And she needs rest. You know, proper prop-your-feet-up-and-curl-up-with-a-book-under-a-big-duvet kind of rest. But every time she's supposed to have a Monday off after a long gallery weekend, she begins thinking of other projects, other ways to help the community, other ways to be outside of herself and keep busy. Maybe keeping busy, not stillness, is her fireworks. Maybe her version of rest is rejuvenation. Or maybe she's just trying to avoid the truth. That she's just a young woman trying to figure it all out in a world where less women her age are choosing marriage. So, she's just trying to fill a void.

Her fingers grasp the locket hanging on the rearview mirror. At a red light, she opens the pendant to look at the two photos inside. One of her mother, Grace, and one of her grandmother, Marie. Her Nan. She kisses it.

And then the person behind her beeps at her to get moving.

CHAPTER TEN

Los Angeles

If newspaper offices could speak headlines, this one might read, "HOPE FLOATS!"

Tom is in before eight a.m. Spooner has showed up promptly by nine. Together, but in their own cubicles, they're researching, talking to various sources on their phones.

On a chair next to Tom is neatly stacked copies of papers from the Margaret Herrick Library, which is the main repository of media from the Academy of Motion Picture Arts and Sciences. There are magazine tear sheets and old interviews that he found archived. Not a single biography is being overlooked either. Anything and everything might reveal a source. He's already read two forgotten biographies written by Marilyn's close friends, Susan Strasberg and Louella Parsons.

Between calls, Tom is continuing to read his old library copy of Noguchi's *Coroner.* He's on the bit about the housekeeper who found Marilyn's "dead" body on the night of her death.

> Mrs. Murray perceived no hint of a suicidal depression. In fact, at 7:30 p.m. Monroe was laughing and chatting on the telephone with Joe DiMaggio's son, Joe Junior.
>
> Yet—and this one was one of the strangest facts of the case—not thirty minutes after that happy conversation, Marilyn Monroe

> was dying. We know this from the report of a telephone call made to Monroe at about eight that night. And the identity of the person who originated the call was another strange face that has provided grist for the murder theorists. For it was Robert Kennedy's brother-in-law Peter Lawford.

Tom sits forward and hits his keyboard to pull up some information before returning to Noguchi's book.

> Lawford didn't reveal the occurrence of that telephone conversation until a columnist who was a personal friend of Monroe's, Earl Wilson, got onto it....
>
> He had telephoned her because she was supposed to join him and friends for a poker game and then dinner. His wife, Patricia, was on Cape Cod at the Kennedy compound.
>
> According to Lawford, Monroe's voice was slurred. She said she couldn't come to dinner that night. Then she added words that were chilling: "Say goodbye to Pat, say goodbye to the President. Say goodbye to yourself because you've been a good guy."
>
> Then, abruptly, she clicked off.

Tom falls back against his desk chair. Stumped. *It doesn't mean Marilyn killed herself after those words, right?* She might have been saying goodbye as she knew she would never see them again. Maybe she was escaping to her life of self-imposed witness protection.

Tom shuffles through his iPod's playlist. "Come Fly With Me" croons out to put Tom into the mindset of the era…to get him thinking…about what he isn't sure…but he can imagine Marilyn taking off for parts unknown. *But where? Bombay? Peru? Sinatra's got suggestions but she could have fled anywhere. Mexico? Europe? China even!*

A courier rounds the corner and drops an Amazon package on Tom's desk. He looks over his cubicle to make sure no one's around. With a scissor blade he slices the box open to reveal a used coffee table book by Norman Mailer on Marilyn Monroe, which is a struggle to fit in his backpack with the other two biographies. Tom's favorite so far is Anthony Summers's *Goddess: The Secret Lives of Marilyn Monroe.* There were only three copies left on Amazon; Tom was fortunate to nail one. But in particular, he's been reading *The Secret Life of Marilyn Monroe* online, which explains that on May 19, 1962, just months before her death, she had whittled down her circle of close friends to a precious few. Tom makes notes of the names in her life at that point. Gladys, her mother; her half-sister, Bernice, the one the world barely knew about; and Ida, who they barely knew either.

Further, the book explains that Marilyn was no dumb blonde; she was much more intelligent than people realized. For years, she had used her intellectual abilities to conceal her most private emotional struggles.

Tom goes back to the coroner's book to highlight some more.

> Sergeant Jack Clemmons, watch commander at the West Los Angeles police station, logged a telephone call from Dr. Greenson reporting Monroe's death at 4:25 a.m. Sunday.

Tom drops the open book on his desk. *Holy Shit! Lolly was right! If the body was found dead just after midnight, then why wasn't the Sergeant called until 4:25 a.m.?* The books all have one thing in common: They present conflicting and muddled accounts of Marilyn Monroe's life…and her death.

Just then Becca rounds the corner to Tom's cubicle, which was neat and tidy despite Tom's racing thoughts. "Mornin' Becca," Tom says with a big inviting smile. "Just give me a second to finish this up, okay?"

She nods. As a photographer, Becca's drawn to a photo next to Tom's computer of a prize-winning Atlantic cod that Tom caught on his grandfather's motorboat. Next to the framed photo, a Gerber multi-tool Swiss Army knife. Tom's hiking boots sit in a duffel bag to take to the cobbler to have the laces and heels replaced. A photo of Tom at his college graduation backyard barbeque with a woman and his grandfather on either side of him. He's never looked happier. Red gown and red mortarboard with a white tassel buttoned to the center. Becca looks to Tom with appreciation. Guys like Tom don't exist anymore. He's like something out of a Norman Rockwell country scene, practically sitting on the bench outside that famous barbershop.

"Is that your mom?" asks Becca, picking up the graduation photo.

"Sure is."

"You don't mention her much…"

"She's just a regular mom."

"Where's your dad?" asks Becca.

"Died in Desert Storm."

"Oh," she says, taken aback. "My bad."

"No, it's cool. I never knew him."

"Gosh," says Becca. "That had to be hard for your mom. She raised you alone?"

"Yeah," says Tom, "But she had my grandparents. Her parents. After my dad died, she packed up the Chevy, and we drove north from Orlando to New Hampshire. I was just a baby. Lived on the lake. I was too young to understand, but my dad was a hero. Had one of those big funerals with lots of military uniforms and decorated sergeants."

"Oh wow," says Becca, her tone of shock and concern. "That's so sad. You never told me."

"Yeah, I don't talk about it much. Only thing I have is that flag…you know…folded in seven military steps."

"I've never seen one," says Becca.

"They give them to grieving war families at the funeral. After they fold it up, the final shape displays a blue triangle with stars on both sides."

"That's nice," she says, "about the flag I mean…" Her voice trails off to some distant place. And then she clears her throat, changing the subject up to a happy notch. "Did you try IMDb?" she asks, leaning across Tom and typing in IMDb—the International Movie Database comes up. Next she types in *Jump Rope Jungle.* Tom politely leans in, and the two scan the actors on the film. "There he is!" says Becca.

Tom studies the name. "Just like Burke said, it's a name with something 'jewelry' in it." They both chuckle. Until now, all Tom could come up with was Goldie Hawn and Ron Silver. Tom clicks off the screen.

"Sterling Powers. What a dumb actor name, huh?" says Becca, "Sounds more like a stripper."

"You're awesome, Becca. Thanks so much."

"What does Sterling have to do with nursing homes, Tommy?"

"Oh, um, Sterling Powers was in a film with one of the old timers at the senior center."

"I see," says Becca, half believing him because Tom's not a good liar, and his face instantly turns blotchy when he's nervous.

Becca glances from Tom's cubicle over to Spooner, who hasn't given her the time of day all morning, let alone this past week. She turns back to Tom, feeling bad she's put him off so many times. "A bunch of us are going out for happy hour tonight if you want to join?"

"I wish I could, but…"

"C'mon. We're all taking Ritter out."

"Really?" says Tom, chuckling.

"Our editor *needs* a drink!"

"Ya *think*?" jokes Tom. "Can't though. Saving for a trip back east next summer. And besides," says Tom, glancing at the now unwrapped red, white, and blue painting, "I have *this* to pay off."

"Sell it on eBay," says Becca. And with that she's off, heading over to Spooner's desk…

The opposite of Tom's space, Spooner's got numerous orange Hermès gift boxes of men's ties cast to the side. An elaborate gold corkscrew sits beside his mocha leather pen caddy, which accentuates a personal breathalyzer just in case he's pulled over by a cop. All gifts from his father to help motivate him along. A cookbook entitled *Man Meets Stove,* which is of zero interest to Spooner except to act as a shelf for his cell phone charger. He always orders take-out food, hence pile of menus in the corner of his desk. On the floor is an overnight bag, just in case. There are zero family photos even though his father went all out to throw a graduation bash at the St. Regis with a brunch at Cipriani the day after.

Becca stands next to Spooner's desk, but he's on the phone. "Got a Marie Morton in Burbank. Age forty-nine. A bit young," says Spooner. "A Marie Morton in Little Rock, Arkansas, died last week, car accident. Could have been her, but too young. College student." He puts the cell to his chest. "Can I help you?" he says to Becca, almost annoyed.

"Oh, I was just seeing if you want to join us all for Happy Hour and…"

"I'm kinda busy just now. But thanks…ah," thinking of her name, "Betsy."

CHAPTER ELEVEN

Tom pulls his Hyundai up to the front of a respectable-size home in Beverly Hills behind an electric wrought-iron gate that leads to a pool, cabana, and guest house out back. He's out of his car admiring the grounds. At the cue of the doorbell, a housekeeper leads Tom to the living room.

Standing in the massive room, the marble floors lead to a spiral staircase, where Tom strains his neck to see all the way up to a wall full of legendary somebodies. He might be young, but he's certain he recognizes some of them from TMZ and the internet. James Dean, Gene Kelly, and whoever else is up there, you name it. Tom turns at a man clearing his throat. "Oh, hello," Tom says, extending a hand and a warm smile. "Tom Hogan. *Hollywood Record*."

"Nice to meet you. Steve Stabler, but everyone calls me 'Stevey.' How ya doin', son?" Stevey wears a long blue velvet robe and a tattered MGM ball cap. He offers a firm handshake for a man in his late eighties.

"So, you represented all of these legends?" asks Tom.

"Nah," says Stevey, "This wall represents all the people I *wish* I represented but who were too smart to go with an agent like me."

"But you did represent Sterling Powers?"

"Oh sure," says Stevey, moving to a glass cart to pour himself a sherry. "One of my biggest clients." Stevey motions to offer Tom a drink. Tom shakes his head no. "But there's no photo of Sterling up there?"

"He never did a picture I liked. Even his eight-by-tens closed in a week." Stevey toasts Tom and sips his sherry.

"Is that why he hired out as a bodyguard? To make ends meet?" Tom points to a photo of Marilyn on a marble table.

"Can you blame him?" says Stevey with a big grin and Groucho eyebrows, picking up the photo of Marilyn. "She was a dish to be had."

"Yeah, apparently a lot of guys felt that way." Tom chuckles inwardly at Lolly saying those exact words. Crazy how Lolly's story has sent him off on this wild goose chase including Gladys Baker and Grace McKee—her mother and her mother's best friend. Then there were Ida Bolender and Ana Atchinson Lower, Grace McKee's aunt—both foster parents at different times. Too bad Gladys Baker died back in '84 in Gainesville, Florida. Another dead-end trail.

Now, standing here with Stevey Stabler, it's clear he might be Tom's only hope if there's a trail to be sniffed out…

Stevey goes to the window, admiring his own built-in pool with massive Italian ceramics full of tropical flora and fauna. A gardener is trimming the bougainvillea.

"What do you think people think of when they think of Marilyn Monroe?" asks Tom, but Stevey doesn't turn.

"A lot of people don't know this, but she was Hefner's cover model for the very first issue of *Playboy*…" Then he sighs. "She was viewed as being superficial. Damaged. Victimized. Some say she represented tragedy. Misery. A woman swallowed whole by Hollywood."

"And others?" asks Tom.

"Beauty, innocence, excessive superstardom. She was a goddess! Greatest sex symbol of all time. A cultural icon! Like Elvis or Einstein, her face is known worldwide, from Paris to Japan. Always will be…" Tom says nothing, hoping Stevey will add to his thoughts. He does: "Funny thing about that girl. I remember a publicity lunch where we were all marveling how she was the queen of generating PR. She was many 'Marilyns' in one. Far craftier than she let on. She could raise the bar to sexy and then turn it down to mousey in a heartbeat. That takes craft. And brains."

"A very smart girl playing dumb blonde," adds Tom.

"Exactly! Always thought she was a tough one to cast."

Tom moves over to Stevey. The two side by side gazing out on the garden, admiring a Bird of Paradise, Tom speaks first. "So where is this Sterling Powers now?"

"Disappeared in '62…Not that anybody in Hollywood ran to file a missing person's report…"

"Same year Marilyn died."

"You ever see *Secretary's Scandal?*" Stevey turns around to Tom, who shakes his head. "Nah. Didn't think so. Lotta folks here probably think he should have disappeared before he made that one. Yeah…I'm certain he went back to New England. To his roots. Small town. I think it was Yarmouth Port. No, no, Barnyard…something."

"Barnstable?" asks Tom.

"You know it?"

"Sort of. Everyone from New England knows Cape Cod. Barnstable is on the inside of the elbow," says Tom, lifting his arm in a muscle pose to form the shape of the Cape. I grew up in New Hampshire. We'd go there from time to time."

"Shame about Sterling Powers," says Stevey. "He was up for the role of Ben-Hur…"

"So, what happened?"

"Chuck Heston said yes." Stevey lights a pipe and takes a big toke. "Yeah, I thought he was gonna be big. But he stayed small. Very small."

"Hashtag sad," says Tom, to which Stevey frowns, while looking up at Tom's features now. That square jaw and ginger hair framed by the sun poking through the sway of a palm tree from the yard. His face lights in an artistic way. "You ever think of acting, son?"

Tom laughs. "There are those who think I'm acting as a reporter."

"Funny. That's a good one. You're a natural comedian." Stevey goes to his desk and removes a slip of paper from a drawer. "Well, here. If you find Sterling, give him this for me, will you?" He hands Tom a yellowed, wrinkled paper. "Final studio paycheck. He never left a forwarding address. Tell him to cash the darn thing already. Fox Studio hasn't been able to balance their books in more than half a century!"

CHAPTER TWELVE

The seats across from Tom's LAX boarding gate to Boston are empty, providing the perfect place to escape, reflect, and write up his research. Maybe his editor was right…journalism matters when it comes from ethical, trusted sources—and darn it, he'd prove himself! Plugging his phone and laptop into a charger, Tom takes a final bite of his turkey sandwich, sips an iced tea, and recalls the last thing Lolly said to him…typing the notes as he remembers:

"And you know why? 'Cause she committed the biggest sin of all. She never grew old. Every fifteen-year-old boy who has his first 'woodie' over Marilyn in '58 is over almost ninety now. But whenever he sees her in his mind, she still looks the same. All the others—they got old. They got gray. But not her. She cheated it. Marilyn Monroe did die that night, but a bigger star was born. Played the role of a fuckin' lifetime! Fooled the entire goddamn world!"

Tom wipes a napkin across his lips, tucks the sandwich crusts into the wrapper, shoves the debris into the paper bag, and tosses it into the nearby trash. The intercoms call his flight.

Getting situated in his cramped middle seat, a last-minute purchase on Expedia, Tom worries about the final thing his editor practically screamed to him through the receiver when he called in sick. "What do you mean you're *sick*, Hogan? We don't get sick! We can't *afford* to get sick! You were supposed to file the Hollywood has-been story yesterday! Who's the *has-been* now? Huh?"

"I'm taking a detour to Cape Cod," said Tom. "Trust me. This story has a lot of moving parts."

"Moving parts?" screamed Ritter. "They're elderly folks in a nursing home! They don't *have* a lot of moving parts!"

❧

The winding line at the car rental stand at Boston Logan Airport is long. Fortunately, he's booked his Toyota Camry on the Hertz website, which allows for a speedier checkout in the VIP lane. The counter girl is chatty, asking Tom where he's from. Turns out she *too* spent summers on Lake Winnipesaukee—*oh my God! No way!*—proud to tell Tom that it's the largest lake in New Hampshire at twenty-one miles long and contains two hundred and fifty-eight islands that are less than a quarter acre in size.

Tom is always up for a geeky-good geography lesson, and besides, he's a good listener.

But, in all the rental clerk's chitter chatter, she neglects to ask Tom if he prefers a car with snow tires or at the very least all-wheel drive. She does offer to toss in a fifth day free, just in case… and all because he's the first one to engage conversation with her all day. "Everyone else has their faces buried in their phones. But listen, you have a safe drive," says the clerk, handing him his documents. "And have a clam chowder for me!"

"Thank you," he says, "I will for sure!" Tom places the documents in his backpack, freeing up his left hand to grasp his luggage handle and, most importantly, leaving his right hand free for a Dunkin' Donuts coffee, double cream, no sugar. There's a stand just ahead past the rental booths. *Ah, New England.*

Home.

He'll need caffeine for the hour and a half ride down the South Shore, especially with traffic. Boston's central artery is always a congested mess where the major routes coincide at I-90, Route 3, and I-93. *Couldn't the Pilgrims have planned for a better roadmap?*

Navigating onto I-93 South, Tom places his coffee in the cup holder, pressing a button on his cell phone. Speed dial. A few rings before the person picks up.

"Hiya, Lolly? It's Tom Hogan."

"You got the Habanos, kid?"

"I'll bring the cigars next time I visit."

"Why you soundin' like you're in a cave?"

"I'm driving. I've got you on speaker phone," says Tom. "Hey, I've got a question. On the autopsy inconsistencies…there's a theory that Jimmy Hoffa had Marilyn killed. Kennedy was a victim of blackmail by the mob. Or, maybe, it was an injection by Bobby Kennedy that killed her…like all those rumors that circulate online about her missing diary."

"Or, maybe, just maybe, the whole thing was a cover up like I told ya," says Lolly. "Don't you listen, kid? It was a fake corpse. The real one got away! Maybe, just maybe, Kennedy *helped* her to get away." Lolly's voice goes tender. "Always had a soft spot for RFK. Family man. He and Ethel were like swans—together for life. Bobby never should have been dragged into that mess. Maybe he felt sorry for Marilyn, is all. Maybe helped her get away. I don't know."

"Didn't you do the RFK autopsy too?"

"Yes," he says, almost embarrassed to admit it. "And sadly, I remember like it was yesterday. Never goes away. Having to perform *his* autopsy in '68 was the worst of 'em that came through. But five years before he died, Bobby was attorney general. Had the power to issue Marilyn an entirely new identity. Her diary mysteriously disappeared that night, sure, but so did Marilyn…"

"And the diary?"

"Probably packed it in her luggage," says Lolly.

"Some say there was CIA information written inside that RFK may have leaked to her," says Tom "So, he *made* it disappear...."

"Maybe. Like I said. RFK was a decent family man. If he made the diary disappear, it was to protect her too. Before *she* disappeared."

"Okay, fair enough. But another rumor claimed that the killers got into Marilyn's bedroom and injected her with drugs directly into her bloodstream rather than pills, which was why her stomach was empty. And the death certificate? The one that's available?"

"Signed by Lionel Grandison, deputy coroner," says Lolly, with the certainty of a Jeopardy answer.

"Yes, I know. But wait? So, you had a corpse?" asks Tom, still slightly confused.

"Jesus, kid. Yes! Some Jane Doe. From another morgue drawer," says Lolly. "Amazing how a platinum wig can turn a dead dame into a Marilyn look-alike."

Tom's throat seizes up and his heart begins thundering, pounding. He almost swerves into another car he's so stunned by what he's hearing. "But why would you *care* to help Marilyn get away?"

"Why wouldn't I? We investigated all types of bizarre stuff. Kinky sex, sadistic shit, you name it. We got tired of it all. She was a beautiful, damaged icon. Made me feel good to help her. Chivalry," says Lolly. "You know chivalry? Today it's dead."

"No, it's not. My grandfather taught me to open the car door for a girl...always pay for a meal."

"Good. Glad to hear it," says Lolly with sarcasm.

Tom switches lanes to ride slower along the shoulder. He wants this conversation to last longer. "Hey, Lolly? I was just reading in Noguchi's book how forensic medicine—"

"Why you givin' that bastard royalties?"

"Just go with me. I was on a plane…nothing else to do but read," says Tom, watching the green overhead signs for the Plymouth exit illuminated by headlights. "Apparently, coroners came to be because in the year 1192 there was a European crime, and because of that crime, a new title was established for certain knights of the English realm. 'Coroner' was the new word. You were the *real* deal, Lolly." A dead silence from the other end. "Lolly? Lolly, you there?"

"Thanks. I'm here, kid. Just busy with my sippy cup." Tom hears Lolly put the cap on his flask. Tom has his doubts that the guy is just an old drunk looking for attention, but there's a part of Tom that wonders why he'd go to these lengths… "Did Natalie Wood accidentally drown or was she murdered?" asks Lolly. "Was Belushi murdered? And so on…"

"That's amazing," says Tom. "All those stories left open-ended."

"Who wants stories left open-ended? Not me! It was my job to *close* them," says Lolly. "You know, not everyone respected us… Sinatra wrote a letter to the Board of Supervisors saying that coroners should be seen and not heard. *Fucker.*"

"As if you chose to have those famous bodies to come through your office…" says Tom, empathizing with Lolly.

Lolly sighs through the receiver. It's as if time moves in one direction, memory in another. "I'd like to see the world go with that fourth or fifth conspiracy…the one that says that Sinatra flew Marilyn's body to Palm Springs from her house in Brentwood during those missing hours before she was pronounced dead. The housekeeper that found her—"

"Eunice Murray?"

"Eunice was on Peter Lawford's payroll all along. You ever hear about Lawford?"

"The one married to Bobby Kennedy's sister, Pat? Yes, she was one of Marilyn's close friends, right?"

"You've been doing your homework," says Lolly. "I like that."

Tom's mind is churning as he approaches the last exit before the Cape Cod bridge.

"Imagine me," Lolly continues, "being in an office with three full-time pathologists, a handful of lab techs, and some part-time residents studying pathology…when supposedly in comes the most famous star of all time. For us coroners, the pay was shit, but we all thought our jobs had meaning. We thought we could make a difference."

"Did you?"

"We did better!" says Lolly with pride in his voice. "She got away, didn't she?" Lolly lets out a hefty chuckle.

Tom's on the entry to the Sagamore Bridge, now crossing into Cape Cod. The road is a bit slick. Some unexpected black ice from the dipping temperatures. He holds tightly to the wheel as Lolly rambles on from his speaker phone. "Ah, it's all different today. You could get away with it back then. Hell, today there's even forensic dentistry…"

"Hey Lolly, I gotta go. The roads are bad…"

"Yeah, sure. Just don't call again til you got those cigars and the Maker's Mark you promised. I miss my bourbon!"

Tom disconnects the call jut as he passes the sign on Route 6. "Welcome to Cape Cod." Part of the knot Tom's been carrying begins to loosen. He's here. He's *really* here.

But is Marilyn?

CHAPTER THIRTEEN

On the windy scenic road of Route 6A, the old black-and-white sign reads: "Entering Barnstable. Established 1639."

Tom's car curves through a corridor of trees with gnarly branches of various maple, ash, cherry, and oak trees. They gloriously canopy the Old King's Highway historic route. Lowering the window, Tom inhales the cold and wintery Cape Cod air. It's as if a fisherman grabbed his best bottle of aftershave and anointed the town with the essence of sea salt, beach plums, and Pitch pine.

Entering the village, Tom senses something poetic, almost spiritual, here. There's not a designer on a Hollywood movie set who could have made this town up.

Barnstable has a general store, a library—though probably not focused on *New York Times*' sensations like Trevor Noah's *Born a Crime* or James Patterson's Alex Cross series. No, this is where locals and tourists find every book on Eastern Shore creatures or *1,001 Ways to Bird Watch.* The old courthouse on the hill stands older and taller than anything else, dating back to the mid-1600s when the legal disputes were things like "he stole my horse's harness" or "my wife plowed *his* field instead of mine."

We see an older gentleman hand-plucking dried winter weeds to eradicate them once and for all from the stone wall. Hearing a car, the gent balances on his cane to glance up, wave. Tom waves back.

Stopping at a crossroad, Tom allows two Bible-clutching ladies to cross, heading up to St. Mary's Episcopal church. The two women wave in rapid gratitude. Tom nods from behind his steering wheel, studying them as they stroll with a skip in their orthopedic shoes. Bundled up from the nipping December wind, they're navy peacoats are secured to the top. Red woolen scarves poke out from their necks, practically covering their faces.

Tom's mind wanders at hidden identities…remembering that every six months Marilyn had to change residence because of the hounding press. She changed her phone number routinely too. Another time, Hollywood couldn't believe that a "dumb blonde" like Marilyn had managed to escape Hollywood to a New York dinner party once, booking a flight under the fake name "Zelda Zonk" and landing in LaGuardia without any reporters. From there, she and her friend Milton Greene drove to Weston, Connecticut.

If Marilyn could do it once, who says she couldn't do it again? Only this time for good.

And maybe, farther east. To Cape Cod. The land of the agenda-free.

She loved the coast. If Manhattan always seemed to beckon, and after living in a fishbowl for so long, maybe hitching a ride with Sterling Powers to this bucolic village was the one place she could swim freely…

Tom drives very slowly past a clapboard structure housing the district attorney's office. Everything seems to be in the singular here. The post office, the drycleaner, the market, the realtor. There's something liberating about the lack of choices. And certainly in the singular for the last parking space. Tom snags it.

Gazing up in his rearview mirror, Tom thinks that there might be this theory or that theory on Marilyn, but none of them matter because he's not looking to rehash her death, he's looking to *resurrect* her life.

Locking his rental, Tom heads onto the brick sidewalk, drawn to a place with a wooden sign swinging on its hinges:

The Porpoise. He studies the building. There's a good chance the Revolutionary War may have been planned at this tavern.

He pulls open the rustic handle, lowering his head to avoid slamming into the overhead beam. His eyes scan the cavernous, wood-paneled room, festively decorated with Christmas ornaments, wreaths, and blinking lights. In the low-lit space of the bar, divided from the dining area, he sees a bunch of old timers. *Great! Like I need another time warp...* He's just had Stevey the agent and Lolly the coroner. *Who's next? President John Adams?* At the least, he's hoping for a *Sam* Adams. Specifically, the beer.

Taking the last stool at the end of the bar, Tom gets the sense that everybody knows everybody here, and it shows. He tunes into a conversation next to him about searching for snow owls down at the Long Pasture Sanctuary.

A waitress, not pretty in the classic sense, brushes her highlighted bangs out of her eyes to display a bit more makeup than face. "Evening. I'm Elizabeth. What'll it be?"

"Sam Adams would be great," says Tom. "Thank you."

She nods, turning to the tap on the wooden bar full of nostalgia. Boston Bruins pennants, Patriots bobbleheads, and Red Sox memorabilia galore. In a corner, some political paraphernalia dating back to a bumper sticker that reads *Reagan Bush '84*. And next to that, an 8x10 photo of John F. Kennedy on his sailboat with his brother Teddy.

"What's your most popular dinner?" asks Tom, scanning the laminated menu and noticing the festive Christmas tree in the corner.

The man on the next stool, as weather-beaten as many of the seaport houses, chimes in. "Chowdah's what folks come here for. G'head Elizabeth. Tell him how you won the Chowdah Fest last year."

"Ah Mayah, it wasn't first prize. It only took the orange ribbon."

"Well, you should've won. Too much Worcestershire sauce in the winner's batch if you ask me." He turns to Tom. "Mayor Herman Bisbee," says the mayor, tipping his beer toward their guest in a toast. "Welcome to Barnstable. How was your Christmas?"

"Tom Hogan, happy to meet you, Sir. Christmas was good." Tom toasts his beer mug back with an added nod of respect.

"You got any problems you come to me," says Mayor Bisbee. "But there aren't any problems here."

"Thank you, Mister Mayor, sir," says Tom.

"So what brings you to Barnstable, Tom? Family?" The mayor slides his side of French fries to Tom, who dutifully takes one.

"No, I don't have family here," says Tom. "Just visiting."

"I didn't think so. And tourist season's long over..." says the mayor, prying.

"Family's in New Hampshire," offers Tom, shifting the conversation. "Grandfather and my mom are up in Lake Winnipesaukee."

"Well, that makes you a Red Sox fan, eh?"

"Always," says Tom, sipping his beer and stealing a couple more French fries.

Two fishermen pull up two stools other side of the mayor. Large men. Craggy. One with a face so wrinkly you could hide stuff there.

"Catch anything out there today, boys?" asks the mayor.

"Nah," says the first fisherman. "Didn't have a swell. Tide's out. Elizabeth, my throat's as dry as a spar yard. What's on tap?"

"Damn you, Scotty Dog, you've been asking me that question every day for ten years, and every day I tell you 'Sam Adams.' So what do you think is on tap today?"

"Sam Adams?" he asks sarcastically.

Elizabeth laughs and draws two for them.

"Boys...meet Tom Hogan," says the mayor, slapping Tom on the back. "Maybe he can help us solve the turtle stranding problem down on the Bay."

The fisherman who inquired about the taps introduces himself as Scotty Harden, then shakes Tom's hand so hard that upon pulling back his arm, Tom has to check to whether it's still there. The other fisherman says his name is Charley Button.

"Now Tommy, don't you let these boys bore you with the big one that got away..." the mayor continues.

"Wait, did you say turtle stranding?" asks Tom.

"Sure did," says the mayor, "got a stranding problem on the shore."

"I *know* about turtle strandings," says Tom with a dose of earnest excitement. "Turtles are supposed to migrate south, but the sudden change in sea temps can cold stun them, so they're carried by tide and wind to the shore. People strolling along the beach might think they're dead, but they're not. They're just stunned. Worst thing to do is put them back in the water. Better to move them to a higher ground, cover them with seaweed, mark the spot in the sand with stones or a stick, and call the Audubon Society."

The mayor's eyebrows shoot up to his hairline. "Well, I'll be...." says Mayor Bisbee. "You really *are* a New England boy."

Tom nods and goes in for a meek sip of his beer.

Elizabeth turns to the fishermen. "So did you call the gatehouse down at Sandy Neck Beach?"

As the men banter on, Tom's eyes inconspicuously glance about...wondering about Marilyn. *What might she look like if she walked through this door?* Not only did she frequently change phone numbers, she also wore disguises. According to multiple biographers, she wore black wigs, no makeup, and clothes that were a size too big. Shapeless. By psyching herself out of Marilyn and back to the girl-next-door, Norma Jeane, she could go incognito. Absolutely and completely unrecognizable.

Apparently, according to what Tom's read, after 1949, not another photograph existed that showed her natural curly and brown hair. As a starlet, there were times in her films she would change her blonde hair to many different tones as variable as

Parisian buildings along the Seine. Ivory, platinum, parchment, vanilla, golden…fifty shades of blonde. *Was she still blonde today? Or had she gone gray?*

"What's your thought, Tommy?" says the mayor. "I don't want these two boring you with arbitration about removing that existing wharf down on Freezer Point."

"And you just be careful, Tommy," says Scotty, "or the mayor will be telling you how he won the Korean War all by his lonesome."

A bowl of chowder and a side of oyster crackers are plopped down in front of Tom, who blows slowly on the first taste before slurping. He lights up. "This is awesome!"

"This is Cape Cod," says Elizabeth, proud face, placing down a small plate of corn bread. It's clear she's taken to Tom, full of respect and appreciation for the small and finer things in life… unlike those demanding tourists of summer.

"Tom," says the mayor, "you're in a tavern that can fix a roast beef and baked bean supper for two hundred at the church picnic and keep every bit pipin' hot! Right Elizabeth?"

"Well, 'cept the ice cream," chuckles Elizabeth.

Tom glances below the bar at his cell phone resting on his lap, watching as it attempts to update his email inbox, but the loading icon just spins and spins. Nothing. The mayor catches this. "We don't get good service in the village. That's what makes us special. Disconnected from the real world."

"I think that's great. I think that Cape Cod is one of those rare places that moves forward by simply standing still," smiles Tom.

The group ponders Tom's sentiment.

"Aw, that's beautiful," says Elizabeth, nodding to the mayor as if to say, *We like this kid.*

Tom leans in. "Can I ask you something?" The mayor nods. "Ever heard of a guy named Sterling Powers?"

The mayor shrugs. "Who wants to know?"

"Just curious," says Tom.

"Never heard of him," says Scotty.

"He was an actor. Went to Hollywood in the fifties," says Tom. "This is supposed to be his hometown."

"Before my time," says Charley Button, who looks to the mayor, who lands his glance at Tom, clearly wondering why he's asking. Tom picks up on it yet is astute enough to know that Cape Cod is and was a breeding ground for famous, reclusive artists and writers—Kurt Vonnegut, Norman Mailer, Edward Gorey…

"I'm working on a novel on old Hollywood," says Tom. "About Westerns, to be exact, so I thought…"

"Oh," says the mayor, a sigh of relief coming over him. "Gee whiz, Tom, you're a writer. Why didn't you say so. You'll need to talk to ole Henry…" *Just what Tom needs. Another old timer.* "Yup, Henry Bartholemew III," the mayor explains. "Town Historian. Every little burg in New England has a Henry, what's left of them. He can tell you the what the weather was on the night the Collins Hotel burnt to the ground. Never forgets a thing."

"Where can I find him?" asks Tom, dipping a piece of corn bread to clean the remnants of the chowder bowl's edge.

"Just missed him. Went up to Vermont to visit friends for the holiday. Not sure he'll be back for the New Year. But you can check the Sturgis Library. They'll have something or another to help you get started."

"Okay, will do."

"And if you stick around a couple days for New Years' Eve, we've got our big costume party," says the mayor. "Sky's the limit on what to wear."

"You should go," says Elizabeth. "Lots of folks there will be able to help you out until Henry returns."

"Okay, I might…" says Tom with a smile and making scribble marks in the air to Elizabeth, suggesting he's ready for his check. She rips a page off her pad and slaps it down, but the mayor grabs it.

"Your money is no good here. I got this one. In the spirit of Christmas, welcome to Barnstable, Tommy. And be careful while you're here, okay?" The mayor stares at Tom for a beat. And another. Then slaps him on the back and exits. Elizabeth watches the slight fear in Tom's face.

"Don't mind him, Tom," says Elizabeth. "Sometimes he thinks he's God. He's probably headed out to the bay right now for walking-on-water practice."

Tom thanks Elizabeth and the fishermen for the evening. He heads out to where the fierce, bitter cold freezes his nose hairs. The street is dark and quiet. Tom can see his breath as he clicks the key fob to unlock his car. Placing his cell phone in the cup holder while clicking on his seatbelt, the service suddenly kicks in. Several texts. There's one from his mother asking how he's doing and saying how much she missed him for Christmas this year but she understands he has to work. And there's another one from his editor back in LA. "Get-eth thy ass-eth into thine office or you're fired. Now-eth!"

With frozen fingers, Tom goes to text back, composing a text, repeatedly hitting the wrong key, deleting, backing up, retyping. But something stops him. It's the music…

Like a strange omen, the car radio plays "Luck Be a Lady Tonight." Tom remembers something Lolly said when he asked him, "Did someone set up Marilyn's life? A trust?"

"Look, kid, I only lifted the sheet from the steel table. I don't know how she financed her life after her death. Maybe her buddy, Frank Sinatra, gave her one sixteenth of a nickel every time "My Way" played on the radio because…she did it her *way!"*

"But that song came out in '69."

"Well, maybe she had a stash of cash under her mattress until '69. Maybe she got a job as a school custodian. How the hell do I know, Clouseau?"

CHAPTER FOURTEEN

New Year's Eve—December 31, 2019

Tom stands in the corner, observing this *absurd* costume party. He's careened his neck in every direction, but there isn't one guest that looks even *remotely* like Marilyn Monroe.

Teeming with kooks and characters, there's a couple of Elvises out on the patio. Tom watches the two elderly impersonators secure their tipsy pompadour wigs. One with a big belly threatens to burst the sequin buttons holding on for dear life. There's a *whole lotta lovin'* going on there for sure.

To Tom's left, there's an outrageous drag queen in Lady Gaga couture, complete with shoulder pads and plumes. To Tom's right is the *fourth* Cher he's counted in forty minutes. Near the fireplace, there's Belle from *Beauty and the Beast* in the classic yellow gown with the hourglass corset. She's tossing back whiskey shots with the Beast.

Tom eyes open wide. *Finally! There she is! Marilyn Monroe!* A six-foot *strapping* man in Marilyn drag. His date, another man, a bit emaciated, in Audrey Hepburn attire; the string of pearls around his neck weighing more than he does.

Tom runs a hand through his hair. *Shit!* He spent the last of his airline miles on his one-way ticket. The car rental was no bargain either. All for this…the land of seaports, flip-flops, clam chowder, and Kennedys. *Cape fucking Cod! On a hunch!*

This time his editor is *really* going to kill him. That is assuming he can get *back* to Los Angeles if his debit card doesn't decline.

Last he peeked, his account had a couple thousand dollars. His auto-deposit paycheck doesn't go in until *next* Friday. Tom gulps. *How long can he keep up this charade of motel rooms and dining out?*

Tom sweats. He fidgets with his shirt collar, clearly *dying* to remove his tie. Glances at his wristwatch, the family heirloom given to him by his grandfather, Herbert Hogan. Tom will have to sell it to make next month's rent after he's fired!

He can see it all now…Tom in a small U-Haul heading back to New England. Grandfather waiting on the porch of his yellow cottage with the white picket fence. *Hi Grandpa, I'm home…your* pathetic *grandson took a risk to chase a story that never existed. So, I just need to crash in your guestroom…for the rest of my life!*

The Citizen watch reads 11:30 p.m.

Eyes darting around the party again, if it keeps up like this Tom will be kissing some Liza Minelli at midnight. Sipping awkwardly from his plastic tumbler, his ice jiggles empty. Navigating his way through the crowd, the room pulses to the band Crazy Town's one-hit-wonder: "Butterfly" about some sugar baby driving him crazy. *Whatever!*

Tom attempts to be inconspicuous, self-effacing, fake swaying his hips to suggest enthusiasm, stalling momentarily to admire two teens dancing the floss. Tom suddenly feels very old. One teen is dressed as Jon Snow from *Game of Thrones.* His date is dressed as Eleven from *Stranger Things.*

Nodding and smiling at the teens—heck, he was just one a few years back—Tom begins doing the math in his brain. Even if he *found* Marilyn Monroe, she'd be like what? Ninety-five? She'd look way different than the world remembers. Certainly not the curvaceous platinum blonde bombshell.

Growing desperate, Tom is certain that there aren't any octogenarian partygoers here, unless you count the two women in the corner window seat. One is dressed as the Notorious RBG in a starched white ruffle collar and hair in a neatly pinned back bun. She's got Supreme Court justice written all over her. Ruth Bader Ginsburg is deep into conversation with *another* notorious Ruth…Dr. Ruth Westheimer, the German sex therapist. Their faces don't suggest even a hint of Marilyn.

Signaling for another gin with a splash of tonic at the bar, Tom catches a glimpse of himself in the mirror behind the server. Turning his chin upward, he admires his jaw. The type of jaw an artist might sketch. Strong but square, like the way he's feeling. He's never thought of himself as particularly handsome or even cool. More that guy from the high school yearbook that won "Most Dependable"—a pimply, ginger-haired friend to the devastated cheerleader just after the star quarterback left her with a broken heart and a neck hickey.

Tipping his tumbler in thanks to the server, a woman steps up for a refill of wine.

Tom tries to place her. She's dressed in a Tehuana dress with a vivid red rebozo shawl, a starched lace headdress, and a string of vibrant Aztec beads. "Let me guess," says Tom. "You're Frida Kahlo."

Frida knits her recognizable unibrow, scanning Tom. "No costume?" she asks loudly.

"This is it," says Tom, speaking over the music, glancing down at his nerdy navy jacket, pressed beige khakis, and red striped tie. "I'm dressed as a reporter," he shouts over the music. "You know…from a thing we used to call a newspaper."

"Ha!" Frida guffaws. "That's funny."

"No. Sadly it's serious." Tom clicks his tumbler to her glass before adding, "Excuse me." He moves on, banging into the arm of a devastatingly handsome young man. Their eyes lock. Recognition. "*Hey,* aren't you…"

"Yes Ronan," he extends a hand. His teeth pearly white and movie-star dazzling. "Ronan Farrow." says the man. "Happy New Year."

Seriously it could be him. Blonde, piercing blue eyes, and his father's dimples. Tom can't seem to let go of Ronan's hand. He studies his features. *Can't be. Could it?* "I saw your father just over there," says Tom, craning neck muscles toward the backside of a man wearing a black wool fedora. Frank Sinatra. Ronan chuckles and moves on.

Just then, something tells Tom to look to where the energy in the room has shifted. At the front door a young woman enters. She like a Polaroid picture getting sharper as it slowly comes into focus. Tom's seeing her like he's never seen *anyone* before.

Her body language is like the popular girl in high school who carries herself with purpose. She's in costume from the '60s, raising a sign with WE SHALL OVERCOME written in bold red caps. *Gloria Steinem, no?* She lowers her tinted Foster Grant aviators and scans the joint. He catches her eyes. She pauses for a moment to examine him. Smirks.

Tom squints from the overhead lights, smiles, and registers the moment.

The party music shuffles to a classic and the voice of Aretha Franklin belts out over the speakers.

Intuition tells Tom that Gloria is about to turn and leave, but somehow their connection is ridiculously poignant. There's an unspoken understanding that they're the only two people on the inside of this party, longing to be on the outside.

As if he's been anointed by this, this, this—um, *goddess*, the room is shrinking, the walls closing in. *He's got to get to her!* Forget that there's something about her that commands respect just like Aretha's song, she's just plain *hot!* All long-leggy in a denim miniskirt, Gloria's long brown hair flat ironed and perfectly parted. She's Tom Hogan's kind of girl.

In an instant, he's bypassing Sonny Bono and Adam Levine—together, *creepy*—to get in range of Gloria. He studies her as he approaches. She's not wearing a bit of makeup. *Au naturel.* Yet, there's something sinfully sexy about her.

Now he's a foot away. Her eyes are sad, pained, and crystal blue. She smiles at Tom. From the nose up, she has a face just familiar enough to be interesting. But that smile. That smile says pure Hyannisport.

Is she…? Nah. She's way *too young to be Marilyn Monroe, let alone the* daughter *of Marilyn Monroe. Heck, she might be too young to know who the hell Marilyn Monroe even was!*

Tom's mesmerized by Gloria. He's in front of her now.

Gloria watches Tom's throat move as he sips from his tumbler, ice awkwardly pushing at the tip of his nose. Tom peers over the rim at Gloria like a nerd in the cafeteria who's just spied the prom queen, wondering if she's out of his dating league. *She is.*

Their eyes lock. They say nothing. Silence speaking volumes.

Finally, the trance is broken when someone slams into his arm, and his ice goes flying. Down his tie.

Her lips part. Her mouth moves gently. Gloria speaks in a kitten purr. "What's a girl gotta do to get a drink around here?"

A moment to process, and Tom says the only thing he can think of, "Um, follow me." She smiles. She has that kind of face that when she smiles the whole world smiles too.

As Tom leads the way to the bar, his nerves trembling, his clammy hand clutching hers, but his mind is pounding like a wind-up toy monkey with a drum. *God, why didn't I dress up? What does this girl have to do with my assignment?*

Yes. The painting! That *damn* painting!

On the other hand, if Tom didn't buy that stupid, *stupid* painting, well, he wouldn't have met the girl of his dreams...Marilyn or no Marilyn.

With Gloria's hand tucked into his pulsing palm, Tom spots another bar on the back porch—a portable card table set up with a floral plastic tablecloth. A couple of bottles of wine in a cooler with soda water, a saucer of lemons and limes, and a bottle of vodka make it official.

"This will do, yeah?" asks Tom, scanning the space. Even though the yard furniture is flipped over and buttoned-up for winter, it's charming enough for Tom and Gloria to carve out a space to sit. For a moment they just gaze at each other. The silence communicates attraction rather than uncertainty. He decides to actually speak. "Hi," his voice quivers. "I'm Tom...Tom Hogan." His smile ignites as his complexion goes beet red with anticipation.

"Tom, huh?" she says. "I'm Penelope. Last name Morton. But you can just call me 'Nell' for short. Everybody does." She extends a hand. "Nell Morton."

"Wait a second, Penelope, last name Morton..." says Tom, "so you're *not* Gloria Steinem?"

Nell giggles. "No, I'm *not* Gloria Steinem. But I am what she represents: Respect. Or is that Aretha?" She motions to the soundtrack playing.

"Aretha."

Over near the heater, Hillary Clinton notices Nell. "Hello, Miss Morton," she winks. "Hello, Mrs. Clinton," says Nell, a sarcasm to her tone, "I voted for Bernie, you know." Hillary is in conversation with Queen Elizabeth about the Sturgis Library book drive.

In the other corner, next to a large red Christmas poinsettia, the other Queen—Freddie Mercury—is in heavy debate with Shakespeare about the marina slip contracts that are due to be paid to the harbormaster by May. When he sees Nell, Shakespeare moves back to his post at the table to pour drinks.

"Hello!" says Nell, unleashing a big toothy smile to the four of them.

Shakespeare winks. "Your usual, Nell?"

"Yes, please," she says, pulling up her go-go boots that are loosely sliding down her silky, long calves.

"To thine own self be true," says Shakespeare. Tom watches the bartender mix Nell's usual. Crushed lemon and lime, some mint sprigs, and sparkling water. No alcohol here. He hands the drink to Nell.

"I'll have the same, please, sir," says Tom, pressing his hands deep into the pocket of his jeans as if trying to dig for something cool to say to her.

"Nell, did you read about the new dinghy storage requirements?" asks Hillary Clinton.

"No," she answers. "Was it posted?"

"Down at town hall," she says. "Decals available starting February."

"Why do you need decals?" asks Tom, waiting on his pummeled lemon and water mix.

"If your vessel goes adrift, the decal aids in recovery efforts," she explains. "But you have to have a mooring to start with…like Shakespeare here."

"The lady doth protest too much," says Shakespeare, and everyone chuckles.

Seconds later, Tom and Nell's eyes meet and they toast their mocktails. "To 2020," says Nell with sincerity. They sip their concoctions. "I don't recognize you from town," says Nell. "Visiting?"

"Yes—ah no, well, sort of," says Tom. "Mayor Bisbee told me about this party." Tom shifts the conversation back on her. "So why an activist?"

"A feminist to be precise," says Nell, circling her straw into her drink.

"Okay. So why a feminist?" he asks.

"Um, because my grandmother always asked if I could write a note to my younger self in two words or less, what would I say…"

"And what would you say in two words or less?"

"Rebel, rebel."

Tom practically inhales her answer. She's emotionally precise. And besides, he loves Bowie!

It's a funny thing about this girl. Somehow her visual beauty subsides as her cerebral emerges. Tom isn't sure what to say next, but an old speaker inside the dining room crackles with a slower romantic soundtrack. Only minutes before midnight, and everyone *ewwws* and *ahhhs* sentimentality.

Shakespeare takes Hillary into his arms, and they sway. Queen Elizabeth and Freddy Mercury do the same.

"Would you like to have this dance?" asks Tom, formal, nerdy—but fairly certain she won't decline.

"Sure," Nell purrs, the other side of shy. She runs her fingers through her hair, tucking the strands behind her ear, before resting her hand on his shoulder, just like at a high school dance. In a matter of seconds, Nell buries her head into Tom's collar. He smells like work, which oddly translates to some sort of stability. A pleasurable sorrow overtakes her as if she's been missing something in her life.

Blood thunders through Tom's chest and shatters down the back of his spine. Whatever is happening is changing the gravity of their space. This party has morphed into their own VIP experience.

As the two move across the threshold and into the thick of the dining room, the people around them can most certainly feel it, too. Here they are, two kids from this generation, completely connected, minus the short attention span of some perpetual internet kingdom…the one that the *outside* world accuses them of being so obsessed with "at their age." No, these two are very much connected in real time.

Nell inhales. She can feel their chakras merging, rising, and then exhaling. Together, they're at an intersection of so many identities.

But Tom feels with her in his arms, he's found his direction… and its straight ahead!

Just an hour ago, Tom was trying to figure out where to find Marilyn Monroe…yet, suddenly the suicidal icon is the last thing that matters. Because *this* thing—this connection—it has no logic. Never in high school or even college did he understand what love might feel like, until this. *This, this*…whatever it is. It might clearly be just starting out, but somehow it feels like they've always been together…right *here.*

The song ends. Silence. There's a beat of awkwardness as they let go of each other, their eyes remaining fused. Tom is the first to break the spell. "That was nice. Thank you." She nods and smiles. With a hoarse whisper he asks, "So, Gloria Steinem, what exactly is feminism today?" This time, Nell takes his hand and leads him back to the indoor porch, plopping down on the wicker loveseat that hasn't been stored away yet. She pats a plaid cushion and readjusts it. Tom turns over a wicker foot stool, resting it near her knees.

"What is feminism?" she asks. "Feminism is the struggle to end all sexist oppression, don't you think?" He nods, figuring that she could say feminism was the Salem witches attending *Disney on Ice* and he'd believe her. She continues, "It doesn't matter what race, color, or religion you are. Not really. It's about equality. But believe me, we have bigger issues right now like capitalism and white supremacy and border policies…"

"Agreed," says Tom.

"I went to my first woman's march a couple years ago."

"Really? Gloria would be proud!"

"For one thing, it was *cold* outside, so we were all bundled up in big puffy coats," says Nell. "It was the experience of a lifetime. I've barely ever crossed the Sagamore Bridge, let alone visit Washington, DC!"

"Sweet!" says Tom. "I watched all those incredible women on TV. It was January, right? Largest single-day protest in US History." Tom's glad he remembers being tuned in.

"Day after Trump's inauguration," she smirks. "It was a very bold statement."

"I'm impressed," says Tom, beyond smitten with Nell.

"What will be impressive is if it all pays off. Equal rights, women's rights, and most of all, reproductive rights. Something my mother fought for..." Nell vibrates with chatter even at the most dismal of topics. "And, I mean, look at the utter feeling of being disenfranchised...and our national debt."

"Gosh," say Tom "I can hardly wait for 2020 to begin."

"It's here," says Nell, leaning in to peck his cheek. "We've managed to miss the countdown with our mini debate."

"Is that what we're calling this? A debate? You're doing all the talking." He winks, his assurance kicking in.

As the folks inside make a big hoopla about the calendar turn, Nell and Tom are more comfortable in each other's zones.

"Happy New Year," says Tom, tangling his fingers into hers.

"Happy New Year yourself," she says, leaning in to take a sip of her sparkling water before carrying on with her rant. "Look," she says, "if men would just give women the same respect as they give gas, gold, and oil through the ages..."

He's speechless. He's sold. *Who's she been reading? Who's she been listening to?* She clearly has texture. The type that chooses to reside in a seaport town with its very *real* people. She's not the type to care for Instagram or TikTok, he just *knows* it, because neither is he...that type. She'd rather involve herself with saving the planet and is far more tapped into what matters then *any* of the girls he's dated. It's beyond refreshing.

"Tommy? Don't you agree about the marshes?" says Nell, but Tom's off in La La Land.

"Huh? Oh, of course," says Tom, pulling a comment out of his ass. "All the marshes with the tall grasses. The ducks can easily be strangled by those plastic six-pack rings that littered about. And what about our oceans? We must save them!"

"Well, exactly," agrees Nell. "So, you'll join me then? Tomorrow? For the Polar Bear Plunge?"

"The who? Um, yes, sure," says Tom, with a drummed-up enthusiasm. He has no idea what he's in for, but he senses that for her, happiness is linked to community and nature. As for him, everything that keeps him stable has now turned to quicksand at her feet.

"Hey, I hate to do this, but I gotta go," says Nell, rising abruptly to leave. Tom rises too. "Don't bother to walk me out," she insists, putting a hand on his chest to stop him. "I can hitch a ride from my neighbor, Cher, just over there." Nell waves and mouths the words "ready when you are" to Cher.

"Wait! Another Cher?" asks Tom. But from behind, the backside of this Cher is a disproportionate, much heavier version with comfort-sole boat shoes under her gown. "Okay, so Polar Bear Plunge…" he repeats, agreeing to whatever it takes to see her again.

"Yeah, it'll be a blast. Besides, it funds the Suicide Hotline… which is why I have to leave now. I'm on call at 6 a.m. and it's already…like…late."

"That's great that you do that," he says, standing awkwardly and debating whether to lean in for a kiss or not.

"Come down to Mill Way tomorrow," she says. "It bottoms out to a residents-only beach. *Tons* of people will be there."

With that, she turns to go, leaving Tom alone, the color draining from his face. As he watches her go, he feels like he might faint. He watches Cher put a coat around Nell's shoulders like a loving aunt might do.

Nell turns to wave goodbye. Cher catches their exchange and nods approval at Tom, as he realizes Cher is Mayor Bisbee.

"Raided my wife's closet!" the mayor hollers out, removing his long black wig. Tom chuckles, before blowing a kiss to Nell. She pretends to snatch it midair and plant it on her cheek.

She's out the door, and Tom is in awe. Nell is a perfect blend of vulnerability and confidence. He can only think one thing…

All his life he believed he would find her. All his life he believed she was there…

Penelope "Nell" Morton that is. Not Marilyn Monroe.

CHAPTER FIFTEEN

Different venue, same players. This is the Seaside Café, a village hot spot for breakfast, where an egg is not *just* an egg. Tom scans the "Benny lineup" on the menu, in awe of the variations on the classic…like the Porto with mushrooms, or the Nordic with slices of smoked salmon. He slams his menu closed, decides on a side of cheesy grits with his breakfast burrito *loaded* with avocados, peppers, mozzarella—*the works!*

A waitress approaches with the coffee. "Cream and shugah?" It's going to take a while to get used to the thickness of the accents here.

"Black, please, thank you." He pushes his cup forward. "I guess I've missed the morning rush?"

"You are the morning rush. It's January."

He chuckles, and the waitress looks to his dining partner, Town Historian, Henry Bartholemew III, back from his visit to Vermont. He shakes his head no on the coffee, too busy doing some sort of equation in his head, mumbling to himself.

One table over is Elizabeth from The Porpoise, enjoying a New Year's morning. She's already acknowledged Tom and Henry.

"So, as you were saying…" Tom asks Henry.

Henry taps his fingers together, a scarecrow come to life. "Course that was back in '58 before the hurricane hit. Or was it… come to think …'59, right after Judith Garnick gave birth to her triplets. But those fishing expeditions aren't what they used to be. Sea bass are *feistier* now. Thornton Wilder once said, 'In our town, we like to know the facts about everybody.' Now what were you asking about, young man?"

The breakfast burrito arrives. Tom takes a bite, then wipes his mouth with his napkin. "Mayor Bisbee wasn't kidding when he said you know everything about everyone. Never met a true town historian until you."

"Aw, shucks, I only go back to about 1961. Or maybe just to '63. Depends who you're asking, but there's times when—"

"Sterling Powers," Tom interrupts before Henry gets off on another tangent. "Actor? Bodyguard? Remember him?"

Henry raises his eyes skyward, making a pyramid out of his fingertips and rests his chin on them. "Sterling Powers? Sterling Powers. Powers. Powers…hmm…." Then, like a computer screen raised from hibernation, he lights up. "Yes, I remember! Real name was Myron Dickman."

"I can see why he changed it," says Tom.

"Had to be about '79 when he passed."

"He died?" says Tom, the sound of disappointment in his voice. Another dead end.

"Yepper," says Henry. "Was out on a date with some girl. She drove him and his car into the harbor. Course she escaped, but she left him there to drown. Didn't report it until the next day. Chappaquiddick role reversal. Shame though bout Sterling. He was going places."

"Yeah, so I've been told," says Tom. "But the date went sour? He tried to rape her?"

"Heck no," says Henry, "She tried to rape *him*! But he was…."

"Batting for the other team?" asks Tom, guessing that Sterling Powers was gay despite Stevey Stabler's rumor that he was romantically involved with Marilyn Monroe. Tom exhales. He's getting nowhere, instead holding his cup to the waitress for a coffee refill. She pours. "Thank you." He leans into Henry. "Did this Myron—ah, Sterling—have any family?"

"We called him 'Horse.' Wait, was it 'Horse' or was it…no, no, it was 'Horse.'"

"Why?" asks Tom.

"Because he left to go to Hollywood, and his first film was a western. Character he played was dragged to death by a horse. That answer your question?"

"Not really," says Tom. "Maybe let's try and focus on his return from Hollywood. Did he have any family here?"

"Sure he did. Few months after his arrival, he had a sort of adopted daughter."

"That's kind of vague…a sort of adopted daughter?"

Henry pauses. Grinds his back teeth to swallow. "Child's name was Gracie," says Henry. "Grace Morton. That Grace was the cat's pajamas. Grew up and ran the local art gallery that her mother owned."

"Wait, she had a mother?" asks Tom.

"Don't we all?" asks Henry. "'Course she had a mother! Marie Morton…friend of Sterling's, I mean Horse's. He even made a neighing nasal sound like a thoroughbred. Or was it an Appaloosa?"

"Henry, stick to the story, please."

"I am," says Henry, slightly put off, pausing to roll the napkin in front of him. "My mind isn't as sharp as it used to be, but I can tell you sure as its church day on Sunday who won the Chowdah Fest last year…"

Elizabeth, eavesdropping at the next table, comments. "That's below the belt, you old bag of bones."

Henry leans in as if he doesn't want Elizabeth hearing him. "The actor Sterling Powers was friendly with Marie Morton. Sweet mousy woman who kept to herself. Opened an art gallery and worked part time at the library. Or did she work full time at the library and part time at the gallery? Well, I can't remember, but one thing I'm certain was how *devastated* poor Marie was, just devastated—we *all* were—when her daughter Grace died in an accident. Marie's only child..."

"That's just horrible," says Tom, feeling bad. "So, you're saying that Grace was the sort of adopted daughter to Sterling before she grew up and died?"

"Didn't I just say that?" asks Henry. "You know Gracie had a baby when she died."

"Did they save the baby?" asks Tom, hopeful.

"Yes. Baby was already born. Only a few months old."

Tom does the math as if drawing it on the table with his finger. "Wait, so you're saying that Marie Morton was a friend of Horse's...er...Sterling Powers, the wanna-be actor. She came here with him from maybe LA. Marie then had a baby girl, named Grace, and years later, Grace died in an accident..."

"Didn't I just say exactly that?"

"In a roundabout way, but yes..." Tom sips his coffee. "How'd Grace die?"

"We don't talk about it much." Henry goes completely tight-lipped.

"Okay, what about the baby's name?" asks Tom, certain of the words that are going to come out of Henry's mouth, so he says it for him first. "It's Penelope Morton, right?"

"Yes," says Henry, surprised.

"But everyone calls her 'Nell?"

"Nellie, yes," says Henry. "You know her? Well, why didn't you just say so?"

Elizabeth glances over at Henry, who glances over at Elizabeth, who glances over at the mayor, who's just entered. It's all just a little too Cape Cod fishy. Elizabeth's wearing a fake smile, and it's as if Henry's saying to Elizabeth, *Don't worry, he'll find a fact or two. Not much to worry about, oh Queen of Chowdah.* As Henry catches on that Tom's studying all their glancing, Henry looks down at his watch. Lighting up like Doc Brown in *Back to the*

Future, he practically pops straight up in his seat. "Oh, shucks! You got a rake?"

"A rake?" asks Tom, baffled by the inquiry.

"A clamming rake?" says Henry as if it's an everyday question.

"No," says Tom, containing a chuckle. "Do I need one?"

"Might," says Henry. "Promised Franklin I'd drop mine off. If you've got a rusty rake or a worn handle, Franklin's fixin' rakes today for clamming season. Gotta be prepared."

"Well, thank you for that information. I'll keep it handy in case I ever need to go clam digging."

"Sure thing," says Henry, eyeing the check and digging in his back pocket for his wallet.

"I've got this," says Tom, grabbing Henry's wrist and staring deeply into his eyes. "Don't worry. You go on ahead and get your rake repaired." Henry rises to go, but it's clear Tom is on to their mysterious behavior. All of them. Because Tom can tell you that the guy to his right is left-handed when pouring the bottle of syrup, and the woman to his left drives a white Honda where thirty other cars are parked in the lot. But what Tom *can't* figure out is how much any of these people might suspect or even know.

Tom does remember reading something about Marilyn. She had a love–hate relationship with reality and truth. She so desperately tried to avoid the truth until she could create her own. Only way to do that was to escape. Start a new life, a family. Her most passionate quest…

Tom stands to go and looks around at the local town folk on New Years' Day 2020. His mind is ticking. Imagine if Marilyn became like so many famous writers and artists that chose to be reclusive. Afterall, Kerouac had his road, Salinger had his mountain, Thoreau had his pond, and Proust had his Paris studio. Maybe Marilyn had her bubble-like existence in Cape Cod. Just the kind of Lobster Festival mentality needed to be inconspicuous. It had to be liberating…

Tom waves to Elizabeth, who nods and waves back.

The mayor calls out, "Will we be seeing you at the Polar Bear Plunge?"

Tom gives a thumbs up without losing the thought he's immersed in.

Bracing for the cold and zipping his parka, Tom realizes that he neglected to ask Henry the most important question of all: *Is Marie Morton still alive?*

Tom glances at his grandfather's Citizen watch. *Shit! Where's he gonna find swim trunks on a New Year's holiday for a polar plunge?*

CHAPTER SIXTEEN

Tom turns left at the blinking light on Route 6A and the corner of Mill Way, following the curve down to the waterfront. His eyes scan the abandoned lifeguard chair. The tattered rope of an empty flagpole whips in the wind. Despite the lack of sunbathers, cars are lined up on both sides of the winding road, just as Nell predicted.

The Arctic-like horizon beckons with familiarity but promises little except frigid winter. The long anemic sandbar segues to a lone and weathered buoy that clanks in the harbor against the constant slap of the waves. Even in all its emptiness, there's something recognizable, longing, in the air's chill. Perhaps it's the knowledge that summer will indeed one day come.

Tom circles his car in the gravel lot of Mattakeese Wharf, glancing at the vessels. He finds himself thinking like Nell, bitten by the bug of environmental issues. If they could just recycle the shrink wrap off all these boats come spring...*well hell, that's a lot of plastic!*

Tom trots down to the beach, hands in his pockets. He can't even feel the cold as his stomach flip-flops over his date with frigid destiny.

A group of cheery townies gather around as if this is some *epic* event, women sipping hot cocoa and wine to the left, with the about-to-plunge men to the right. Some are dressed in swim trunks and heavy fleece, their legs long gone white from last summer's tan. Some wear long-sleeve T-shirts with their sponsors' company logos on the back. There's Kinlin Grover Real Estate, Barnstable Insurance, Nirvana Coffee Co., and so on. Sips of warm whiskey keeps them spirited for the task at hand.

Tom moves through the thick crowd, sandwiched like a mussel in a shellfish harvest. He turns at the sound of a familiar voice. "Hey there! You showed up!" says Nell, her face and hair windwhipped. Her smile electric white.

"Of course, I showed up," says Tom, hands on hips and a grin that reads his soul is hers to steal. A sudden surge of warmth makes even the ten-below-wind-chill-factor air feel tropical.

Nell taps playfully at his arm. "Of course, showing up won't exactly win me the Mercy Otis Award, but I'll take whatever I can get."

"Mercy who?" flirts Tom, tapping back, but he's eyeing Scotty Harden, the fisherman, a few feet away and clearly the smartest guy for arriving in a wetsuit.

"Mercy Otis Warren," says Henry, coming up behind Tom, "born right here in 1728, or was it 1729? No…it was '28."

"Mercy's my Barnstable hero," says Nell. "She was a playwright, a historian, and a pioneer in women's rights."

"And a true Barnstable patriot," adds Henry. "Now c'mon you two…Tom here has to get in the lineup."

Tom can only stare at Nell. Nothing in her behavior lets on a clue of who she might be. A tap on the shoulder turns Tom around.

"Been looking for you," says Charley Button, the other fisherman from the tavern. "I think we're about the same size." He holds up a pair of swim trunks to Tom's waist. Baby blue with a whimsical lobster print and drawstring.

"Awesome, thank you!" says Tom, snatching them, and practically sprinting to the public bathroom just off the boardwalk.

He returns only a few seconds before the foghorn sounds *Go*!

Seconds later, the plungers are off and running—men in all shapes and sizes, some gym-fit, but most with white bellies flopping in the cold, yet all running for a good cause and bracing like crazy to plunge into those rousing waves.

Tom leads the pack, slim, lanky legs leaping up high as if he'll dodge the bone-chilling temperatures. No such luck.

Distant seagulls caw like mad, as the men dunk in synchronicity. A round of hollers and swears. The crowd cheers for the brave—or is it the crazy? Depends on how you look at it. Then the men reverse out, rising from the waves, moving slower this time with their frozen limbs. As they touch the shoreline, red legs are evidence of their insanity.

"Oh my God! It's frickin' *freezing*!" hollers Tom, teeth chattering, and blowing hot air on his hands. He jumps up and down in one place.

"Woo-hoo!" says Nell, "You did it!" Elizabeth and Nell are there to pat him down with a towel, as he shakes his sopping head of hair.

"Over here!" shouts Scotty, his voice carried into the wind from where he's hopped into the warmth of his truck, engine running.

"Go on, go join 'em," says Nell, tossing him an oversized ivory cardigan. He takes it, tries to fit into it, but takes notice of the print. He's seen this before...but oddly, he can't place it. Ivory with bulky black cable, a chain-link design from an over-zealous knitting needle. "It's Nan's," says Nell, registering the confusion on his face. "It's for good luck."

"I could use your grandmother's good luck." Tom shivers before adding, "Say, what a guy's gotta do to get a dinner date around here?"

"If you're asking me to dinner, I'd have gone even if you *didn't* plunge into the January water."

"Now you tell me."

"Yes, we're *very* date-friendly here," explains Nell. "Barnstable was recently voted number ten of the best small dating towns in America."

"According to who?" he asks, circling Nell and still jumping about to keep warm.

"According to AARP," she says.

"Great, I'll remember that when I'm sixty-five," says Tom, kicking sand at her. "So where were the other towns?"

"Brentwood Tennessee was number one," she says, kicking sand back. "Followed by two other Tennessee towns. I think Charlottesville was number five."

"Sweet! I like Charlottesville," says Tom, teeth chattering, "UVA was one of my reach schools."

Tom nestles his frozen nose into the bulky woolen sweater, still fixated on its Mexican design, because whoever was previously wearing this is in a vague photo right there in the forefront of his mind. He can see it, *right there*, but he can't place where he's seen it before. "Yeah, your Barnstable might be great for dating," he says, snapping back to the moment, "but it's even better for lots of fish-and-chip shops. All claiming to be the best, the most original, and the oldest."

"Well, I know one that claims to be all three," says Nell. "If you're lucky I'll tell you which one."

Suddenly, and from seemingly nowhere, a scream is carried through the wind, catching their attention. "What the..." Nell stretches her neck to the shoreline. "Is that...Joan?" she says squinting, before heading back to the beach as she picks up her pace with realization. "Joanie! Joanie!" But, Tom, who's already surmised the situation, tosses the big ivory sweater to the ground, dashes ahead of Nell, sprinting through the sand, to where Joanie hollers out, "Winston! Winston!"

The crowd turns to see the fuss, but Tom is waist deep, carving his arms through the waves, and navigating the hefty current, one hip at a time. He spies floppy ears. Winston—a Cavalier King Charles Spaniel—is struggling to paddle back to shore.

Without hesitation, Tom scoops Winston into his arms, all tail and paws, splashing and flapping about. Tom is like a big collie...gentle and strong. A lovable Lassie. A savior.

Channel 5 news, having covered the race, captures the rescue on camera. Winston gulps and whines relief, as the crowd can be heard at the shoreline screaming, "Tom is a local hero!" *A hero! A hero!*" The word *hero* reverberates across the sand and the seashore.

CHAPTER SEVENTEEN

A "Closed for Lunch" sign suspends from a rope on the back of the gallery door.

Tom jiggles the handle before glancing up to the side of the building to double check the number. He's certain he's got the right place because Nell gave him the address after he saved the dog. "Come by the gallery tomorrow around noon," she said. "It's up in Wellfleet."

Is there another gallery? Tom cranes his neck up and down the street, but he can't spot one. He jiggles the handle again, before knocking on the glass. Nobody answers, unless a series of eclectic paintings can speak. Various themes of oils, watercolors, and then…

A pair of eyes, behind a sculpture peering out at Tom, who flinches at the sight of a person watching him.

Tom taps on the glass and motions for the eyes to come to the door.

The eyes move forward from behind the sculpture. A nose, then a face, then a hand, lifting a spoonful of yogurt to his mouth. It's a man we recognize as Frederick, dressed very festively from head to toe. Except—wait a second—he's wearing Nell's sweater over his ensemble…the one Nell gave Tom yesterday when he was shivering. The ivory bulky Mexican one now accessorized with a big cowboy belt through the yarn loops of the waistline.

Placing his yogurt on the counter and sauntering toward the door with the exaggerated motions of a dancer, Frederick's arms swing to unheard music. He grabs the doorknob with his thumb and forefinger, swinging it open like Fred twirling Ginger.

"Hellooo," says Frederick, "We're sorry. But is English not our native tongue?"

"What?" asks Tom.

"Were we perhaps frightened by some mean old librarian when we were little, and we haven't read a single word from that day to this?"

"Okay, I'm lost," says Tom.

Frederick takes the sign off the door, and holds it in front of Tom, pretending to spell out the words in a childish sign language. "Closed…for…lunch. Closed for lunch! Get it?"

"Right. Well, I can read. I can even write. Look, I need to see a girl about Horse."

The man's expression goes sly. "Ew, doesn't one see a *man* about a horse? And usually after hours in some smoky East Village joint in the company of other macho fellows?"

"No, Horse was a person. Goes by Sterling Powers. Sorry, I was hoping to find the owner? Nell Morton? She told me to meet her here at noon?"

"And we would be?"

"Tom Hogan."

"Oh my!" says Frederick, covering his mouth with his hand. "You're our stud hero."

"Huh?"

"Talk of the town. Saved Joanie's little dying Winston with your bare hands from that monsoon!"

Tom runs a shy hand over his head and then extends his hand to shake. "Well yeah, thanks. But honestly, it was hardly a monsoon."

The man eyes Tom's hands. "Oooh, what lovely, *large* dog-saving hands you have." He takes Tom's fingers, studies them. "Frederick O'Keefe, gallery manager. Pleased, I'm sure."

"Can I come in?" says Tom, moving past Frederick into the doorway and admiring the beautifully lit space. The pine plank floors are high glossed while the walls are white, offsetting the art collection in a very ethereal way. "This place rocks," says Tom. "Does it always look like this?"

"We're working on an abstract installation. Got a big exhibit sale coming up."

"You have a show in January? Off-season?" asks Tom, admiring a series of orchid paintings.

"Darling boy with big dog-saving hands, we must prepare for May. Nothing like the present," he chirps.

"I see," says Tom, putting his hands in the safest place he can come up with—his pockets,—and spinning back around to Frederick, who's eyeing him like candy.

"So listen, Fred…"

"Erick. Fred hyphen Erick," he corrects.

"Yes, Fred-erick. May I inquire when Nell will be back?"

"It's our lunch hour." Frederick points to a container of yogurt on the counter. "Our probiotic is losing its culture as we speak."

"Well, what time will you *all* return?" asks Tom, sarcastically.

"Two p.m. Maybe," says Frederick, nibbling at a hang nail with big doe eyes, his tone as if egging him on to ask more questions.

Tom can only shrug. "Okay then. I'll go grab lunch myself." As Tom turns to leave, his eyes dart about to see if there's any artwork that might mean anything to him, like the painting he bid on at auction, like the one Lolly had. He sees a couple portraits, kids at a beach, some abstracts with pastel colors, and a couple of metal sculptures in the corner. He comes out with zero. "Thanks a bunch," Tom exhales. "Will you tell her I stopped by?"

"We will. But you may want to call her first…she's rehearsing at five."

"Rehearsing? As in a play?"

"Yes," says Frederick, very know-it-all. "Summer stock theatre."

"But it's only Janu—" starts Tom, stopping, and then remembering. "Ah, better to practice. Memorial Day is just around the corner."

"Now we're talking, big boy," says Frederick, sauntering back to his yogurt. "She's trying out for *The Vagina Monologues*, you know."

"I've never seen that," says Tom.

"Well, technically I haven't either," says Frederick, "but apparently, it's *only* the most important piece of political theater in *decades*. I suppose I'll have to just *suck* it up."

"Why is it that everything involving Nell has a political bend?"

"We know," says Frederick, winking.

Tom knits his brow. "Well, thank you for your time, Fred-Erick." But Frederick only bats his eyes as if he's holding back the world's biggest secret.

Tom is out the door, debating whether to turn around. When he glances back, Frederick is sucking on his yogurt spoon from inside the picture window, keeping a hungry eye on him.

CHAPTER EIGHTEEN

At the backdoor porch of The Porpoise, Tom wraps up a phone call while standing in the one spot that allows cell reception. He's been chatting with the rental car clerk in Boston to extend his car rental. She thinks he's such a nice guy that she's giving him the extension with the employee discount rate. He punches a silent victory fist into the air. "Oh, thank you *so* much," he says into his receiver. "I owe you dinner in New Hampshire sometime. Maybe our families can all meet at Shibley's at the Pier." He listens to the clerk, then, "Exactly! The gnocchi lobster n' cheese. Me too." She says something else, and he adds, "You're awesome," before they hang up.

Tom visually inhales the horizon beyond the empty parking lot, surrounded by salt marshes. The ice hangs on cattails flattened by the elements and the golden light softens the edge of the branches. If this winter's symphony had a name, it might be called "Silence."

Tom moves to the edge, hands in his pocket, inhaling the crisp, dry air. In the words of Kurt Vonnegut, "I want to stand as close to the edge as I can without going over. Out on the edge you can see all the kinds of things you can't see from the center." Those words may not necessarily apply to Tom, but in a strange way they could. He could learn to love it here, away from the hustle and pretense of LA. In Los Angeles, the energy is low. Bodies never touch—they're all in *cars*. Yes, at the heart of him, he's a New England boy who loves earning the seasons.

Tipping his face to the blue skies, where the late afternoon winter sun feels inviting despite the calendar's determination to end the day at 4 p.m., Tom will take what he can get. He turns, heading up the steps to the backdoor of The Porpoise, where sunlight streams through the panes. The bar is empty except for Henry Bartholemew on the seat near the kitchen and Mayor Bisbee to his right. Just the two of them.

"Greetings, Tommy," says the mayor, glancing up from the sound of the cowbell jingling on the door frame.

"Hey, Mayor Bisbee. Hi, Henry!"

"See you survived the Polar Plunge rescue," says Mayor Bisbee.

With a massive portion of fried clams in front of him, Henry comments, "Why you're the first one to save a dog since 1953 when ole Josh Miller saved a stranded sea pup." Henry slurps his soup, and pauses mid-spoonful, "Oh, no, wait a second. It was '58…'"

Tom slips into the bar stool other side of the mayor. "Hey, I've got a question for you guys."

"And I've got an answer," says Henry. "Maybe."

"Nell Morton…" says Tom, watching Henry's expression change from whimsical to more serious. The mayor's face stays neutral. "Now, don't laugh. Promise? But what can you tell me about feminism?" Tom observes the look on their faces. The mayor chuckles a loud belly laugh. Not the kind of question he was expecting. "In general, I mean," says Tom, laughing too, but the laughter sounding very nervous and goofy. "I like Nell."

"Kind of figured you were sweet on her, Tommy," says the mayor. "Not sure what she has to do with all that research for your book on Hollywood Westerns…" His tone drops off, suggesting it might all be a big fat lie.

"In every Western, doesn't the guy get the girl?" asks Tom. The two men shake their heads no. "Well, then, I'd just like your perspective."

The mayor taps Henry on the shoulder and sighs. "Feminism, eh? Not my cup of chowdah. I'll let you boys ponder that one, Henry." He messes up Tom's hair as he bypasses him. "Besides," adds the mayor, "I've gotta head over to the hospital to greet our town's first newborn baby of the year." The excuses keep coming. "Then I'm headed down to the Senior Center. Doing a lecture on whether the old Crocker Tavern is still haunted." And with that, he's gone.

Tom slides over in the seat next to Henry, dragging his placemat with him. Henry stares straight ahead at the bar, where a 1978 Red Sox team photo hangs. "Sox finished second in the American League that year," says Henry. "Record of ninety-nine wins and sixty-four losses if I got my numbers right. Don't suppose you remember?"

"I wasn't born yet, Henry," says Tom, "But getting back to feminism…"

Henry nods, looking up to the ceiling a moment. "I've seen a few waves on the analysis of feminism but let me try to sum up my glimmers of understanding those waters."

"All ears," says Tom, asking the waitress for his own cup of chowder.

"The waves of feminism… Well…" says Henry thinking and slurping chowder sips. Then speaking with what sounds like one big long run-on sentence without a second to breathe: "First there was the years of Mary Wollstonecraft, the Seneca Falls Convention—Elizabeth Cady Stanton, cresting in some ways with the disappointment of women not being included in the Thirteenth Amendment to the Constitution in 1865 when it extended the vote to African American men. Then…well…"

Tom chimes in: "Then you had the suffragist campaign that led to passage of the Nineteenth Amendment in 1920, establishing nationwide the right of women to vote. And then the movement catalyzed by Betty Friedan and others…around '63 or was it '68, yes?"

"No, wait a minute…yes…no…yes, '68, I think?" says Henry, "when women were protesting about making and carrying coffee to their bosses."

"The *Mad Men* era," interrupts Tom.

"Don't know it," says Henry nodding to the bread pudding dessert on the menu. "And I thought I was supposed to be teaching you…"

"I was just reading that the first wave of feminism crested in the sixties, and that the second wave of feminism emerged post-sixties in fields like literary and gender studies. I mean, what do I know?"

"Hmmm…" groans Henry, perhaps surprised that the kid might be smarter than he looks.

Tom talks like he's spent the night at his motel room studying and memorizing a book word for word. Tom leans in and says, "I do think that the suffragist fight for the vote, with its pattern of political organizing in the US, drew heavily on the experience of the abolition movements of the 1800s, and it deserves to be recognized as the second wave."

Henry just stares.

"I'm just saying…" says Tom, polishing the chowder with bread, against the swipe of the bowl.

"I think you lost me at…golly," says Henry. "You just lost me." He's taken aback. Way back.

"And it was 1982 before equal rights for women finally stuck," adds Tom. "Maybe you could advise me in a more contemporary way on feminism? You know like the sexual revolution when women said, *I'm not going to be subservient. I'm not going to service JFK sexually…*"

"JFK?"

"You know, all the Marilyn Monroe kind of stuff..." he says, hoping to hook him.

Henry takes a huge intake of breath before pushing it out. "When it comes to women's rights, my better half, good rest her soul, used to say, 'Henry, just remember: Take out the trash and don't patronize me by calling me "Sweetie," and we'll be just fine.'"

As Henry speaks, Nell enters through the back door. It occurs to Tom he can imagine taking the trash out for Nell for the rest of his life.

"Hi Nellie," he calls out, all smiles.

"Freddie said somebody was looking for me?" says Nell, with ethereal sunlight streaming across her angelic features. She looks like she's stepped out of a classic movie. A period drama kind of face. She just glows.

"Yes, *we* were looking for you," says Tom, imitating Frederick, but Henry is still dumbfounded by their discussion.

"Henry, you okay?" asks Nell. "You look like you've seen a ghost. What you boys talking about?"

"Feminism," says Henry.

"Feminism?" Nell bursts out laughing. "Yeah, sure." The boys' faces remain stone cold serious. "Okay, whatever," exhales Nell. "Like I'm supposed to believe that."

CHAPTER NINETEEN

Los Angeles

The newsroom is much darker than usual. Desks are empty and the pound of computers has gone silent. There is noise, though, coming from Spooner's cubicle where a chair has just been knocked over.

Breathless, Becca stops at a desk, hoisting herself up on it and crossing her bronze legs in a flashy and suggestive way. She picks up a stapler, pointing it at Spooner, who's been playfully chasing her. "I'm Super Staple Ninja," she jokes. "Don't come any closer!"

"Very funny," says Spooner.

Becca snaps the stapler in the air. "I've got ammunition here, and I'm not afraid to use it. So, take *that,* and *that*!" She clicks the black device rapidly. Fake violence.

Spooner, her pursuer, chuckles. "I've already been circumcised."

But her sudden take-charge attitude is enticing. As she snaps the stapler towards his pants, his cell phone dings with a message.

"Maybe I'll just staple on a little extra to make up for your shortcomings," she teases.

"Shortcomings, huh?" says Spooner, getting closer, but instead of straddling her, he opts to peek at his text.

This is her chance to dash out of the space, and she does.

Dashing down the hall, giggling and breathing heavily, hoping he'll be on her heels, Becca keeps glancing back over her shoulder, but Spooner's stalled. To read his phone. How does

Becca know this? The light from his screen is the only thing that can be seen in the office.

Spooner opens the text, which is just a link to a YouTube called "Baby It's Cold Outside." When the video pops up, he sees a guy running frantically into the ocean to rescue a dog. Spooner is stunned. He watches it again. Is it? *Holy Shit! It's Hogan! And he's trending with over three million views for saving some mutt. WTF?!*

Spooner's mind spins in ten directions, but he sees Becca waving from Tom's cubicle. He weighs it out. Tom can wait five more minutes, and besides, Betsy might know just where he went to bond with a dog on a beach.

Spooner tosses the phone on his desk and heads to Tom's cubicle. He rounds the corner. Becca shimmies up on Tom's desk this time, knocking Tom's auction paddle and program onto the floor along with his caddy of pencils and paperclips. Spooner eyes Becca like a devil as he unbuckles his belt. "I can get you promoted, you know. Ritter listens to me."

"You've been telling me that for a month now." She rolls her eyes.

"Well, good things *come* to those who wait...but remember, I'm not into commitment..."

He pins her arms behind her and kisses her, almost violently. She pulls away and grabs his face, smooshing its features in her hand, speaking straight into his eyes. "Did you ever think maybe a woman likes to *fuck* for the sake of having sex too? Just like a man. And it doesn't mean you have to call me in the morning. I really don't care. I'm too solid to be *your* girlfriend. You wouldn't know *how* to have a girlfriend...so get over yourself."

It's clear Becca has her limits. Spooner pauses on that thought. "I like that," he says, biting at her neck. He parts her lips, their tongues attacking each other. Becca turns her head to the side.

"No, Stan, not here."

He pulls back. "Stan? My name's Sid. Not Stan." Spooner's wounded.

"Stan, Sid, whatever…" Two can play at that game. Her tone cool with revenge for all the Betsy name-calling.

Spooner grins. He's liking this new Becca. So much so he's officially pissed off. He rips her blouse open like a teenager. She's braless. He grabs her breasts roughly.

"Take me, Stan the man," she screams out, chuckling and liberated.

"It's Sid! It's *Sid*!" Spooner picks her up and replants her on Tom's desk, her back landing *hard* against the cubicle wall. As he does, her body slams right into the painting, tearing through the center of the canvas.

"What the hell was that?" asks Becca, jumping off the desk and rapidly turning around.

"Are you okay?" asks Spooner, examining her backside. The look on Becca's face says she's skeptical of his concern. "No, really," he asks again, childlike, "you okay?"

"Oh shit!" says Becca. "Tom's stupid painting." The painting isn't completely ruined, but it's no longer something you could bid on. Or hang. She puts her blouse back together as best she can since most of the buttons are on the floor.

"What do you mean, Tom's stupid painting?"

"This *is* his office, you know."

"Why does he have this?" his mind already ticking the possibilities from all the recent nursing home secrets. Becca primps at her hair and pulls her skirt back down around her knees. She still doesn't answer.

"C'mon Betsy. Why does he have this?" Spooner's turning the painting over and sees the frame is cracked too.

"I don't know," says Becca nonchalantly. "Some auctioneer said it belonged to Marilyn Monroe." Becca brushes at her blouse. "I mean, really, who cares…"

He breaks open the frame, revealing the signature previously concealed under its border. Spooner brings the painting closer to his face, eye level to the corner writing. Close up he can read "Marie Morton 1961."

Spooner slowly lowers the painting. His eyes narrow. His mouth tightens, his jaw ticks with a hard swallow. *Marie Morton? Marie Morton!* Tossing the painting onto a side chair, he rips through Tom's office, papers now littering the floor, the drawers, all of it.

"You know, Marie Morton has the same initials as Marilyn Monroe," says Becca. But Spooner is a madman, and it's scaring her. "Hey, Sid, I don't think you should be doing that," says Becca not appreciating the invasion.

"Shut the fuck up, Betsy!" says Spooner.

"No, *you* shut the fuck up!" declares Becca. "And it's Becca. Becca Busa. Not Betsy, or Betty, but Becca."

"Yeah, I know. I'm sorry, Becca," he appeases, but doesn't stop demolishing Tom's space. "But this Marie Morton is *my* assignment. Someone hired me to find his ex!"

"And her name was Marie Morton too?" asks Becca, confused.

"So, tell me," he asks, his tone gentler, "what has Hogan told you about this Marie Morton?"

"Nothing," says Becca, completely oblivious. "Why? What's it to you?"

"He's stealing my job."

"I don't think so," she says, confused about what someone named Marie Morton has to do with any of this.

He barely acknowledges her input. "And, why the fuck is Hogan saving some mutt on YouTube?"

"Oh, you saw that too?" says Becca. "Yeah, he sent me the clip this morning. He's up on Cape Cod. A little out of season for tourists but hey, rates are cheaper, I guess."

"What does Cape Cod have to do with the nursing home story?" asks Spooner, hands on hips, and out of options to snoop. "What's the story about? And why does he have all this Marilyn Monroe stuff everywhere?"

"Am I supposed to be telling you this?" she asks, heading back to her own cubicle.

"Sure, why not," he adds, following her.

"Just keep it on the down low," says Becca. "Apparently some old coroner sent him on a mission over some old movie star, Sterling Powers. The whole thing sounds ludicrous if you ask me." She grabs her purse, camera case, and cell phone. "Um, are we done here, Sid?"

"Yeah, yeah, we're done," says Spooner, his tone kinder to Becca now. Hands still on hips, but his mind racing. He's confused. Almost vulnerable, if you can believe it. "Hey, Bec," he says. "Look, I'm sorry. I think you're actually awesome. I'll call you. We'll do dinner. A *real* dinner. I really mean it this time."

She stops in her tracks, surprised. "No prob, Sid," she says, turning back to him. "Just don't hold your breath."

CHAPTER TWENTY

Cape Cod

Barnstable Market is the only place that sells just about everything from beer and wine to homemade soup and ready-made dinners, but it's the ice cream that's caught Tom's attention. He pays for himself and Nell at the register.

"Thank you," says Nell, taking a bite of a frozen yogurt. She turns back to Tom. "Remind me why we're eating ice cream in the middle of January?"

"Cuz' we're *cah-razy!"* he says, circling around her to open the door for her. As they stroll side by side, he asks, "Hey, where's this Crocker Tavern that the mayor says is haunted?"

"Just there," she points. "And it *is* haunted."

"You believe in ghosts?" asks Tom.

"They believe in me," she says, deadpan. Tom smirks at her sassiness, pausing at the stone wall. He finishes off his ice cream and gazes up at a stately house, with gray weathered clapboard siding and two chimneys. An American flag flies out front at the door stoop. Up on the roof, a majestic gull with chalk-white feathers stares into the distance.

"And just up over there…" Nell points across the way, "Is the house my mom was born in. Horse and my grandmother lived there when they came to town. He was my grandmother's best friend. Now, it's just a big old boarded-up sea captain's house. Still has the original widow's walk around the roof." Her voice trails sadly, as though the roof might reach up through the sky and touch her mother in heaven. "Nan—that's what I call my grandmother. Well, she always gave me head rubs and told me that Horse had eyes bluer than the desert sky."

"Horse?" asks Tom. "Odd name."

"His name was Sterling. Sterling Powers. Nan, well, she had a thing for men with blue eyes..."

"Blue-eyed men have all the luck. Paul Newman," says Tom, and then tossing in a line of bait. "Frank Sinatra..."

Nell continues, oblivious, "Nan used to tell me if we looked up at the stars, we'd see Horse, *and* my mom, so we did. Together. Every night." Nell stops to look up at the setting afternoon sun. She gets very serious. Performance mode. "'When he shall die, take him and cut him out in little stars, and he will make the face of heaven so fine.'"

"*Romeo and Juliet*," says Tom with a beat of melancholy, studying her stunning beauty.

"My grandmother loved *Romeo and Juliet*." Nell swallows hard, holding back tears.

He doesn't dare ask if she's still alive. Instead, he cautiously asks, "Tell me about your mother."

"I long for her," says Nell, like a frightened child. "A love I never knew. She died, you know?" He nods with an empathetic expression. "I was always happy until I was ten years old," says Nell. "The year Nan told me the true story of my mother's death... because some kid in school was making fun of me."

"I'm sorry, Nellie." says Tom.

"I guess you don't know what you don't have," she says in haunted and hypnotized tone. "Nan used to always tell me that all little girls should be loved and live in a big house with a mommy and a daddy. Nan would understand. She told me she was moved around in foster care a lot as a kid." Nell's bottom lip quivers. Tom squeezes Nell's arm. They're face-to-face. "My mom was in a moped accident with a tourist. She was on the moped. The car hit her." Nell's eyes water up with the refusal to discuss any more details.

"That's awful," says Tom. "I don't mean to pry or upset you…" He tosses the last of his cone into the town barrel, licking a sticky finger and then taking her hand into his. "I just really like you and I want to know about your life."

"I know," she says kindly, her voice still crackling. "It became this big conspiracy thing in the town. Some say it was an accident, and some say it was deliberate…that she *killed* herself. Put herself out in front of that car…"

"God," Tom whispers. "I'm so sorry…I—I don't know what to say."

"Nothing *to* say," says Nell, with a huge intake of air.

Tom stops in the middle of the sidewalk. "That just sucks. It had to be so hard for your Nan to lose her only child and for you to lose your mother. And then to have everyone speculate…"

"Depression runs in our family, according to Nan. She taught me about suicidal ideation and how it can stem from depression. Though, so far, I'm positive in my outlook on life." Nell kicks at a pinecone with her foot. It tumbles into a winter garden as they stroll. "But it's why I volunteer with the suicide hotline. In case I can save some other girl's mother, I guess. Even just one."

"It had to be hard being raised by a grandmother, no?" asks Tom while navigating the crooked sidewalk, the hundred-year-old elm tree's roots bursting through the pavement.

"My grandmother? Nan filled Mom's shoes just fine," Nell says defensive-like. "Nature or nurture, right?"

"Huh?" says Tom.

"Are we a product of nature or nurture? Old theory. Is it biological or psychological? If its biological, then I'm destined for suicide. But I don't think I'm the type. The nurture is in how Nan raised me. I felt safe."

Tom's realizing her story matches the town historian's account. It fits in with his investigation to date, yet somehow he's more interested in the humanizing of her pain rather than the fact checking. He's genuinely sad for Nell.

"Nan raised me because I didn't know my father," she continues. "I mean, what I learned is that in order for a kid to survive—to be resilient—it's vital for them to have one dependable person in their life. No matter how many babysitters or fake aunts and uncles, you still need that one person."

Tom is touched by how effortlessly she opens up to him

"I never talk about this, but Nan always felt that God was punishing her in some way for my mother's death. I don't know what to believe except that if it was suicide, well, it was a cry for help. It's a crime of loneliness...." She gulps. "Did you know the words 'silent' and 'listen' are spelled the same with the letters inverted?"

Tom remains quiet, swallowing hard, before placing an arm around her shoulder as they walk, which is tricky on the narrow and winding sidewalk.

"I often wonder what my mother was thinking in that final moment," adds Nell. "Whatever it was it must have been bigger than the both of us."

"You know it's not your fault," says Tom. "Right?"

"Right, but didn't she love me enough to stick around? Was she mad at Nan? It's never added up. And Nan, well, she never wanted to discuss it. Like I said, a kid doesn't know what they don't know about not having a mother...but I'd have liked to *know* my mother's final story."

Tom finds irony in this. Here Nell is wondering about her mother's death. Was it suicide or an accident? And here *he* is looking for Marilyn who died or *didn't* die by suicide or accident.

Tom knows one thing for certain...this is *not* the time to tell her why he's here. He gently squeezes her delicate fingers, stops on the sidewalk, facing her full-on. "It's so sad, Nellie, and I kind of get it." Tom tips his head to the side. "I lost my dad as a baby, so I mean, I kind of know."

"You did?" she says, with a thrill of connection.

"Yes, in the war. Desert Storm. He was shot. My grandfather practically raised me the way your grandmother raised you because my mom worked all the time. But I always wondered what his last minutes of life were like. Did he think of me back home? Did he think of mom?"

"Oh my God, you totally get it," she says, coming in for a big hug. They hold each other for a long moment. Swaying as the wind picks up a January bite. Then they pick up their stroll again. "Nan said mental health issues ran in our family back to her own mother's clinical depression."

Tom studies Nell as they walk. Taking in her gorgeous profile. Tom knows if he spills his story to her, all her pieces, all her stories both very far away and very present, will somehow fit. *Won't they?*

"So yeah," Nell continues. "What we learn at the suicide prevention center is that it's not about death. It's about maintaining life. How we can help people in need be able to cope in their lives. I mean, suicide is a permanent solution to a temporary problem."

"Like hating a holiday because you're alone?" says Tom.

"Or being angry because your wife walked out. It's all temporary stuff. You have your entire life ahead of you."

"Gotcha. Wow, Nellie," says Tom. "That's really kind of deep work that you do. I'm so impressed and proud of you too." He goes quiet. Their silences between their words are kind, not awkward.

"Thanks. I'm glad someone's proud of me," says Nell, carrying on up the road, their pace previously slowed by the intensity of their conversation. "I've logged about five thousand volunteer hours. Did you know that statistics say that sixty percent of women between the ages of forty-five and sixty-five had the highest suicide rate in the years from 2000 to just last year? My mom died in '93 when she was only thirty. I wonder what the statistics were back then."

"I can help you find out." Tom can't help putting together the pieces of Nell's life. He longs to be sensitive to this beautiful, kind, and giving creature in front of him. But there's no denying it. Lolly and that agent's story all factor in here. He swallows hard. Runs a hand through his hair. "It's kind of selfish to kill yourself, don't you think?" he asks, but she looks stunned at the comment. "What I mean is that the person committing suicide is both the perpetrator and the victim," says Tom. "And those left living...well, they're always left with the burden, just like you and your Nan."

"It's funny you say that," she says, but with empathy not as a challenge. "To those left living, they're angry and confused."

Nell takes his hand in hers as they cross the street.

"What do you say when a suicide victim calls?" Tom asks with genuine concern.

"I ask them their name for starters. I tell them mine."

"So, like, you humanize the call," says Tom. "Makes sense."

"Then I ask them if they've hurt themselves."

"What if they've got a gun and say they're going to end it all?" asks Tom.

"Luckily, I haven't had that yet," says Nell as she slows in front of a certain house. "I guess I would validate them first. Then remind them I've just picked up the phone on my end, so maybe they can convince me why this is the day it should all end right this second, you know?"

"So it's about getting them to talk," says Tom, looking up to the home they've just stopped in front of.

"Yeah, it's how I was trained to handle calls. Once they hear themselves, sometimes it gives them clarity. I hope I've saved enough people..." she looks ahead at the cottage fifty feet from the road. "And on that note...I'm home."

Tom turns to take in her house. A rambling spread of land, with massive pine trees and a long seashell driveway that leads to a pleasant backyard tumbling into a garden shed. A big stone stoop is festooned with vintage and primary-color pottery. The summer remnants of an herb garden and rows of dried hydrangeas still present.

"Sorry, I'll invite you in another time," she says, letting go of his hand as he escorts her to the front door. "I've got to rehearse lines for the show."

Tom has a million more questions but he's certain he's met his quota for one afternoon. But he's still a bit disappointed.

"But how about lunch tomorrow?" she asks. "And maybe—"

Tom cuts her off, leaning in on impulse for a kiss. A real kiss. Slow at first, he tenderly tastes her sweet lips before deepening the kiss.

She finally pulls back, touching her fingers to her lips. "Well, um..." she blushes. He blushes too. "We were saying?"

"Lunch," he reassures her, his fingers now dangling playfully with hers at their sides.

She lets go, awkwardly fumbles to fit the key in the front lock. It finally turns.

As she opens the door to the living room, Tom spots a massive abstract painting of red, white, and blue hanging on the wall. It's just like his—except it features an American flag draped around what looks like a body. A strand of blonde hair peeps out from the flag.

Trembling, Tom says, "Holy shit, where'd you get that?"

Nell looks from his expression to the wall. "Oh, that? It's nothing. My Nan painted it. Years ago," she says. As if it's nothing out of the ordinary.

Tom swallows hard. This moment is poignant, irrevocable, struck by a bolt of historic reality. If what Lolly said was true, and Marilyn painted these close-to-identical pictures, then Marilyn

Monroe is clearly Marie Morton, and Marie Morton is clearly Marilyn Monroe…Nell's grandmother. And she clearly didn't die on August 5, 1962!

"It's gorgeous," he chirps, barely audible. "But I gotta um, go." He trips off the front step, turning and awkwardly heading up the driveway.

Nell frowns and calls after him. "Tommy, you okay?" He nods and gives her a thumbs up but keeps walking until he hears her door click closed.

At the top of the driveway, he turns to look back at the property nestled up on a slight hill. Placing his hands to his knees, he tips forward, inhaling gulps of air.

He stands straight up.

Starts walking.

Fast.

What the fuck? What the fuck! Tom who barely ever curses, is practically delirious crossing Route 6A back to the other side.

All he can think of is the fact that Nell just opened the door on what was once just her regular life and closed the door onto her future life. The one from hell.

This information is about to change everything…

CHAPTER TWENTY-ONE

Tom sits on the bench at the laundromat. The dryer cycle has him under a spell as jeans and socks rumble round and round, but tears stream down his cheek. He's half humming and half singing Sinatra's "All the Way" to himself. He's certain that if he's going to love Nellie, he's going to have to love her all the way. Through it all. The good times and the bad. *Sigh.*

He moves to the table to fold his whites. He's visibly broken. This situation isn't fake news. This is *real* news. And it's also harmful news. As a journalist, he remembers a college professor lecturing him about integrity and the written word.

"As writers, we work very hard to earn the right to be a public voice in newspapers and in online presence. It doesn't happen overnight. Anything that goes out, especially online, should be kind, should be honest, should be researched…and most of all should offer something necessary to the world. Otherwise, what's the point?"

Does the world have a right to know about Marilyn Monroe? Sure, yes. No. Maybe. Tom's head bounces with ethics. It's not about what's possible, it's about what's morally permissible. He worries how it might change Nell if she learns. Worries how it might change *them* as a couple—or the potential to *be* a couple. *And hey, who says she doesn't already know, right?*

Yanking his jeans out from the dryer and shaking them out, Tom feels everything compounding. He figures she *must* know. Short of being raised under a rock—although let's face it, Barnstable is close to being as off the grid as you can get—

how can you *not* know if your grandmother is Marilyn Monroe? Though come to think of it, if Tom's grandfather was Tony Curtis who'd suddenly colored his hair blonde instead of dark brown and worked in a library, he might not know either.

On the other hand, if she *doesn't* know, and he's the one to tell her, she might hate him.

And what if it messes her up for life? Just like her mother... spending her life always preparing for the next catastrophe. Just like her Nan.

But how could he possibly have an open and honest relationship with her without the truth being out there? Even if the truth is only between the two of them...he could *promise* to keep her secret.

Moving the dark-colored clothes into a pile with his whites, Tom thinks back to his research about Marilyn's family. Marilyn's father was a biker. He deserted her mother before Marilyn—born with the name Norma Jeane—even existed. Apparently, he died in a motorcycle accident. Norma Jeane's mother, Gladys, became a basket case and was committed to a mental institution. And Norma Jeane was moved to one foster home and then another. No wonder Nellie had said that her nan felt every little girl should have a home with a mother and a father. Because Nell's grandmother *is* Normal Jeane. And *she* never truly had one.

Tom folds his dress shirts like they've just come from the department store, and thinks about Stevey Stabler, the agent. *"Hard to believe that little Norma Jeane, the girl from nothing, ended up in Hollywood as Marilyn Monroe. One of hundreds of girls with a dream. Little Norma Jeane finally got a break. A walk-on part in a gangster film called* Asphalt Jungle. *She was electric! So sad she had all those personal disasters, one after another—failed marriages to miscarriages. Doctors told her she'd never had a child."*

"Except she fooled them all..." Lolly had said.

She certainly did. And now here was Tom, standing in the middle of Barnstable, about to destroy three generations of women's lives, by blowing up their *entire* story…

Pulling his cell phone out of his jacket pocket, Tom presses in a number on speed dial and waits for the person to answer.

"Grandpa! Happy New Year! Sorry I didn't get back to you and Mom…but I'm working on a story." A pause and then, "It's so big Grandpa. Will change our financial lives forever…" As his grandfather talks, Tom notices a blue sock he dropped on the floor, picking it up to add to the pile, and scouring the dryer for its twin. "No, no, I can't talk about the story just yet. But I've got a question… You still believe honesty is the best policy?"

The expression on Tom's face tells us that the answer is *yes* but the bigger question is: *Does honesty only apply when telling the story to the world? Or just when confronting Nell?*

Or both?

CHAPTER TWENTY-TWO

Los Angeles

Spooner yanks open the door of the nursing home, slamming it rudely behind him. He pounds with certainty down the hallway, practically knocking over a feeble man with a walker. "Hey," shouts Spooner, "watch where you're going!"

Spooner scans the joint, but nobody is around, until an old lady approaches.

She's dressed to the nines in a lovely chiffon peach-colored ensemble. "It's you!" she says, hopeful. "Have you seen my movies?"

Spooner eyes her and guffaws. "Your movies? Sorry, lady, I only watch movies in color."

"You're very rude," she snaps.

"Right, well, if you can just point me in the direction of someone who actually runs your cinematic experience…"

Miffed, she raises an arthritic finger toward the end of the hallway.

With a nod, Spooner hustles toward a busy nursing station.

Until something stops him.

Sunlight streaming through an empty room…

The bed is made, and the sheets are tucked tight. Leaning on the wall is a red, white, and blue painting. A landscape. "What the…"

Spooner enters the room and goes to the painting still in its frame, collecting dust and resting alone under the window. It's similar to the painting in Tom's office. Spooner tilts his head sideways, eyes it over to be sure, and then picks it up, placing it on the bed. Carefully, he cracks a piece of the worn frame off the bottom right-hand corner. As clear as day: "Marie Morton, 1961."

Someone touches his arm.

"May I help you, sir?" a nurse asks.

"Oh, hi, yeah…I…" She looks at the broken frame in Spooner's hand. "It just sort of broke," he says. "Where did this painting come from?"

"It belonged to one of our patients."

"Oh, that's nice," says Spooner, struggling to maintain a polite manner while feeling ready to burst out of his own skin. "And who was the patient?"

"Mr. Wagner Lutz," she says, squinting her eyes and smiling.

"I need to see this Lutz right away," says Spooner, overly anxious, heart pounding.

"I'm sorry," she says, taking hold of his forearm. "Lolly passed away two days ago."

"Who the hell is Lolly?"

"Mr. Wagner Lutz. Lolly was his nickname. Were you a friend of the family, or…?"

"Is any of his other stuff here?" asks Spooner, scanning the room, his eyes falling on a box in the corner.

"Those are the last of his belongings. He was such an entertaining man when he wanted to be."

Spooner ignores her and immediately squats to rummage through the box.

"Were you a friend?" she asks again, this time her tone a bit stern as if to suggest he really shouldn't be going through the man's personal belongings.

Spooner pulls out an old compass, a wristwatch, a deck of cards, and an old photo of a few people in a graveyard. He tosses everything back in the box.The items clash on top of the metal flask, bottom of the pile.

The nurse persists. "Sir, were you family? Because—"

"No," says Spooner. "I wasn't family. Let's just say I was a distant friend…." His voice falls off, deep in thought, trying to figure out what Marie Morton's painting has to do with Tom on Cape Cod. Perhaps Tony Spits hired Tom too—to find her.

"Funny thing about this painting," says the nurse, running her fingers across it, "in the past month, he started telling us that Marilyn Monroe painted it for him. Can you imagine that? Poor ole bugger."

Spooner takes a moment for his brain to catch up. He remembers what Spits had said in that Italian restaurant, "*Story of a lifetime if you find her.*"

Spooner bolts from the room.

The nurse follows after him. "Sir? Sir!"

CHAPTER TWENTY-THREE

Cape Cod

Nell's swings her front door open to greet Tom. "Hello, there," she says flirtatiously. "C'mon in. I was just stretching on the sundeck." Tom follows Nell inside, keenly aware that she possesses a certain pedigree despite her casual yoga clothes and trippy dreadlocks.

"I'm digging the funky hair," says Tom, his lip turning up to form an involuntary grin.

"Yeah," she says, spinning back, "a friend studying cosmetology came over last night. I was her guinea pig."

Tom takes in the room. Imagine Martha Stewart breeding with a mad Bohemian decorator. Overstuffed chairs, flowers on the table, and tons of books. You might call it "homey," but one more throw pillow would make it a disaster.

"I'll put the kettle on," says Nells, "but first, a little lunchtime music." She heads to her stereo, shuffling through her old CD collection. "Spotify is spotty here, so…"

"Maybe that's why they call it Spotify," says Tom.

"Yeah, and my iPhone is dead, so no Apple Music, but…" He watches her load an old CD. She presses the button and classical music pours out.

"Rachmaninoff!" they both declare, taken aback—*ha!*

"The *Best* of Rachmaninoff," says Nell in a sexy tone, one-upping him. "Prelude in C-sharp Minor, I'll have you know." She winks.

She gestures for him to step into the kitchen as he shyly hangs back at the entrance. "Yeah, I love Rachmaninoff," she says. "I guess my studies of Russian literature paid off to some degree… no pun intended."

"Rachmaninoff? Russian Literature?" says Tom, with a wide grin, finally moving toward her. "So you're a wicked *smaht* New England girl."

"I try," she says, blushing and offering a giddy laugh that's way out of character for the Nell he's known so far. "C'mon, let's head to the porch." She grasps his hand, leading the way. "Lunch is ready. I can render you numb with thoughts on Nabokov and Fyodor Dostoevsky."

She leads him down a long, crooked hallway. The house feels timeless. Even its willowy wallpaper permeates a scent of roses, fresh mint, and nostalgia. Tom wouldn't be surprised if his own mother's favorite singer, Carly Simon, might appear from a back guestroom singing about her famous secrets.

As they move through the yellow kitchen, pots and pans hang clustered above a wooden butcher block island. An idle blender is ready for smoothies on a Mexican-tiled counter, along with a coffee maker, toaster—nothing out of the ordinary. Under the window is a deep stainless steel industrial sink. Overhead, herbs dry, suspended from the ceiling by thin string.

Tom turns to the table in the kitchen nook leading to the porch, where a wall greets him with a row of paintings. A collection of the red, white, and blue ones, just like the others, but in smaller sizes. He feels very lightheaded. A bead of sweat begins to form at the nape of his neck. *Is the room swaying…or is he?* He's about to faint. He closes his eyes attempting to inwardly calm himself.

"We're having salad, sprouts, quinoa, shrimp, and avocado. Because everything can be cured by avocado," says Nell, busying herself with plates at the counter. She turns to see his expression.

"What's wrong?" He moves in front of the paintings. He can't take his eyes off the canvases. "Oh, you like those?"

"Yeah. Yeah, I really do," he says, choking on his words.

"Nan painted those," says Nell. "She never thought they were good enough to hang with 'real' artists. That's why they're not in the gallery. Though it's time I did a private installation of her art. And Frederick, well, he can be difficult about the gallery, but he's kind of forcing me to show them. You know Frederick, very opinionated."

"Yes, *we* know," says Tom flapping his hand to his chest, attempting humor to squelch his nerves at every pulse point.

He turns back to the paintings, worried his expression might give himself away. Nell moves up behind him, placing her arms around his waist. He abruptly pulls away from her and spins so she's facing him. The look on his face is one that says an entire power plant, not just a light bulb, has gone off in his head.

"Nellie, listen, I have to—"

"I know what you're gonna say," she says, cutting him off and moving to the counter, busying herself with setting cutlery at the table. "Listen yourself," she says, "and grab those glasses over there. Sparkling water is chilling in the fridge." He dutifully does as he's told. "That stuff we were talking about last night…I know it's hard to discuss it," Nell continues. "Let alone with some guy who just drifted into town." She begins to tear up again.

He places the glasses down on the table, taking her into his arms. "I'm not some guy who just drifted into town, Nell." He wipes her tear-stained cheek with the corner of his plaid shirt. I mean, I was. Or I guess that's what I wanted everybody to think. But I was here to actually, um…" The moment of truth. He's got to say it. Tell her about the story he's investigating. But he can't. He just can't. Not here. Not now. Not yet. "I was here to um, research—a novel thingy…a Hollywood western."

She pulls away from him. “Right? I know that.” She places the forks down.

“But I didn’t find what I expected here.”

“And just what did you find?” she asks, her arms gesturing for him to sit at the table.

“You. I found you.” Tom stands, holding onto his chair. He swallows loudly. Harder than he’s ever swallowed in his entire life.

“That’s really sweet,” says Nell, flickering her fingers at his hand on the chair, evident in her desire to sit and eat, as well as finish their *other* conversation.

She sits, and he takes a wicker chair to her left, placing a fiesta-colored cloth napkin on his lap.

“Thing is, it’s a very tough subject. I mean, Nan used to panic,” says Nell. “She’d be at work down at the gallery, hear an ambulance, and worry it was headed to the house for my mother. Honestly, I think Nan might have had a little PTSD herself, but from what I don’t know...she always kept quiet about her past. Didn’t want to affect how she raised me, I guess.”

Tom says nothing because in order to say anything he’ll have to breach the subject of Norma Jeane, who transformed into Marilyn Monroe, who became Marie Morton. Instead, he wears a tight-lipped smile, eyeing the food in an inviting ceramic-colored bowl.

Nell picks up on this. “Oh, please, allow me,” she says, taking the two large salad spoons and filling his plate.

“This house is cozy,” says Tom, taking a bite of avocado, looking around.

Nell looks around herself and declares, “Yes, I am the accumulation of all that I am. And I am exactly what I am because of what happened up to this point in my life.” She exhales with relief. “I’m supposed to be right here. Right now. Barnstable, Massachusetts. In this moment, with my new friend, Tommy. *This* is my purpose.”

"That's very nice. And very esoteric," says Tom.

"That's what mindfulness has taught me," she says, with a lovely slow smile, completely in yogi control. "Well, that and a morning of yoga stretching on the back porch," she giggles.

Tom feels this could be his complete purpose too. This beautiful woman and this beautiful seaside town. She begins talking about the summer garden, and he studies her face as she speaks. He's also studying her behavior for evidence. Nothing is apparent, except that Tom is clearly falling head over heels for the purity that Marilyn has instilled in this young woman from a time when she was just Norma Jeane herself. Tom can't put a finger on it, but he would say he feels almost pedestrian next to Nell.

"And look! This is Sylvia, my cat," says Nell, as a big golden tabby leaps from above the cupboard and circles around their chair legs, purring.

"Hi, kitty," says Tom, wiggling his fingers at her whiskers. "It's unusual to see an orange female, you know. They're usually only male." Sylvia smells at his wrist and rubs against his calf.

"Wow, clearly you read," says Nell. "She's almost thirteen and the most *glorious* creature always lying around in the sunshine. The other cat, Ted, is over by the heater." Sylvia gravitates between them for whisker rubs.

"You named your cats Sylvia and Ted?" he muses. "Like Sylvia Plath and Ted Hughes?"

"Nan named them. She loved Sylvia. Said Sylvia made even her *dying* an art."

Tom swallows hard as the food travels to his stomach, and he thinks of Marilyn's stomach pumped empty of pills. She made dying an art too. And she would have been alive to know of Sylvia Plath's death in February of '63, just months after her own supposed death.

"And she's very Zen," says Nell of Sylvia, tickling her hindlegs. "I learn a lot from her. Sometimes we rise and fall on the mat of life together. Breathing in the *nowwwww*."

"You mean the *meowwww*," says Tom, forming his hands in prayer pose under his breastbone.

Nell chuckles. "Yes," she says, very matter of fact. "Together, the human Ted and Sylvia had an erotic and literary love affair. Not so sure I envy that type of love with a bit of insanity." Her words hang as if to suggest she's looking for a lifetime partnership to be yin and yang, art and acting, passion and plight. As one.

As if Tom can understand what she's proposing, and not sure he can ever meet her artistic match, he offers his own original inspiration. "Maybe someday you'll visit an ashram," says Tom. "In India." His tone full of kindness. Free of ego.

"India? Ha!" says Nell coyly, surprised by his offbeat but gentle suggestion. "I can't even get myself to Boston!" She exhales and smiles at his constant thoughtfulness. "The Dalai Lama says 'Once a year, go someplace you've never been before,' so I'm way behind on his advice." Her eyes wander to a thinking place. "But I hear there's a good one in New Hampshire."

"I'm from New Hampshire."

"I know," she says biting her bottom lip to stop the unleashing of a smile.

"Maybe we'll go together," he says, unleashing a bigger smile on her behalf. "You can meet my mom and grandfather."

"I'd like that," she says tenderly, staring into his eyes and giving off a certain frailty that only an orphan can exhibit.

He reaches for her hand and stares back. Is he falling in love or is this *already* love? Truly, the idea of falling suggests you've already landed. Of course, he's dying to ask *Can I meet Nan?* But he's petrified to shine the flashlight into the empty cave. Because the moment he does, there's no turning back from the ghosts of Marilyn Monroe. He'd rather go at this as organically as the salad in front of him. He's going to "live in the now," just as Nell has been preaching. *But hell, it ain't easy!* He's on the edge of the ledge without the luxury of just jumping off into the freedom of truth.

"C'mon," says Nell, popping up to clear the plates. "let's have coffee in the living room." He begins to gather the silverware to the counter at the sink. "Oh, no, I've got it," she says. "But thank you. You go on. Check out my shelf on Russian literature. Some first editions there." Then she whispers, "I'm like a closeted librarian."

A sigh of relief comes over Tom at being dismissed to the living room, where he's again greeted by the red, white, and blue painting and a massive bookshelf. The books are haphazardly shoved into the spaces. Upon closer inspection, he realizes they're actually separated at least by fiction and nonfiction. *Kind of like Nell's life at the moment.*

Scanning the collection, Tom recalls reading in one of the Marilyn biographies that Philippe Halsman photographed Marilyn's apartment in 1952, and he "counted two hundred books on her shelf." Tom steps back, estimating with the drift of an eye...easily two thousand books. Enough to take her from 1952 to the present. Books on psychology, books on poetry, and a shelf on—*holy shit*—Kennedys to Clintons. And wait, oddly a lot on Abraham Lincoln. Tom remembers reading in Lois Banner's book, *Marilyn: The Passion and the Paradox,* that Marilyn wanted to be intelligent enough so she might understand the world around her.

Tom's fingers trace across some philosophy books. Plato, Saint Paul, and the Book of Revelations—clearly among her favorites, old and rabbit-eared from decades of reference. It's as if the old is mixed with the new, the before and after. Marilyn BC and Marilyn AD.

It's all so surreal.

A glimpse into a world *beyond* Marilyn Monroe...

Tom squats down to a lower shelf, force-filled with paperbacks shoved two rows deep. He pulls forward the one hardcover, *Paintings in Proust*. Just behind it, he spies a row of others. Dusty, in the back, he pulls out more to reveal a backrow: *Marilyn Monroe: The Biography, Goddess, Marilyn: Norma Jeane, The Last Days of Marilyn Monroe,* and so on. The same books he's ordered for himself on Amazon.

Footsteps approach from down the hallway. Tom quickly places the art book back in its place to cover the evidence. Standing up, he briskly rubs his dusty hands together.

"Find anything good?" asks Nell, placing down the coffee pot with a tray of cookies. "They're vegan, don't worry. No white flour, no eggs, no sugar, and no chocolate chips. I use carob."

"But it's still a cookie, right?" he jokes, taking one and nibbling. He munches for a second, his eyes tossing back and forth to judge the taste. "Okay, you win. I could live with these…" his words linger to mean *I could really live with you.* Because the cookies are just dreadful.

"Did you come across my first editions of Leo Tolstoy?" asks Nell.

He shakes his head. "No. But there's a lot to read here, for sure."

She moves to a shelf just above the Marilyn books. "The entire set includes *War and Peace, Anna Karenina,* and *Resurrection.* Cool, huh?"

"Really cool," says Tom, attempting to go along with her enthusiasm for Russian books.

"Shouldn't they be in a glass case to protect them?"

"Never," snaps Nell. "Nan bought them for me for my high school graduation, and they'll be with me until the day I die. I'm not worried about handing them off to someone else. I want to enjoy them."

"You have a point," says Tom, putting his hands in his pockets as if it might keep him from trouble. "I mean, why do people worry about preserving things instead of enjoying them? But just a thought…have you considered googling them? Just to see what they're worth."

"I don't google. It opens us up to so much noise and pollution," says Nell, standing up and handing him *Anna Karenina*. "They're worth what they're worth to me. Priceless."

Tom cautiously fingers through the book's pages, remembering it was required reading in his eleventh grade English class. He stops flipping pages and hands it back to Nell, asking, "The world is always more fascinated by the fall of a man than the survival of a woman, don't you think?"

"I never thought of it that way," says Nell, seaming her lips together in thought. "Yeah, I think that's right. Except Anna didn't survive."

Tom knows this is the perfect time to say *Yeah, but Marilyn Monroe, did…* but he can't. He just can't. Not yet. He can't risk it. So, he offers, "I often wondered…if my dad got home from war, would he have survived being back in civilization? Or maybe he would have left my mother for some seven-year itch." Tom looks for a reaction from Nell's face at the allusion to Marilyn's most famous movie. Nell doesn't flinch.

She places the volume back on the shelf. Grabs at a book by Sylvia Plath. "Look at this…"

He takes it. Opens it. In the corner of the title page are the initials "MM" penciled inside as if to suggest she owned it.

"Nan's favorite shelf was this one," she says. Tom catches the *was* her favorite shelf, but it doesn't mean Nan's dead. It could have been her favorite shelf in her younger years. Like you might say "chocolate was always my favorite ice cream," right? Because maybe you don't eat it anymore.

The next shelf is like a communion of women who spoke out and stood up. Laura Tetrault's *The Myth of Seneca Falls*, Erica Jong's *Fear of Flying*, Simone de Beauvoir, and even Colette, the iconic French writer who broke every rule.

"Nan's heroes," says Nell, her voice proud. "She wanted to be more like them."

He turns to her. "Thank you for sharing your life with me," so profound in his tone, which of course seems a little odd to Nell. They're only books, after all, but to Tom, he's just stepped into the portal where Marilyn slept, ate, and read the very books that occupied her life in the hereafter.

Nell pulls a really rabbit-eared copy of *The Feminine Mystique* from Tom's hand and places it back on the shelf. "Nan's superhero. That book. Don't ask me why," says Nell. "But she always taught me how Betty woke up all these stay-at-home housewives and would-be feminists." Nell nods her head at the memory. "When I was a little girl, Nan was always quoting Betty Friedan. And Gloria Steinem and Erica Jong. And Florynce Kennedy. But not Jackie Kennedy, so much."

The words *Jackie Kennedy* come at Tom full force just now. He stands perfectly still. Egging her on, he asks, "Why not Jackie Kennedy?"

Nell walks with the book to the window, gazing out through some quiet void in her mind. "I don't know," says Nell. "What's so wrong with Jackie Kennedy? I know Nan hated that bloody pink suit. She said it was gross that Jackie continued wearing it after her husband was shot. Wasn't ladylike. But that never made sense to me. Jackie was known for being a lady in history, right?" She turns back. "I mean, I believe the point of wearing the suit was to show the world the tragedy." Nell shrugs. "We were watching that movie—what's it called? *Jackie*, I think. One-word title. Natalie Portman starred. But she thought Jackie was so pretentious."

"Natalie or Nan?" says Tom, gulping.

"Nan did," says Nell. "That strange, elegant accent. I mean, look at my grandmother. She's always been so simple. A water baby by the sea."

It's at this moment that Tom realizes Nan is alive. Marilyn Monroe aka Marie Morton is *alive*!

Nell lifts a photo off the coffee table, handing it to Tom. He sees a woman dressed as Rosie the Riveter, the World War II icon. "That's Nan at the annual costume party a few years back."

Tom studies the woman with a red polka dot bandanna wrapped around her head, a blue worker's shirt, and her arm lifted in the infamous muscle-clenching pose. The face is that of an older Marilyn, her love affair with the camera barely evident, but if you didn't know it was Marilyn Monroe, and you weren't *looking* for Marilyn, why would you think anything else of this woman in big horn-rimmed glasses and graying brunette hair? She could be just about anybody.

"See what I mean?" says Nell. "Nan is full of chutzpah, but she's just your average Jane."

Tom's face goes white. *But this woman is no average Jane or even some* plain *Jane, she's Marilyn* f-ing *Monroe!*

"I want to meet her!" Tom blurts out.

"Sure, sometime," says Nells, creasing her brow at his enthusiasm. "I'd like that…but in due time. She's very private."

CHAPTER TWENTY-FOUR

Los Angeles

Spooner plucks his Tumi overnight bag from the backseat of an Uber. He hops the curb and begins heading toward the departure doors of LAX, scrolling his phone for his boarding pass just as it rings.

The name on the screen: "Dick Head Boss."

Spooner answers the call and doesn't even say hello. "Before you rip me a new asshole, just let me explain because—" Spooner starts, pulling his cell away from the screeching voice on the other end. It's Ritter for sure. We know this because we can hear him too. So can the entire airport.

Finally, his boss takes a big breath, then speaks very slowly as if talking to someone with limited capacity. "What day of the week were you planning to tell me you're leaving the paper?"

"You know the story you gave Hogan? Well, I've got a live lead on the old timers—"

"How'd you get a live lead? They barely have a pulse!"

"Well, ah…" Spooner can't divulge his story or Spits will kill him.

"It was for the Weekend Edition!" screams Ritter. "A punishment piece for Hogan, the other little screwup!"

"You aren't kidding, it's a punishment piece…" says Spooner, glancing up to the flight board for the updated info into Boston. All of the east coast–bound flights are blinking *Delayed* as a storm moves east through the Great Lakes. Spooner sees a second caller on his phone. It's Tony Spits. "Look, boss, I'll write. I'll even send a postcard. But I gotta go." He hangs up on his editor and clicks over.

"Spits? It's me—"

"I know who it is, kid, I just called you," says Tony Spits.

"Right," says Spooner, stalling at the security checkpoint.

"Your message said you found my beautiful Marie because of a painting?"

"I think so, yeah..." says Spooner, wondering whether he should tell Tony Spits that he *thinks* Marie Morton is Marilyn.

"You hear me?" says Spits.

"Yes," says Spooner, having zoned out.

"So, you're off to Cape Cod?" asks Spits.

"Yeah. I'm not sure Tom knows who he's found, but I'm gonna cut him off before he finds out any more about, ah, your Marie Morton." Spooner paces in front of the security line.

"Well, just remember, you're traveling on my money, so this ain't no damn vacation. And remember another thing—"

"I know, I know," says Spooner. "If I find her or your kid, I talk to you first."

A sound of the phone fumbling on the other end. Spooner can hear Spits mumbling something to his cronies. He returns to the conversation with Spooner. "I'll find out about this Hogan," says Spits. "I've got *people* in Boston."

"It's Cape Cod."

"Yeah, I got people there too."

The board flips over to *Cancelled*. "Look," says Spooner, "I gotta go. How about that...they're calling my flight..."

The two hang up, and Spooner slams his phone against a trash barrel. He brings the phone up to look at the screen, scanning the front and back. It's fine. Not a crack in the glass. Spooner exhales, moving his neck and shoulders in mini circles to calm himself. Then he goes to a nearby bench, drops his bag on the ground, and goes to the internet to find another airline that might have a flight, even if it's a connecting one.

With little luck and all flights delayed, he scrolls his Instagram account. It's gonna be a long night.

CHAPTER TWENTY-FIVE

Cape Cod

It's a crisp winter day. Sun is shining despite frigid temperatures. A sunny and happy Tom breezes through the front door of the gallery, but not before flipping the "Out to Lunch" sign over to "Open."

Frederick sees him. "Oh, dear. Where is our mind today?"

"Hello Fred-erick. Is Nell in?"

"Indeed." Frederick stares at Tom with a long pause.

"Well, may we see her?" asks Tom.

Frederick suppresses a smile at Tom imitating him, then glides across the floor like a runway model to see if she's available.

Tom stands in the space, inspecting the various works more cautiously this time. Seascapes, cranberry bogs, July Fourth scenes in watercolor. Real New England Currier & Ives stuff has replaced the contemporary wall. Clearly Marilyn Monroe's patriotic series are better than any of those.

"Isn't that one upside down?" asks Tom, surmising a lone abstract.

"We're not sure," says Frederick, tipping his head to figure it out.

Nell appears behind him. "Hey you…" She leans in to kiss him on the lips. A pleasant surprise, he reaches out to take her fingers in his hands.

Staring at her with a puppy-struck look he says, "I wouldn't think of going even one day without seeing you. But please explain to me why anybody would want illustrated charcoals." He points to a series on the far wall.

"We're going to pretend we didn't hear that," says Frederick.

"He's joking, Frederick," says Nell, eyes glued on Tom's. "You are joking, right?"

Tom shrugs. "So, you want to celebrate our newest artist?" asks Nell. "Susan Maguire."

"Let's have champagne!" says Tom, certain that after celebrating he'll have to be straight with her. He can't deny her the truth another second. *Whatever* that truth is going to turn out to be.

"What are you doing tonight?" asks Tom.

"Whatever you want..." says Frederick.

Nell turns to Frederick. "I think he meant me."

"Well, of course he did," says Frederick, fluttering his hands about as if dismissing the entire idea.

"Maybe we could go to our favorite restaurant," suggests Tom.

"We already have a favorite restaurant?" inquires Frederick.

"It's a very short list," chuckles Nell, with an added snort. Tom does the same, and they giggle at their own joke.

"How about someplace other than The Porpoise," he says. "I'm turning into a bowl of clam chowder as we speak."

"Gotcha," she says. "How about Haruto? Just down in Yarmouth Port. You like sushi?"

"My middle name is 'California Roll.'"

❧

Parking along the curb of Route 6A, Yarmouth Port, Tom exits the driver's side and scoots around to open the passenger's door to Nell. Rising statuesque onto the sidewalk, Nell wears a black wool dress that hugs her form.

Tom glances down at her boots. "Aren't those?" he asks.

"Yes," she professes. "My Hogan boots. In your honor."

"Sweet!"

Arm in arm, they walk toward the small white historical house with black shutters. It's done its best to disguise its typical Cape Cod features with a Japanese garden of aesthetic and philosophical ornamentation, camouflaging the otherwise barren trees on the street.

Inside the cozy space, a waiter seats them at a small table. Tom glances around at the minimalist style, though a hint of history is apparent in its ceiling rafters. Delicate Japanese music plays in the background.

"How about that Boston weather?" asks the waiter, handing the two their menus. "Flights cancelled in and out of Logan."

"Is it heading south?" asks Tom.

"Don't think so," says the waiter. "Salt air tends to dissipate the snowflakes." And then, "Can I get you anything to drink?" The two opt for sparking water and hot sake.

"You're going to love the food here," says Nell, studying the menu as Tom studies her with a connoisseur's eye—her long shiny brown hair now free of dreadlocks, her blue eyes glittering off the candle's reflection. Pure perfection. She glances up, then back down to her menu somewhat demurely. Perhaps Tom and Nell have fallen into role play. They've created a discreet reliability in one another. Or not. The big secret still hangs. Yet there's a silent truth between them—*just them*. If only this Marilyn Monroe situation didn't exist. *Can they have trust?*

And maybe, for all he knows, Nell knows about her grandmother. Maybe she's trusted him this far to carry on this code of silence. Maybe she trusts the organic chemistry of boy meets girl, boy falls for girl, girl falls for boy. Perhaps it's how she *wants* this to remain, so that for once in her life she's not attached to the quasi-Hollywood mystery of a sex bomb grandmother gone MIA.

Tom wrestles with timing and truth. Because for whatever reason, he just knows tonight is the night he *must* confront her about her grandmother. His grandfather always taught him that the truth will set you free.

"I bet you'll love the *tako no sumisoae*," says Nell, glancing up over her menu, breaking the silence. "It's bite-size octopus tossed with miso sauce. To *die* for."

"Awesome," he says, glancing at the menu prices. Steep. He swallows. Good thing his grandfather deposited that thousand dollars as a Christmas gift. He hated to ask for cash, but he told his grandfather he needed it for something work-related since he's eating up all his sick days on this investigation.

"The Hijiki salad is my favorite," she says. "Cooked seaweed, carrots, and tofu."

"Sounds perfect," says Tom, glancing at all the options. But his mind is elsewhere. On the truth again. *Because the truth will set you free…the truth will set you free…the truth will set you free.* "Hey," Tom asks, "how did a single grandmother support you?" He's expressionless, hovering over the menu.

The look on Nell's face suggests his question is out of left field. "She owned the gallery," says Nell. "But I suppose it's a good question," she twists her lip into a thinking pout. "I never really asked. "How did your mother afford to raise you?" she puts it back on him, a bit of sarcasm in her tone.

"She worked menial jobs. Grandpa took care of me on the farm."

"So, she had backup then," says Nell, her eyes squinting as if she's searching the memory banks of her mind. "I think Nan made some investments out in LA years ago."

"Oh?" Tom prompts, sipping his sparkling water with as much self-control as he can muster, despite wanting to gulp at her mention of Los Angeles. This is as close to Hollywood that they've come in their discussions.

"Yeah," says Nell, "She was raised out there. Adopted. I mean, how much of your grandmother do you know?"

"Not a hell of a lot. Just the usual immigrant stuff. Irish ancestors."

"I'm thinking one of these days I'll do one of those Ancestry DNA tests," says Nell. "I think you do it with a cheek swab."

"That's not a bad idea," says Tom for lack of a better comment.

"Yeah, I mean imagine if I found out my father was some famous scientist that I didn't think he was, or that my mother had a bit of Italian in her and hailed from some two generations back…the child of a Venetian opera singer, or even a really cool American Indian or—"she stops as the waiter arrives to take their orders.

Tom's mind is still on the financial element. It's been said that Marilyn was in financial straits at the end of her life. Her lawyer, Mickey Rudin, told her she had all but about thirteen thousand dollars to her name. Sounded like a lot in '62. Enough to get her started and pay the rent, maybe, until she could get a job at the local library. She had to be getting money from another source. And perhaps Horse helped.

"Although…I promise I won't ramble," says Nell, as he tunes back in. "I do that a lot. You're always a good listener, Tommy Hogan. A really good listener."

"I have to be," says Tom. "I'm a journalist. If I don't listen, I don't get the story."

Nell giggles. "There's no story from me. Trust me. Just a boring girl raised in Barnstable by her equally boring but occasionally vivacious grandmother."

"I don't believe she was boring…"

"Okay, maybe bad choice of words. I guess at the heart of her was some sixties rebel with a deep mistrust of the corporate world."

"None of that here in Barnstable."

"Yah think?" Nell teases. "Heck, even the shop signs have to be carved from wood."

"No neon here!" says Tom. Though he feels like he's glowing the words *liar* in every word he says, every move he makes. "And I noticed no chain stores either."

Now it's Nell that's studying Tom...as if she's the one gathering information on what he might be thinking or feeling. He stares at the wall behind Nell's head as if wondering what to say next.

Silence.

After a few moments, Nell reaches for his palm. Rubs it. "I'm in Cape Cod, but you're somewhere else."

"Oh, I was just thinking," he says.

"About what?"

"My family was so old fashioned. Kind of like the people here. I mean, I couldn't go online until I think I was in high school. Did your grandmother let you go online?"

The waiter places a bowl of salted edamame between them. Nell plucks one, sucking on the pod before she speaks. "I didn't have a cell phone until I was fourteen. It had limited call ability—I think I was allowed three calls to my Nan, *her* best friend, and my best friend. Add that to the fact you can't even *get* reception here, though you can get reception in Hyannis. That's where Barnstable High is—where I went to school. But yeah, she still monitored my calls. She kind of monitored everything I did. Probably just to protect me."

"From what?" He, grabs an edamame from the bowl.

"Child predators? Cranky fishermen? Sharks? *Jaws*!" she jokes, imitating the soundtrack.

"Cracks me up how our parents' generation were so frightened of that movie," says Tom. "It was a mechanical shark. So stupid."

"I know," says Nell, "It's wacked."

Tom wants to ask who Nan's best friend is or was, but he doesn't want to push the inquiry.

The food arrives, and the presentation of salads, sushi, and tempura is mouth-wateringly beautiful. For a moment they're silent, busy organizing their plates. At the unfolding of chopsticks and positioning the soy sauce to wasabi, Tom says, "If you had a famous dinner party who would you invite? Five people."

"Oh, that stupid game." Nell rolls her eyes. "Dead or alive?"

"Your call."

Nell places the chopsticks at the side of her cheek and thinks, "Michelle Obama…Beyoncé for sure, because she's such a smart businesswoman. Then a toss-up of either Gloria Steinem, Erica Jong, um…another significant feminist in the sixties…"

"What about twenty-first century? Sarah Jessica Parker with *Sex and the City?*"

"No way," says Nell. "That's when feminism stalled out. I've watched those reruns. Those women were self-indulgent and hysterical. PMS was okay but so was everything materialistic. It all just denigrated into hedonistic. I mean, I couldn't even tell you what a Birkin bag looks like."

"Fair," says Tom. "But you still have one more dinner guest. I said five."

She ponders. "I guess someone when it was a real challenge for women…"

"There's Marilyn Monroe," Tom blurts out.

"Yeah," says Nell, forgiving, almost sing-song. "I don't know enough about her. She was just a sad movie star. Killed herself, didn't she?"

"Yeah, I think so," Tom says casually, then attacking a Hamachi roll. "I mean, who knows…myths, I guess." He shoves the yellowtail sushi into his mouth, preventing him from saying more, allowing him to gather his thoughts. Nell picks her chopsticks at her plate. Tom wonders if maybe Nell's a very good actress, just like her grandmother, and is pretending not to know about Marilyn Monroe.

"Maybe Joni Mitchell?" says Tom. "There was a great story on her in *The New Yorker*."

Nell nods. "You read the *New Yorker?*"

He nods. "It said something about how her music was for falling in love, over and over, while defending her sense of self. Something like that."

"Maybe, but I think I'd go with someone like Jane Goodall—"

"The gorilla woman?"

Nell nods. "Yeah, or even Daenerys Targaryen."

"*Game of Thrones*? Emily Clarke's character?" asks Tom. "Now you're talking!"

The waiter stops by to check on everything. They nod with mouthfuls of delight.

Tom sips his sake. He's got an idea. Maybe he can figure out how her mind works through her value system…how Marilyn may have influenced her. "Nellie?"

"Mmm?" she looks up.

"What's more important for a man to possess: fame or money?"

Nell thinks on it—*hard*—before offering an answer. "I'll go with fame."

"Why?"

"Well," Nell says, staring at the wall behind him as if figuring out what she wants to say. "If the guy has talent from fame, it's far more attractive than if he just has a hefty bank account. You want the man who *invented* the widget, not the one who *invested* in it."

Tom dares, "Fame, huh? So…like a politician or maybe a Pulitzer winner or even a baseball player?" He's referencing JFK, Arthur Miller, and Joe DiMaggio. All of Marilyn's exes.

"Sure," she says, completely innocent, "I guess any of those guys might work…" But then she frowns her forehead as she reflects on his odd and old choices. "Or Steve Jobs, John Legend, or…how about Jordan Peele, that really cool director?"

Leaning in across the table, Tom asks, "What about me? I'm a guy, and I have neither to offer. Fame nor money."

She leans to meet him and pecks his lips. Then lowers her arm to pluck a piece of sushi, bringing the chopstick to his mouth. "No, you don't have fame or money, but you have a big heart. You're kind." She squiggles her nose. "And kindness is so underrated, Tommy." Her voice goes breathy. "Don't you know that…" her voice trails off to a sensual place of suggested euphoria.

They share a look. A look that says, *Let's get the check and get the hell out of here.*

Tom's lip curls in a triumphant smile.

CHAPTER TWENTY-SIX

A stack of old CDs are scattered across the living room floor. Music permeates the walls. Tom is playing air guitar while Nell dances on the coffee table to Ariana Grande before the disk player shuffles to a golden oldie…KC and The Sunshine Band blare from the stereo…

"Oh my God, I love this song!" says Nell with such sentiment, crossing her hands over her heart, then changing-up her moves to the beat, dance-skipping, happy-go-lucky…

"Watch this!" says Tom, moonwalking to perfection and gliding right into the kitchen. He disappears for a moment and then reverses back dancing the "awkward robot." He's nailed it.

"Oh yeah?" sneers Nell. "Well, watch this!" She leaps from the table and starts the elbow-to-knee classic. Tom joins in. They trip and knock into each other, losing their balance. Silly laughter ensues.

Nell raises a hold-it pointy finger as the music changes to rap. Turning her back on Tom, Nell marches across the room to the fireplace where she starts twerking…adding in the perfect booty pop.

Tom stops short, staring at her in awe. "Damn, girl! You had me at *booty*." She giggles, moving around him. "You win," he says. "Like, I completely, totally surrender."

With a confident flair, Nell "Egyptian" moves around Tom, who tosses her onto the sofa in jest. They face each other, breathless.

"That was fun," says Nell, messing at her own hair. "Nostalgia is *way* cool, don't you think?"

"You mean the music?" asks Tom. "Or crazy shit like that?" He points, rises from the sofa, and—still dancing—sashays to a shelf full of tchotchkes. Bobbleheads span the cupboard from Snoopy to Queen Elizabeth, Elvis to the Beatles, Jesus to Joe DiMaggio, Muhammad Ali to Superman. And, just behind all of them, Marilyn Monroe. Tom points to the plastic bobbles, cocking his head sideways in sarcasm. "You collect these?" he asks, his tone a bit off.

Nell snickers. "Those stupid things? *No way.* But Nan always thought they were hilarious. *She* collected them. I just don't have the heart to take them down."

"I like this one," says Tom, picking up Jerry Seinfeld. "Ever watch his show?"

Nell nods her head. "It's always streaming." Nell stands up and goes to place Seinfeld back in his spot. "Nan used to say, 'You know you've made it when you're a bobble head.'"

"Oh, yeah?" The perfect segue: "So which one was she?"

"None of them, silly," says Nell. "So, I guess she never made it." Tom holds the moment. "Nan was something else when I was little," says Nell, topping off their wine glasses. "I think she *knew* she was *gorgeous,* but she downplayed it, you know." Tom goes to sip, instead gulping from her comment. "I mean, I tried to get her to color her hair once from brown. Put some highlights in it…get my friend to give her a sassy bob, but she never wanted to experiment. It's all so strange because whenever we were alone, she was *so* experimental. Dancing, singing, putting on shows in our living room."

"Quasi Broadway musicals," Tom chimes in. Imagining it to be true.

"Yeah," Nell snickers. "Exactly." She moves closer to him and sips from his wine this time. "Sometimes, she'd have all this weird bossy energy. Telling me, 'No, head up high, move more to the left' or 'Say it like you mean it,' as if we were auditioning for a big feature film. Maybe it's why I joined the theatre workshop."

"Sounds fun to me," he says, his voice quivering.

"Maybe she was a little bipolar. I mean, we'd go from gold foil stars and coloring books to dramatic productions with musical numbers. It was a bit much."

Tom places his wine on the table and plops back down on the sofa. "Did you ever watch old movies?"

"Yeah, sometimes," says Nell, plopping down next to him. "But she was very selective. She always chose which ones."

"Did she have any favorites?"

"Um," Nell's eyes do a calculation. "Jerry Lewis? Yeah, anything with Jerry Lewis."

"Oh, yeah, I heard of him. Any others?" He hears his own question. It almost sounds like he's prying.

"*Guys and Dolls*," says Nell. "There's a scene I know by heart, where a group of guys are singing 'Luck Be a Lady Tonight.'" She looks to Tom. "Do you know that one?"

"Um, not really," he says, half paying attention, since it's not helping him move into Marilyn territory. Until she says…

"It starred Frank Sinatra. Nan just *loved* Frank Sinatra. Anyway, some character in the movie says something like, um, 'to love and be loved is the greatest gift a woman and man can have on this earth.' I think it was someone in a red butler's uniform. It always made Nan sad."

"What else did Nan say?" asks Tom, relaxed, sleepy.

"She hated the way women quiver when they spoke in old films. How they folded their arms like this," says Nell, folding her arms as if she's serious and angry. "They always raised their voices and pouted in those classic movies. They're either all high-pitched whiners or little bitches."

"Your Nan said that?" chuckles Tom, snapping back.

"Yeah," says Nell, "She could be pretty direct."

"Did she—"

"Enough about my grandmother," says Nell, nuzzling into Tom's side. She looks up, and he goes to kiss her. Tenderly at first, then really exploring her lips with consideration. They kiss gently for a long time as though every touch of their mouth is a forever kiss.

Nell pulls back first, running her fingers through her hair. "I turned the light off in my heart."

"Why?" he asks gently, turning into her.

"Heartbreak in high school. Boyfriend cheated on me."

Tom falls back against the sofa, his eyes lifting to the ceiling. "My ex-girlfriend cheated on me too."

Nell gets comfortable, hands resting on her chest and staring up to the ceiling as though it has stars. "That boy was the one I lost my virginity to, so you know what that means?" Tom shakes his head *no*. "Well, you always remember your first. So, I'll be in his head for the rest of his life too," she snickers. "I've got a bad track record with men. The college one—well, he was a player. Really hot. A poet. Pretended to be the love of my life. Then he vanished," she says, with longing. "And then there was the stage-five clinger."

"Why a clinger?" asks Tom.

"On the third date he was ready to pick out names for our kids. Is that a good reason?"

"Can you blame him?" he says, turning into her, and now he's running his fingers down her nose and chin. He can practically inhale her beauty.

"He recently tried to get me back, you know."

"He did?"

"Sent me dick picks."

"Seriously?" asks Tom. "That's gross!"

They both burst out laughing, making it funnier than it is, probably because they're unusually drunk. And extremely nervous.

Then, Nell gets serious. "I went to talk to a therapist once. Wondered if not having a father or a mother was fucking me up in relationship choices."

"But you had your grandmother," says Tom, reaching in to kiss her again, yet wanting to respect her need to talk. Nell kisses him again for a little bit and then lowers her head into his chest, inhaling his shirt. He gently strokes her hair.

"I love having my head rubbed. Nan used to do that," she says, her voice sounding hypnotized. "But she never gave me the sense that she trusted men. She was so fierce in protecting me. Taught me to find strength that isn't found in a man."

"How did that work out?" he whispers, kissing the top of her head.

"So far so good," she mumbles. There's an awkward pause where Tom is processing the way Nell uses words in the past tense when referencing her grandmother. Nell keeps saying things like, "She *was* so fierce in protecting me." He was certain she was alive, but well, maybe not. And, if she *is* alive, Nell could be referring to her behavior in past tense—meaning how she might have acted years ago or last year as opposed to in the present, when she's an old woman. He's drawing a blank. Too much wine. A hunger for sex. And his heart is superseding any logic that his head can produce at 11 p.m.

"Don't you agree?" says Nell.

"Um, what? Yeah, sure. I agree," says Tom, going along, mesmerized by this complete experience. Nell is the most gorgeous woman he's ever been with.

"Yes, she really did teach me to be independent." Nell goes to snuggle in more, but Tom sits forward to grab his wine and take another nervous sip. He should just ask her straight out if her Nan is alive or dead, but he's utterly petrified to know. Knowing… well, it will take away from the organic unfolding of falling in love with Nell.

Instead, Tom blurts out, "Did she have money?"

"Nan? Some."

"From where?"

Nell knits her eyebrows. "You already asked how she had the money to raise me. But come to think about it, she invested. Stock tips," she says, now sitting up straight. "Why are you so interested in my grandmother?"

He puts his wine down and goes to take her in his arms. "I'm not. I mean, I am. I'm interested in *all* that is you." He attacks her mouth full-throttle because he knows if he's not kissing her, the next words out of his mouth are going to blow his entire cover.

Nell surprises him. She suddenly wants to be kissed. Hard. Her tongue penetrates his mouth. They float into their orbit creating their own sexual vortex. It's as if whatever the outcome—the mystery—is irrelevant. The universe is conspiring in their favor just now.

All that matters is tonight. The two of them. As one.

The CD player moves to the next disc. X Ambassadors' "Unsteady" pumps through the house. The lyrics holding the note as Tom wants to hold onto Nell and as the lyrics reflect he's feeling a little bit unsteady himself. Without even heading to the bedroom, Nell and Tom slide down to the Berber rug, lips still attached. Nell sweeps the CD cases away to find space to lie comfortably. Before long, they're tearing off sweaters, dresses, jeans, panties, bras. All of it.

Entwined naked in each other's arms, exploring each other from head to toe…these are two young lovers moving into heavy adult territory.

The music owns the room.

And they own each other.

This is serious.

This is *really* serious.

CHAPTER TWENTY-SEVEN

Tom's breath barely catches up with his thumping heart as he falls back on the carpet, exhaling euphoria. So this is love. An odd mix of happiness and anxiety

His mind travels back in time…daydreaming…

He was a little kid at the Craftsmen's Fair of New Hampshire. Every little boy had purchased a ticket to win the Tickle Me Elmo doll, one of the most iconic and simultaneously *annoying* toys of its time. But his mother could only afford one ticket. It was highly unlikely they'd win the darn raffle, and every toy store shelf was sold out. The fuzzy red doll was such a fad that she couldn't even *buy* him one without paying $1,500 on some black market. For her, that was more than a month's salary.

Tom remembers watching the farmer near the snow cone machine calling out a series of numbers. "17, 7, and 26!" *His numbers!* Tom's eyes nearly popped from their sockets. *The winning ticket!* He looked up to his mother, who had tears in her eyes. She pulled him in. *"You've won, honey, you've won!"* He stood in utter denial as she nudged him, *"Go on, get your prize."* The neighbors all clapped, turning around to watch little Tommy Hogan, the big winner, as he made his way to the front of the crowd like Moses parting the Red Sea.

At the counter, Tom's heart was beating so hard. He lifted his arms to take the gift box from the farmer, staring in awe at Elmo beneath the plastic cover…the red plush Muppet with oversized white eyes and arms spread wide as though he'd been waiting for him all his life. Tom felt a swell of pride. He knew he'd take such good care of Elmo forever. He was the luckiest kid in the world…

Tom glances over at Nell. He won the prize all over again. He's the luckiest man in the world. And he'll take good care of Nell until the day she dies. If only she'll let him.

"Where'd you go?" she whispers. Tom shrugs, swallows hard, and tries to speak but nothing comes out. "Come on, then," she says, rolling backwards with a smile. "Let's go to bed."

"Is this a sleepover? Because I didn't bring my pajamas."

"Yes," she laughs, raising a brow. "And we sleep in the nude here." She heads to the bathroom, disappearing around the corner, her giggle like that of a mouse, a mere miniature squeak, just like her grandmother's famous laugh.

Moments later, Nell reappears in boy shorts and a faded tee shirt that reads *The Future is Female.* She puts out her hand and pulls him upright. "I'm wiped out. Have to be up early tomorrow. Volunteering at the senior center."

"That's cool," says Tom, standing beside her now in just his boxers.

"Yeah, all the old ladies give me their history, and I give them energy and undivided attention." Nell turns out the lights downstairs and blows out the candle. "I guess I have more connection to my emotions than they did as young women back in their day." They head upstairs, Tom following behind as Nell speaks. "The shitty bit is that a lot of them were once these *gorgeous* women with husbands and careers, and they are so well-traveled, but men just don't look at them anymore. It's like they're invisible now…"

Kind of like your grandmother… Tom's thinking.

But Nell banters on. "They're used to being cut off in the middle of a sentence before their ten seconds are up by someone younger and too busy to listen to them. It's sad."

Tom's mind immediately thinks of Lolly. He loved to listen to Lolly. Got a kick of out him. But when Tom rang Lolly just two days ago to tell him he thinks everything he said might be true, he learned the sad news that Lolly had died. Such a shame he didn't live just a bit longer to see his story come to fruition, but now Tom felt even more compelled to bring Lolly's truth back to life.

As they ascend to the top of the stairs, Tom sees a light coming from the attic. The pull-down steps are suspended just above Nell's bedroom door, with a string almost begging to be pulled.

Maybe it's where Marilyn is hiding out? Tom looks at Nell and knits his brow. "Is this the part where I find out you're not so perfect because you have a crazy aunt living in the attic?"

"Yes, and she's got a peg leg." Nell play-punches him in the shoulder. "Nah, nothing like that. I was up there today going through some of Nan's things."

"Really?" says Tom, torn between wanting to devour her some more and wanting to just know the truth. About Nan. About *Marilyn.* About all of it. The lit space beckons for discovery. "Okay, so, prove to me that there's not some creepy ghost in the haunted attic."

Nell makes googly eyes and does creepy-crawly fingers. As if she's a witch luring him into her candy house, she asks, "You really want to know, little boy?" He nods with certainty. "Fine. C'mon, but only for five minutes," she says, her voice back to normal. She gestures for him to climb up first. "Go on."

The two climb the narrow steep steps to get to the top, where Tom suspects he's entering a magical, private time warp.

Glancing around at the unfinished attic, ceiling insulation exposed, he's not sure what he's about to see, but he knows that whatever he's in for, he'll be dancing on the edge of a volcano.

To his left, he spots old Carole King, Beatles, and Carpenters albums lining the walls. To the right, there's worn record sleeves of Sammy Davis Jr. and tons of Tony Bennett. Above, a handful of winter coats and simple dresses are suspended from a ceiling rack. Boxes of shoes are neatly stacked and labeled on the floor. Hat boxes in a corner.

"Wow! Look at all this," says Tom, staring around. To him, it's apocalyptic.

Nell frowns. "It's just some dusty old junk that Nan asked me to donate."

Yeah, but they're Marilyn Monroe's*! Don't just donate them! Put them in a museum!*

Tom turns to Nell, lighting up like a young boy who's discovered a pirate's treasure chest. "Nell, I just want you to know…no matter what happens, I'm really crazy for you."

"Okay," she says, taken back by his strange admission. "That's nice. I'm kind of crazy about you too." She moves to a corner under an attic window. "Come here," she says. "Wanna see something cool?" Leading him to a 1950s-style cedar hope chest, she kneels to its side and turns the key in the lock.

He kneels too, trying not to tremble. *Here he is, little Tommy from New Hampshire about to open the hope chest of Marilyn Monroe. Way bigger than Tickle Me Elmo!*

"Isn't it crazy that women had hope chests before they got married?" says Nell, lifting the lid. She pulls out a pair of Jax black-checkered pants…ones that Tom has seen in countless research photos. Supposedly Marilyn had several pairs. Tom recently saw a pair on an auction site. Black satin ones claiming to be handed down to Dr. Greenson's daughter because they were too large for Marilyn. The Jax label sewn inside. *Stay calm, Tommy, stay calm…*

No sooner Tom catches his breath, Nell double-whams him with her next thought. "They were her favorites, but she can't fit into them anymore."

"She can't fit into them anymore." Anymore. Oh my God, she's alive! Tom digs his fingers into the cover of the hope chest for support. *He's just found out Marilyn Monroe is truly alive! Really.*

Truly. Alive. To this day! His fingers tremble as he takes a shallow breath, enough to brace himself. And he didn't even have to ask. Nell volunteered the information. The look on his face says he might cry, but instead he smiles.

"Are you okay?" asks Nell. "You look like you've seen a ghost."

"Kind of."

"Nan had a lot of ghosts," says Nell, standing up. "I don't know what happened in her life that was so dark, but she used to love to come up here and look at these things from some happier times."

"Maybe you should just come out and ask her?" says Tom.

"Maybe when the time is right. She's old. I don't want to upset her." Nell lifts more items out of the chest. A pink Pucci blouse, carefully wrapped in plastic, the liner smelling of cedar and moth balls. A neatly folded full-length scarf. Nylon purple gloves, sheer and sexy. Beneath the clothes, a stack of tattered *LIFE* magazines. The first dated December 6, 1963—price 25 cents—with "Mrs. Kennedy, Caroline and John Jr. wait to join procession to Capitol." Underneath that issue, the "John F. Kennedy Memorial Edition Including His Biography and His Most Enduring Words."

Tom wants to ransack the chest, but he patiently lets her do it her way, lifting out each piece with care. October 2, 1964: "The Warren Report." *Look* magazine's "The Dramatic Conclusion of the Death of a President" from March 7, 1967. Tom says nothing, waiting for Nell to speak. "I think because these were about the Kennedys, she thought they might someday be worth something."

"And a book," says Tom. Unable to help himself, he reaches in to lift *Science and Health with Key to the Scripture* by Mary Baker Eddy. "Christian Science?" he says, fingering through it. "Wonder why it's not downstairs on her bookshelf?" As soon as the words leave his mouth, he comes across a hand-written note: *"Norma J, my dear, read this book. I do not leave you much except my love, but not even death can diminish that; nor will death take me far away from you." —Ana Lower.* He glances up to see if Nell is reading and she is.

"Hmmm…wonder who Norma J was?" asks Nell, shrugging her shoulders. "Guess Nan bought it secondhand in a yard sale." Now Nell reaches back into the chest, so Tom shuts the book quickly, gingerly placing it onto the floor. Tucked in the corner, wrapped in tissue paper, Nell releases a lone tattered baseball. She lifts it out. "Here, you want it?" asks Nell, tossing him the old baseball. "You're a Sox fan, right?"

"Yes," says Tom, rolling the ball in his hand. "But it's from Yankee Stadium, I'm afraid." Upon closer inspection, his eyes bulge. It's autographed by Joe DiMaggio. *Fuck! Fuck! Fuck!*

"You know what Nan used to say when she saw this baseball?" Tom is frozen, speechless. "That life and love are everything. Whoever steals life steals it all…whatever the heck that meant."

"Maybe stealing home base?" asks Tom sarcastically, but he knows exactly what Marilyn meant. She stole her life away. She *got* away. Her only crime was loving the wrong men.

"Who was the love of her life?" asks Tom, barely able to balance on his knees.

Nell sits back on her shins, lowering the lid. "Hmmm… she used to talk about a really good friend named Bobby, and a woman named Pat. Oh, and then there were guys named Sammy and Frank. But I don't think it was a who, it was more a what. She loved the arts," says Nell, rising and wiping her hands of the dust. "Literature, movies, theatre, singing, and dancing. And she just loves nature walks. Her garden. The birds."

Tom runs the names through his head…Bobby *(Kennedy)*, Pat *(Lawford)*, Frank *(Sinatra)* and Sammy *(Davis Jr.)*. He realizes he wouldn't think twice about these common names either, unless of course he was investigating the life of Marilyn Monroe! *Maybe she's playing me? Maybe Nell knows all of this, and she's seeing how I'll respond.*

Tom stands now, but the room is turning slightly blue—or is it in his head? Because he might literally faint, but he doesn't know what fainting feels like because he's never actually passed out. Moving to the banister, he takes a few gulps of air, standing upright, "Sorry, I'm just tired."

"Me too," says Nell. "I said we'd look at this yard sale stuff for five minutes, and I've given you ten."

Tom makes the *after you* gesture, and she moves to the stairs. *I can't let her sell this stuff in a garage sale. Someone will catch on…*

"My grandfather used to carve cedar chests as a hobby," says Tom, looking around one more time. "Sold them at the fair. My mother has one passed down from a great-grandfather that's lasted like two hundred years. She never 'hoped' for my father to marry her, but she hoped he'd come home from war."

"I can't imagine being a widow," says Nell, squeezing his hand. "It sounds so devastating." Nell climbs first back down the stairs, careful to hold the makeshift railing on either side, looking up to Tom climbing behind her. He holds the DiMaggio baseball in his hand for dear life. As he gets to the ground floor, Nell carefully pulls the light switch off, and Tom tucks the staircase back up, pushing until it with force, three times, until it finally locks into place.

As he does, a Yeats poem, framed, near the bedroom door, reveals itself.

Never give all the heart, for love
Will hardly seem worth thinking of
To passionate women if it seem
Certain, and they never dream
That it fades out from kiss to kiss;
For everything that's lovely is
But a brief, dreamy, kind delight.
O never give the heart outright.

Tom knows this poem—he read somewhere that it was one of Marilyn's favorites.

"That's going in the garage sale too. Seeing that every time I go to bed?" Nell chuckles. "And you wonder why I'm afraid of love."

"Please don't be afraid of love." He touches his lips to hers, clutching the baseball in his left hand. "I'm here. You can trust me."

CHAPTER TWENTY-EIGHT

Spooner's red-eyed arrival to Boston's Logan airport plays out hastily; he's one minute away from exploding on the car rental clerk…the one we recognize from Tom's car rental counter.

"*C'mon, c'mon,*" snaps Spooner, grabbing at the paperwork and initialing the contract pages in record speed, shoving them back at her, crinkling the pages. "I already told you, just give me all the extras," he says. "Car insurance, navigation, full tank, return low, all-wheel drive, everything. You got it?" She nods. "Except the car seat."

She obliges, robotically typing like mad into her computer, adding his license and other pertinent info, backspacing on her keyboard in error and nervousness.

"*Jesus,*" he says. "Can't you type any faster?"

Next, she opens a road map, circles "You are here," and turns it to his side of the counter. Spooner pushes the page back in her face. "Just tell me which way to go to pick up the damn car," says Spooner.

Directing him to an escalator, she calls out, "Please drive safely." But he's gone, taking the escalator steps two at a time, leaving the counter clerk to wonder if all LA people are so rude.

~

Tom wakes to a *ding* sound coming from his phone. He ignores it. Doing a happy dance in his heart, he groggily turns to snuggle

Nell. Her head should be on the pillow, but instead he finds a note that reads: *"Morning sleepy head. Detox tea brewing on the counter. Front door locks automatically. Call me later. Xo Nellie. P.S. Last night rocked."*

Tom realizes that the best gifts of life are those never imagined. He falls back on the pillow with a big exhale and ear to ear grin.

Moving to the bathroom, Tom places his cell on the sink ledge. It continues to *ding* with text messages, but the house has unreliable cell service. Splashing water on his face, he examines his complexion. He sees himself as much more handsome and confident than he was just yesterday. That is until he tastes his morning breath. Anticipating the need for a toothbrush, Nell's left a sticky note to the mirror. *"Spare toothbrush in the cabinet."*

He opens it to an array of all natural and herbal products, tampons, and a five pack of Oral-Bs spotted in the back next to what looks like a very old bottle of copper-colored liquid. The letters on the black-and-white label read Chanel No. 5.

Marilyn's signature scent.

Tom's eyes widen. He removes it, careful not to clank the other items, and brings it to his nose. It could be any scent whose chemistry can only be brought to life when it plays on *her* flesh. Tom can only imagine how the delicious aroma miraculously transformed on the nape of Marilyn's neck.

His phone dings a text again, startling him to almost drop the bottle in the sink basin. Carefully placing it back, albeit with a clank, he moves to the kitchen to get two bars of cell service. Now the texts come pouring through. One from his boss, one from a friend about a sports event, one from his mother, and quite a few from Becca back at the LA office.

Becca's texts arrive in this order:

Hey, how's Cape Cod? Call me. Followed by a smiley emoji.

Then: *Call me! Spooner knows about Sterling Powers and the painting. He's on his way to find you.* With a shocked yellow face emoji holding its cheeks.

Next: *Where are you? Did you die or something?* A yellow face emoji wiping a tear.

Next, late last night LA time: *I don't know what's going on but he's going to find you!!!! Some story about a woman named Marie Morton.* An angry face emoji. And a red devil emoji repeated several times in the text message.

Finally, one very last text even later last night: *Fine. Don't call. Just run. Xo.* A prayer hands emoji and a big red kiss.

CHAPTER TWENTY-NINE

Spooner revs up the engine of his rented black BMW x5, blowing down Route 93, weaving in and out of lanes. He bypasses Scituate and Plymouth in record time and crosses the Sagamore Bridge into Cape Cod. A rap song vibrates through the vehicle and can be heard outside. His cell phone rings. He fumbles quickly to pick up.

"Mom?" His voice is like that of a frightened child stuck at the bottom of the escalator watching his mother already at the top. A pause as she speaks. A stunned Spooner says, "You did? Wow, I don't know what to say." Because his mother has informed him that she's just remarried…to a man Spooner has never even met. "Well, as long as you're happy…" he says, feeling left out.

Maybe it's best to change the subject. "Hey Mom, I'm on a *huge* assignment. Biggest one of my life, and I'll be able to—" He's interrupted. "What's that?" he asks. Another pause, longer than the look on Spooner's face. "Oh, okay, sure, I understand." And with that, she's gone...dashing off to Bali with her new husband. Spooner disconnects the call feeling no better than he did before she rang. "Fuck, fuck, *fuck*!" he screams, cranking the music back up to max volume. Sure, Spooner could be identified as a human with a bratty frailty that translates to ugliness, but there's a vulnerable side of him that just needs to find someone who feels compassion. Someone who might take Spooner into their arms, hold him, and rock with him. Who could tell him it will all be all right…even if it never will be.

Exiting at Route 6, Spooner signals left into Barnstable. That's where Becca said Tom was hanging. At the blinking light, he blows down Route 6A, winding his way into the village. Spooner glances left and right at the clapboard houses. The look on his face tells us he's not into seaside towns, lighthouses, or lobsters.

He slows at an old inn in a 1740s barn set back from the main road. The carved wooden sign The Lamb and the Rabbit. Spooner twists the wheel, turning left with little consideration of other drivers, speeding past the carved wooden sign for the inn. His BMW is definitely out of place amidst the family vehicles and SUVs. Slamming the car door, he heads to the front office where a sign reads: *One of the Top 5 B&Bs in Coastal Massachusetts—Boston Magazine.*'

He plucks a brochure, scanning it: wood-burning fireplaces, suites with kitchenettes, a covered horse stable, a courtyard with a solar heated saltwater pool, year-round hot tub, and lounge chairs. A woman stands at the counter. He doesn't even look at her. "Yeah, I'll take any room. But Wi-Fi is a must," says Spooner, dropping his platinum card on the desk.

Moments later, Spooner turns the key in the room's lock, and his eyes dart around the quaint warm yellow walls and a framed bird print. There's an outdated TV and DVD player. A private bath. Tossing his jacket on the four-poster bed, he whips out his laptop to sign in for messages. To most Americans looking for a bit of nostalgia, this room with a potbelly hearth would be charming. To Spooner, it's all wrong.

"Hey Spits," says Spooner into his cell phone, his laptop opened. "I made it… Can you hear me? *Spits*? You're breaking up. *Spits!*" Spooner tosses his cell phone to the bed, where it bounces safely off the quilt. "Fucking small town! Fucking worthless Pilgrims!"

He heads to the shower.

~

A quiet motel room nearby, where a blank computer screen sits in front of Tom. He types the bold title word.

"*BOMBSHELL!*"

A subtitle follows:

"*Marilyn Monroe's granddaughter alive and well in Barnstable, Cape Cod.*"

His byline:

"*Tom Hogan.*"

Scattered around him on the desk, on the bed, and on the floor are a full morning's research…books, biographies, articles, and a handwritten list of the proof he has to support his theory on the night of Marilyn Monroe's disappearance:

1. Don Hockett, son of the man who owned Westwood Village Mortuary, wheeled out the zipped black bag that carried Marilyn's body from her address at 12305 Fifth Helena Drive. *Yet, who saw the body? Was he paid off? Or was it already "zipped" when he arrived?*
2. Multiple prescriptions were found near Marilyn's bed. However, not a glass of water to swallow the pills was anywhere in sight. Further, there was zero residue of pills in her stomach.
3. Housekeeper Eunice Murray claims she saw a light under Marilyn's bedroom door, yet the carpet pile under the door of Monroe's bedroom was too high to cast even the slightest of shadow.
4. Why is it that five hours elapsed between the time Eunice found her body and authorities were called? Were those five hours enough time to plan her escape to self-imposed witness protection? Why was her fam-

ily therapist, Dr. Greenson, called first instead of the police? *What kind of botched investigation was that?*

5. Why did the first coroner's report magically disappear?
6. *LIFE* photographer, Leigh Wiener, was supposedly the only one allowed inside the coroner's office. Claims he had photos of dead Marilyn. Claims to have taken three rolls of film and they're in a safety deposit box in LA. *Why is it nobody ever saw them?*
7. In Donald H. Wolfe's book, *The Last Days of Marilyn Monroe,* there is a photo of Eunice returning to Marilyn's home a few days later. Before she leaves, she gazes into the guest cottage, to the floor just beyond the window where Marilyn died. *Could she be thinking, "Thank God. She got away..."?* Further, years later, in a 1983 BBC interview, Eunice lowered her head in her hands and kept asking how long would she have to cover the truth?
8. Joe DiMaggio refused many friends and family access to the funeral, thus keeping the service small and intimate. *Were the few funeral attendees (including her physician, Dr. Engelberg) all in on the plan?*
9. And the biggie: Cedars of Lebanon Hospital is where Marilyn supposedly had an abortion six weeks before she died, yet there's no record of any surgery. *Did she and her baby get away?*

Tom's face glows off the computer screen as he sits staring at the facts, almost catatonically. Finally, he takes a deep breath and holds it before exhaling loudly through pursed lips. He's nailed this story, but his stomach is churning with nerves. Reaching for a bottle of water, he unscrews the top and chugs. His eyes never leave the screen. Placing the bottle down, he circles his neck around his shoulders to release tension. Finally, with a tortured certainty, he begins typing his story:

They say legends die hard, that myth beats reality every time. But there is that occasional point where myth and reality intersect. Such is the case with the legend and reality of Marilyn Monroe.

One of the problems surrounding her death—aside from the bungled police report and the flawed and inconclusive coroner's report—were the swirling conspiracy theories. Did she take her own life, or was it a murder? Over fifty years later, we find out neither theory is true. Turns out on the night of her "death," she escaped. She lived. The thrice-married bombshell movie star, whose biggest desire was to mother a child, lived and thrived in Cape Cod with her daughter, Grace, and her granddaughter Penelope, under Marilyn's new identity: Marie Morton. Yes, Marilyn Monroe lives on…

Glancing at his grandfather's Citizens watch—12 p.m. in Barnstable and 9 a.m. in Los Angeles—Tom's core is whispering to him. And what he's hearing is his grandfather's lifelong advice about integrity and honesty. Tom stares blankly at what he's written, but reflecting on the rules of ethics in good journalism once more:

> *Is it true?* Yes.
>
> *Is it researched?* Yes.
>
> *Is it necessary?* Um, sure, maybe, yes, I don't know.
>
> *Is it kind?* No.

His cell phone rests idly to the left of his computer.

Life can be incredibly tough and challenging, but there's so much we can't control. Yet, what we *can* control is how we respond and react to information.

In a situation like this, he could control it either way. If he doesn't tell the story, there's no assurance he'll get the girl for good, and no assurance Spooner won't blow his cover anyway. But even if he *doesn't* tell the story, he knows he doesn't want to destroy Nell's life with the paparazzi and intensity her grandmother left in Hollywood after Spooner leaks it.

Except it would be far worse. Social media would make this go viral in seconds. Crazy people would be camped out on Nell's doorstep by tomorrow at noon.

On the other hand, if he *does* expose the story, he'll be rich! Not that he only values money, because Tom doesn't. But paying off his crushing student debt, being on time for his always-a-month-behind car loan on a vehicle that doesn't run, and helping his mother have a guaranteed lush retirement? It's tempting. Heck, he could go home to New Hampshire—a local hero like his father—and take over the farm.

He'd been trying to convince his grandfather to franchise into one of those hydroponic shipping container farms. With Tom's forthcoming payday, they could afford one of those high-tech greenhouses for community vegetation. He could even grow multiple crops and distribute all very simply via Tom's tablet or smartphone. His grandfather would be so proud of him…*wouldn't he?*

Tom rises from his desk and begins pacing his tiny room. He longs to call his grandfather to garnish his advice on this entire mess. But he realizes he can't tell a soul, let alone even get good cell service even if he *wanted* to call him. This is one of those times he'll just have to "pull up his bootstraps and be a man," as Grandpa might tell him. Except Tom's not even certain that he can afford the *boots* anymore!

Plopping back to his desk chair, he clicks onto a records site. *Find digitized birth certificate online: Just enter a name to start…Start now! Solve Family Mysteries. Join 100 million users. New Records added Daily. Make Instant Discoveries. View their birth record online. Get started today! Billions of records. Start a free trial. Services: Family History, Family Trees, DNA Testing, Genealogy Records, record Search.*

Tom's mind moves to Nell saying she'd love to someday do one of those DNA tests. His thoughts reminisce last night, their dancing, their laughing, their lovemaking, and their secrets. *But their trust. Damn! Their trust!*

Tom begins humming along to Frank Sinatra's "Under My Skin" playing from his earbuds on his iPhone.

Clicking to his recently-imported photos, Tom looks at Nell's stunning face. Nell on the porch doing yoga, sitting in lotus position; sharing ice cream—her hand covering the lens playfully; the two of them doing selfies in the car—her tongue even flipped up to her top lip, similar to a photo of Marilyn standing next to Joe DiMaggio.

Another photo of Nell in a white hoodie, her face angelically framed, just like the photo of Marilyn on the beach in a white hoodie, feet wet in the sand all the way to her knees. The resemblance is uncanny. And his favorite…the one of Nell at the sushi restaurant holding a drinking glass next to her right cheek, her left fingers covering her lips, deep in thought. It's practically *identical* to the black-and-white one of her grandmother with Simone Signoret and Yves Montand, photographed in 1960. The photo and copy editors will love assembling this story when they see the photo-op comparisons. This is the biggest story of a lifetime! *Everyone's* lifetime!

Tom scans the article once more before hitting the send button...before sitting back in his chair and rocking. All the while he's staring at the screen, the cursor blinks.

He hears Nell saying, "Nan always said the web is a horrible place to visit. Especially google. It takes away the chance of meeting someone organically before they can explain about themselves. It's just not fair." Tom stares harder at the screen while her words reverberate in his head loud and clear. Nell had also said,

"Nan worried about the possibility of being alone and then the possibility of never being alone, you know what I mean?"

When this article runs, he knows his editor will think they hit the jackpot, but he knows he'll turn Nell and Nan's carefully calculated world upside down. *And for what? So, somebody local will be wrapping their fish bones in the newspaper the day after?*

Tom hears Ritter... "You're all closing in on me! Your apps may be the way of the world, but you're losing touch. All of you! Where's your soul? Your *humanity*?"

Tom remembers the look on Nell's face when she pulled those clam digger pants out of the hope chest. "Nan used to say that 'people are like shadows. They disappear when things get dark.' Do you think that's true? I hope not. You won't ever disappear, will you, Tommy?"

Tom returns to the blinking cursor, reaches his fingers to the keyboard, and highlights all that he has written.

And then, in a second, the story is gone.

He's hit the delete key.

He's wiped it all away.

He rises from the desk, grabs his jacket from the closet; the empty hanger is left swinging wildly. As Tom locks the door to his room, his mother's words consume him: "You'll never go wrong if you go at everything from a place of love."

CHAPTER THIRTY

Spooner opens the door to Town Hall, practically *tearing* it from its hinges. In front of him, a chalkboard on the counter reads: Marriage Licenses—Monday; Building permits—Tuesday; Fishing Licenses—Wednesday, Thursday, and Friday.

Tapping the counter bell relentlessly, Spooner stretches his neck to get someone—*anyone's*—attention from the back room. Finally, two elderly women appear together and make their way to the front. Slowly. Very slowly.

"Can you ladies snap it up a little?" asks Spooner. "I'm kind of in a hurry."

"Listen, pally," says Joanie, the first lady, "we opened this department especially for you. It's not usually open today. Didn't you read the sign?" She points to it.

"That's right," says Annie, the other woman, "Today is our fishing permit day. It's winter striped bass season, you know."

"And floundah," says Joanie proudly. "Good fishing this time of year."

"Ladies," says Spooner, "I don't want to offend your delicate New England sensibilities, but this isn't a department, okay? It's a goddamn file cabinet! So put your bony little hands in there and just get me what I called you for, and then you can go fillet your flounder!"

"Sir," says Annie, her tone stern, "I do not appreciate your attitude. We have strict rules here. The birth certificate department is only open until noon on Mondays, Tuesdays from ten to two, and Wednesdays it's closed for choir practice. Mrs. Miller took the day off from organ duty at the church. So why don't you come back tomorrow, at nine—"

"You're kidding, right?" says Spooner, leaning into the counter. "Look, I know you two know your way around here. I bet you probably issued the marriage license to Captain Smith and Pocahontas." Spooner bites his lip to suppress a laugh. "And I appreciate your devoted service to this community," he says, putting his hand to his heart. "If I had two gold watches, I'd give you one apiece. But I don't. So just get me the birth certificate for Grace Morton. Please."

The women look at each other. Joanie reaches under the counter and pulls up a sign, which she slams on the countertop. "Out to Lunch."

"Ladies, *ladies*..." Spooner exhales calmly. "I just flew all the way across the country from Los Angeles after multiple cancellations and two connecting flights. Now, I know my journey was nothing compared to what you two must have endured coming over here on the Mayflower, but I'm tired. I'm very impatient, and I want you to find the birth certificate. *Now*!"

"We don't care for your behavior, Mister..."

"Spooner. Sidney *fucking* Spooner!"

"Well, Mister *fucking* Spooner. If you keep on like this, I'll have to get my supervisor."

Annie's eyes shift to the door of the supervisor's office. Spooner looks over to spy a man older than the two women at the counter. He's reading a newspaper and sipping his coffee. Spooner contains a grin and raises his hand to them in defense.

"Okay, ladies," he says, "I don't want you calling Hellboy over here. I apologize for my language. I just need to find information on Marie Morton and her daughter, Grace Morton."

"Good, because you're acting like a spoiled child," says Joanie.

Spooner lights up. He grins at the motherly reprimand. "I'm sorry," he says. Gently. He'll take whatever motherly attention he can get.

The two women lean under the counter and remove their lunch bags. Annie reaches inside and pulls out a yogurt and a spoon. She begins to set up her lunch. "*Awww,* c'mon, ladies," says Spooner, his tone growing desperate. "Somebody in this sweet, quaint, godforsaken little town must know where I can find Marie Morton? She's a painter, I think?"

Joanie pulls out a napkin, carefully unfolding it. Then she pulls out a tiny container of salt, pepper, and a hard-boiled egg, which she taps on the counter.

"We're out to lunch, Mister Spooner," says Annie. "We'll be back in forty-five minutes."

Spooner tosses back his head in laughter. He must admit he's not used to being put in his place.

Nonchalantly, he reaches over to one of the brown bags and looks inside. Giving Annie the puppy eyes, she nods approval for him to remove a banana, which he does. He peels it. With a big mouthful, he mumbles, "I bet you have a pretty tough union…"

CHAPTER THIRTY-ONE

Tom, winded from sprinting, bounds with purpose up the walk to The Porpoise, looking for all the world like he's lost his bearings. Tugging open the door, he scans the joint. It's only 3 p.m., but there's Mayor Bisbee and Henry Bartholomew with the two fishermen, Charley Button and Scotty Harden, at the bar.

"Hey Henry!" calls Tom impatiently, breathless, not even greeting the others. "I need to talk to you."

The mayor holds up a hand. "Now hold on, Tom. Henry is in the middle of a serious debate. Been going on since lunch hour. Whatever it is, I'm sure it can wait."

"Fine," says Tom, agitated. He turns to the bartender. "Elizabeth, double shot of Jack."

"Don't you think it's a little early?" asks Elizabeth. "You okay, there Tom?"

He nods. No sooner the shot is in front of him, he gulps it in one swallow, slams the glass on the bar, nods to Elizabeth for another, and tunes into the debate.

"He was only a twenty pounder," says Charley. "The world record is seventy-eight pounds, for Christ's sake!"

"Who says," says Scotty, sipping his beer. "Only striped bass that big was the *fifty* pounder I caught last summer!"

"Only bass you can handle is that Bass Ale in front of ya!"

"Henry," says Elizabeth, eyeing Tom with concern. "Just go on and settle this, because Tom here needs to talk to you."

"Only fish ever caught in these waters that big was back in '63. By Jack Garvey," says Henry. "No, no, wait a minute. Yes, yes, it was Jack Garvey. That's who. And that fish was a beauty. All thousand pounds of her—giant bluefin tuna!"

"Henry!" demands Tom, running his hand through his bangs. He's sweating profusely. "I have to ask you a question. It really can't wait."

"C'mon then, boys," says Elizabeth, listening in. "Let's move it down that end of the bar and let Tom here talk with Henry." The mayor and the fishermen oblige, sliding their beers across the bar towards the kitchen and moving a few stools down.

"What can I do for you Tom?" says Henry. "Done all I can for those fish mongers."

"I need to know some more about Horse."

"Back to him again, eh?" says Henry. "Look, Tom, you're a nice young man, but I already told you all this historical brain of mine can possibly hold."

"Tell me about the woman that was his best friend. The one he brought from Los Angeles..."

"Okay," says Henry, "But my mind's a little rusty." He looks to his empty beer mug, then to Tom, then back to the mug.

"Elizabeth!" says Tom, pointing to Henry's mug. "Refill on me."

"Coming right up," she says, pouring from the tap, listening in on their conversation.

"Well," says Henry, "Sterling Powers's, er, Horse's woman friend...she wasn't much to look at. A quiet, little mousey brunette. Think she was four or maybe five months pregnant. Didn't see much of her though. Lived like a hermit. Worked at the library for a long time before she finally opened that gallery."

"Where did the brunette come from?" asks Tom moving his stool closer to Henry's.

"California, I suppose."

"But you said he was gay, so he couldn't have had a girlfriend."

"No, she was just a pal." Henry lights up, "Wait, it's coming back to me...Horse claimed she needed a place to start a new life where nobody would recognize her," says Henry. "Can't imagine who could recognize her anyway underneath those big dark sunglasses and that kerchief she always sported. Only saw her at the grocery store and the post office. And that's when she *did* go out in public. Kept her head low."

"How old do you think she was?"

"I don't know," ponders Henry. "Mid-thirties at best."

"Jesus," says Tom, exhaling hard and rearranging his shot glass on the bar. "And you're sure nobody knew who she was? Not a single person in this town?"

"Yes! We all knew who she was," says Henry.

Tom's heart skips a triple beat. "You did?"

"Yes, I already told you," says Henry, agitated. "She was Marie Morton, Horse's friend!"

"C'mon boys," calls out the mayor from the other end of the bar. "What's the big secret? Get back over here. We're takin' bets on Scott's next catch."

Henry glances up at them and comments, "Well, let me tell you...Scotty Dog couldn't catch pneumonia running naked through two feet of snow in Harvard Square on Christmas, let alone catch a big fish." The men chuckle, slapping each other on the back. Henry turns to Tom. "Right, Tom?"

But he's already gone. He's left two twenties on the bar.

CHAPTER THIRTY-TWO

Tom stumbles to Nell's front doorstep, pounding a hard fist instead of using the brass knocker. Pacing the small stoop, it seems like an eternity before she finally answers.

"Hey, *you*," says Nell, pulling the door open, a script in her hand. "I was just running lines. Thought you were coming by at seven? I was baking a—"

Before she can finish, Tom has already made his way past her, standing in front of the red, white, and blue painting that first petrified him.

"What's wrong?" she says, knitting her brow. "You smell like whiskey."

"Nellie…my *beautiful* Penelope Jeane Morton," he slurs just a bit, dropping his arms to his side, as if releasing a boulder, yet coherent enough to be reminiscent of Lolly's confession. "We gotta talk."

"Worst three words in the English language 'We gotta talk,'" she says, bracing herself by sitting on the arm of the sofa. "Is this the part where you tell me you have a girlfriend in California?"

"No," he says, "I wish."

"You do?"

"No, that's not what I mean," he says. "You're the only one for me. I mean I wish *that* was the problem."

"We have a problem?" she asks.

Tom moves to the painting, pointing to it. He inhales deeply and turns to her, his voice going uncharacteristically low. "Did she really survive?"

"Did *who* survive?"

"You know who."

"Do I?" she asks, perplexed.

His eyes remain fixated on Nell. "Nan, Marie, your grandmother…" his tone annoyed now. "The person who painted this painting."

"My grandmother?" asks Nell. "*Again,* with my grandmother…" Nell heads towards the kitchen as the oven timer dings. Pulling on two mitts, Nell bends over the oven to remove a zucchini cake.

"Nell, look, you don't understand. This isn't a joke," says Tom, forced to find sobriety, tapping impatient fingers on the counter where the cake pan now cools. "There's a reporter who's going to show up and tell your grandmother's story to the entire world."

"Wait, there's another one of you? Really?" she asks sarcastically, placing her oven-mitted hands to her hips. "Oh, Tommy, I can assure you that my grandmother is hardly breaking news."

"Yes, actually, she is." Tom says flippantly before moving in front of her.

"Why are you acting like this?"

He takes her square by the shoulders. "Nellie, I'm talking about Marilyn Monroe."

"Huh?" she asks.

"Marilyn Monroe! She was your grandmother. How can you not *know* that?"

"She was?" asks Nell sarcastically, expelling a burst of laughter. "Right." She backs away from him. "And who was my grandfather…Elvis Presley?"

"Maybe, possibly, I don't know," says Tom, circling around her now. "All I know is Sid Spooner is going to blow this town out of the water. Your simple little clam-chowder existence is about to be history!"

Nell moves away from him, shifting her glare out the window. Arms folded. "God, and I thought you were one of the normal ones, Tommy." She spins back. "So, what exactly is your point, Mister Tom-the-Reporter Hogan?"

"There is no point except to warn you. I'm trying to protect you." He goes to her side. "Nell, look around. Look at the Yeats poem on the wall upstairs, the—the, um, bobble heads in the living room, the clam diggers in the attic..." his tone is growing desperate. "You handed me Joe DiMaggio's baseball!" He moves to the bookshelf and pulls some books forward with force, until he gets to one with the initials "MM" inside. "Look!"

Nell places her finger on the page, lowering her neck to read. "Yes, MM. Marie Morton."

"A.k.a. Marilyn Monroe!" says Tom. "And mirrors. You have practically *zero* mirror in this house. Why is that?"

"Nan hated to look at herself. She thought she wasn't attractive."

"That's almost comical. The most beautiful woman in American history. Ugly," says Tom, running his hand through his hair. "Don't you get it? It all adds up. Nellie, I'm telling you. Just tell me where she is? You can trust me. I want to protect you! *Both* of you!"

"Can I? Trust you?" asks Nell, hissing under her breath. "Is that what this is all about? Where my grandmother is?"

"Yes—I mean, no—I mean, not anymore." He's back to her side again, but she nudges away, keeping her shoulders squared and grasped at both elbows as if in a straitjacket of self-protection.

After a moment, Nell moves down the hallway, calling back, "Well, Nan isn't available anymore."

"What does that mean?" Tom follows behind her. "Not available how? Did she *die* recently? Are you just saying that to protect her?"

"It's none of your business. But protecting my grandmother *is* my business." Nell spins around. "Where's your grandmother, huh? Alive or dead?"

Tom's look tells us he's surprised she's flipping this on him. "My grandmother died of heart failure a few years back. God knows I miss my Gram. Made the best apple pie—"

"I don't appreciate sarcasm at a time like this," says Nell.

"A time like what?"

Nell heads the towards the bathroom speaking as she walks. "It just *figures*. Every time I meet a guy, and I start to believe that maybe just *maybe*...but this one...boy, you take the cake *and* the candles!" She's sitting on the tub edge now, her eyes watering up. Tom stands in the door jamb saying nothing. "I mean, why would some guy want to stalk my poor grandmother. She's a nice, old, retired lady who makes a mean *blueberry* pie, so there."

"And she loved a good ole grilled steak," adds Tom.

"How did you know that?" she asks, surprised.

"It's been written about," he says matter-of-factly. "Are you kidding me right now, Nell?"

"No!! Your questions are out of line," she says with the astute attitude of a trial lawyer. She pushes by him and walks back down the hall.

"Nell, stop!" He grabs her arm. They're back in the middle of the living room now. "This is serious." They're in a staring match. Her face conveys complete and utter innocence. "Oh my God," says Tom, "You really don't know, do you..."

"I know that I think you're nuts."

"Come here," he says, putting out a hand to hers in complete surrender. "Let's sit down."

She refuses his hand, so he sits, rubbing his hands down his knees before beginning. "In old newspaper talk, this story would be called a 'bombshell,' which is ironic because Marilyn *was* a bombshell. Gorgeous. Your grandmother lived a life of fabricating the truth. She escaped the night she supposedly committed suicide. I mean, they don't even have *those* facts straight, let alone the part where she got away. I mean, in all my research—"

"Oh, you've been researching me?" she snaps, feeling exposed, humiliated.

"Please, give me a minute to explain," he pleads, putting up a hand. She just stares. "In all my research, my guess is that somebody gave her a new identity that night, allowing her to escape and have the thing she wanted most. A daughter. Your mother. I'm thinking Horse wasn't the only one in on it, but he was the friend who brought a pregnant Marilyn Monroe here to Barnstable, where she could raise her baby in complete safety and—"

"Okay," she says, chuckling nervously. "I've heard enough. This is just crazy shit you're talking. You're insane." She revs up. "You know what? You can just leave now." She heads to the door.

Silence stretches between them as Tom looks up at Nell because there's always a pause when the jury goes out to deliver their verdict. But not in this case.

"Why?" says Tom, rising dutifully, but wounded. "Why do I have to leave? I want to help you."

"*Help* me?" she asks, with a look like she might slap him. "You're just trying to use me to get some story. Fake news, fake news, *fake news!*" she rants as if she might stick her fingers in her ears like a hysterical child. Then she stops. Gets in his face now. "Let's face it. If you're a reporter looking for a story, well, this crazy notion will go viral in two seconds."

"No, it won't," he says, "I don't want it to. Not anymore."

"Oh *really*," she says, tripping him up. "But you wanted it to."

"Yes—um, no!" he shoots back, his voice strangled. "I'm in love with you!"

"Oh," she says taken aback as he stands there looking helpless. "Well, you have a funny way of showing it."

"*Fuck* Marilyn Monroe," he begs.

"Right, because everybody else did."

"I didn't mean it like that," he says, touching her arm. "You *know* I didn't mean it like that. I mean fuck Marilyn because I love you and that matters more than *that* truth—"

"Well, whatever," she says, pulling her arm back to herself. "But I don't believe that Marilyn Monroe was my grandmother."

"Believing and knowing are two very different things," he says, gently. "I happen to know."

"Okay, great, you win. But I don't have time for this," she says, moving back toward the door. "I'm just a simple Cape Cod girl who cares about women's issues and making a difference in my community, so if you think I need or *want* to be the granddaughter of some ditzy blonde showgirl, you don't know me at all." She pulls the door open, fuming mad.

He says nothing. Defeated.

At his silence, Nell says, "Thank you for your time," which of course sounds stupid, but she's clearly at a loss for words.

"Fine. I'll leave," he says, bypassing Nell. He turns at the threshold. "I know this is a lot of information. I know you need to process this, and I'll happily walk you through it when you're ready. But before I go, just think about this...okay?"

Her expression says she's waiting for his end-all comment as her tone turns authoritative. "Go on," she says.

"Nellie, if you're so #MeToo, well, *fuck's sake,* wake up! Because your grandmother was Marilyn Monroe! She was the biggest victim of all! Except she wasn't really a victim. Because she was a *survivor.* That's so much better and so much what every women of every generation would want to hear. She survived!"

With that he's out the door, leaving the comment suspended in midair.

Nell feels chills crawl her arms. She clearly sees that he has a point, but she can't believe it. *Won't* believe it. It's all some crazy nightmare.

Closing the door, Nell leans against it and slides down to the floor, clutching her kneecaps, rocking in her tiny space. Tears begin to form in the corners of her eyes. The twist of what he's just said comes at her repeatedly, practically knocking the wind out of her. But the biggest question of all: *If it's true, why hadn't Nan ever told her?*

CHAPTER THIRTY-THREE

The front door swings open at The Porpoise, and Sidney Spooner immediately moves his way through the locals to pull up the one stool available. He tosses his keys on the bar. "Yeah, can I get some service here?" Elizabeth is behind the bar—double shift today—servicing the usual crew for dinner and drinks. She nods to the mayor, who nods to Henry.

She sets a handful of beers down in front of a group and turns to him. "I'll be right with you, sir. Is there a problem?"

Spooner shrugs his shoulder as if to suggest the entire town is the problem. He picks up a menu from the counter.

"Hi, I'm Beth," says Elizabeth. "Now then, what can I get you?"

"Uh, yeah, I'll take the nut-crusted filet of Cod," says Spooner.

"Favorite here," says Elizabeth. "You're gonna love it! Almond crusted with a cranberry citrus butter."

"Great," he says, glancing around, uninterested in what she has to say. "I want it simply grilled. A little oil. That's it."

"Cup of chowdah to start?"

"I don't do chowder." says Spooner, still sizing the joint up and not even looking at Elizabeth as she speaks to him.

Spooner slams the menu closed to find the mayor at his side. "Mayor Herman Bisbee here," he says. "Welcome to Barnstable." He extends a hand. Spooner extends a hand too.

Spooner knits his brow. "Sid Spooner. Charmed, I'm sure."

"Oh, Sidney Spooner from Los Angeles," says the mayor. Spooner suddenly tunes in with interest. "You're the lad who was upsetting my gals over at Town Hall this afternoon. Annie and Joanie said you had the place in a tizzy."

"Yeah, well, if Annie and Joanie can't handle the heat then they should really get out of the town hall."

The mayor continues to study Spooner's face, searching for some sign of decency. He comes up blank. "Kindness is a skill, Mr. Spooner," says the mayor, digging into his back pocket for his wallet. He hands his check and some bills to Elizabeth. "Keep the change, Bethie. You're gonna need it." He glances over at Spooner. Then leaves.

Spooner calls out to Charley Button and Scotty Harden on the other end of the bar.

"Hey, you guys know where I can find a town historian named Henry?"

"Yeah," says Charley. "You must mean Henry Bartholmew."

Spooner's eyes scan the fishermen. "You been out after orca, the killer whale?" He laughs at his own joke. The fishermen scowl.

"At least fishing is a decent way to earn a wage…wasn't always gonna be a fisherman," says Scotty, his expression wounded. "I almost became an accountant."

"And I almost became a surgeon," says Spooner, "and my parents were almost proud of me." Spooner nurses his drink. Hard.

A couple hours have passed, and the joint is practically emptied out except for some empty beer mugs surrounding Spooner and Henry around the bar.

"Yup, she was a beauty," says Henry. "A dame to be had. Every man wanted her."

"Really?" says Spooner, hopeful.

"Oh, yes! Sure did," says Henry. "What a knockout. A beauty! Had a finish like a 1936 Chris-Craft Runabout. Smooth and shiny. What a sail."

"Yeah, that's great, Henry," says Spooner, propped on one elbow. "I'm truly fascinated by the entire history of every boat in the harbor. But can I pick your brain about Marie Morton?"

"Oh right," says Henry, glancing at his empty mug and then to Spooner, then back at his mug again. "Was that where we were?"

"Hey, Ellen," Spooner says to Elizabeth, snapping his fingers. "Two refills, pronto. Put 'em on *Harry's* tab here."

Elizabeth refills the beers, placing them down. "His name is Henry, and mine is Beth," says Elizabeth, giving Spooner a dirty look and sharing a look with Henry that says this guy is nothing but bad news. Henry takes the cue.

"Now then, where were we," says Henry, sitting up straight and stretching his arms on the bar, reaching for his beer. "Ole Horse never wanted to go back to Hollywood after that. Surprised too. Knew everybody. All those stars. Was a bodyguard for Clark Gable, Gloria Swanson, even some of them Rat Packers. Why he even got to guard Marilyn Monroe! Imagine that?"

"Right," says Spooner, "Now we're getting somewhere."

"Last we heard, Sterling and Marie drove up to Syracuse," says Henry. "Or was it Niagara Falls?" Henry winks to Elizabeth.

"Ah, maybe it was Lake Erie," adds Elizabeth.

"Music to my ears!" says Spooner, pulling out his cell phone, raising it in the air left and right, then spinning his stool backwards. "Hey, where can I get cell service around here? I gotta call someone."

"Might have to cross back over the Sagamore Bridge," says Elizabeth, wishing to be rid of him. "On your way to Syracuse."

"Great. Thanks Ellen," he says, "And thanks, Harry," says Spooner to Henry, bolting out the door.

CHAPTER THIRTY-FOUR

Raw, bone-chilling rain pounds on the panes of Nell's cottage windows. Only the seaports of Cape Cod could deliver such a dismal alternative to a Boston snowstorm. Nell paces her hallway, to the kitchen then back to her desk, rubbing her arms briskly, the hearth sparking warmth.

But Nell's face is withdrawn. Silent. Tapping into her yogi and meditative control, she suddenly forces her body to be still. Focusing on her breath. Her eyes stare hypnotically in a debate with the flame. *What is the worst scenario? That the man she's falling in love with had pursued her all along for a story? Or that her precious grandmother is really not the woman she always believed her to be? But why would Tom tell her that Nan was Marilyn Monroe if she wasn't?* Nell's body might have stopped moving, but her mind races with questions.

She longs to pick up the kitchen phone and ring her Nan middle of the night, seeking an explanation, but the practical and Zen-practiced Nell knows it's after midnight and she must live in the moment of this journey. *But had her entire life's journey to this point been a lie?* Nell stares at a photo of her mother holding her as a newborn baby. *Did my mother know? Did she take her own life because she couldn't handle the truth?*

Nell ignites the burner for the kettle. *It's all too far-fetched! Too crazy!* Yet, for the blink of a moment, there's a part of Nell that believes that the pieces fit. For a woman named Marie Morton, this was pure bliss. This was a beginning—a tiny cottage, a garden, a gallery, a granddaughter—a getaway. The thoughts pour out of Nell like Nan's spigot to the rose garden.

Nell's hand is unsteady with the teapot, pouring the whistling hot water over the lemon and ginger tea bag. Methodically, she dunks the teabag up and down, up and down, deep in thought. *Were there* no *choices for Nan? Are there regrets where there weren't choices? Was Nan* pushed *into obscurity?*

Tom's words are in her head. *"She was the biggest victim of all."* Nell knows that Nan was much more than a victim. Nell knows nothing of Marilyn Monroe, but she knows that Marie Morton was a mother, a grandmother, a caretaker, a neighbor, a friend, an artist, a gallerist, a gardener, and the occasional usher at the Episcopal church. Nan covered the local bake sale, volunteered at the shelter for abused women, and deeply cared about her community. No, Marie Morton is not the question at all—it's Marilyn Monroe. Because Marie Morton was a survivor.

Nell slings the tea bag into the trash, warms both hands on the mug and goes to her computer, firing it up from its dormant state, the blue screen igniting the room. Clicking to the internet, Nell types "Marie Morton" into the Google search bar.

Nothing comes up except her grandmother on a float in the July Fourth Parade waving with the Rotary Club.

Next, she begins to type, backspacing with several nervous mistakes, "Marilyn Monroe."

The internet loads.

Over 122,000,000 results come up.

Nell guffaws a breath of shock. She begins reading the first entry from Wikipedia:

Marilyn Monroe (born Norma Jeane Mortenson; June 1, 1926–August 4, 1962) was an American actress and model. Known for playing comic "blonde bombshell" characters, she became one of the most popular sex symbols of the 1950s and early 1960s, as well as an emblem of the era's sexual revolution.

Nell feels the gulp settle in her throat. June 1, 1926, is Nan's birthday too! The joke had always been that Nan's birthday was always just shy a day or two too *late* to celebrate on Memorial Day weekend.

To the right of the wiki entry are photos. Nell clicks on them. The woman is a young, gorgeous, pillow-white blonde. She almost portrays the energy of a stereotypical Americana girl next door, but her sultry eyes and playful mouth seem to say *Come hither*. She could be a L'Oréal lipstick advertisement with the whitest teeth and a dazzling smile. The kind of face women can only *dream* of possessing.

But there's something in the photos that Nell can't ignore. That tousled hair and that widow's peak...Nan's.

Nell enlarges the photo. This woman *could be* Nan's in her younger years. Christ, it could be the makeover she tried to get Nan to *do* for *years*! And Nell had never seen Nan as a blonde, not even in pictures. She remained defiantly brunette. Nell glances at the photos on the shelf, her eyes darting to each one. In all of them, Nan's mouth is closed, expressionless, with the slightest crow's feet. Even the picture of Nan and her daughter, Grace, when she was a little girl, finds Nan a good distance behind her daughter as Grace learned to walk. Nell can see the baby's features—but not Nan's.

She named her daughter Grace—the very name of the woman Marilyn most adored, according to Wikipedia. Grace McKee, the best friend of her biological mother, Gladys. The woman who was a *constant* in the life of little Norma Jeane before she became Marilyn Monroe. And wait, the spelling of her middle name *Jeane* with an *e* at the end. It's Nell's own middle name too.

Nell huddles back over the computer, searching "I am the daughter of Marilyn Monroe" to see if anything on her *own* mother comes up. An obituary doesn't even exist for her mother since she died before there was internet, really. Instead, the computer loads to the thump of Nell's heart, so intense it practically renders her fingers numb to the point of paralysis. As she hits news, she sees this:

"WOMAN CLAIMS SHE IS THE DAUGHTER
OF MARILYN MONROE AND JFK."

Nell scans it with disbelief. Then another woman comes into view. And yet another! It becomes apparent that Marilyn's love life and alleged pregnancies continue to regularly make headlines. Even her gynecologist, Dr. Leon Krohn, suggested she'd become pregnant again in 1961 and gave birth to a baby girl in June 1962, which would have been impossible given her filming schedule and surrounding media hounds. Nell quickly realizes that there's little evidence to back these allegations.

Another California woman wrote a biography claiming to be the lost daughter of Marilyn Monroe, but her claims were immediately dismissed as a publicity stunt. DNA tests continue to prove that no child ever existed.

Nan falls back against her chair. *Maybe Nan escaped Hollywood? Maybe she got away? Maybe Grace* was *the baby she ended up having?* As Nell reads on, she sees that if any of these imposters' admissions turned out to be true, anyone claiming to be Marilyn's child could be the natural heir to the estate of Marilyn Monroe, which was estimated to be worth only about $7.5 million back in the day but over $100 million today! *And*... makes another $5 million every year.

Nell sits upright at this information. *If Nan had all that money, where was she hiding it? Why did they live so meagerly? To avoid exposure?* Nell types in "who handles Marilyn Monroe's Estate?" and the same answer comes up. Even over fifty-years later, amidst the posters and refrigerator magnets, the multimillion dollar "brand" was handled by her acting coach, Lee Strasberg, one of the few at her funeral. He and his wife, Paula, were like surrogate parents to Monroe. But when Paula died, Lee's second wife, Anna, inherited the estate, eventually hiring a professional company familiar with managing the worth of famous dead people.

The legal jargon goes on for pages and a variety of lawsuits, which eventually led to Strasberg selling the estate to ABS for an estimated $30 million.

As Nell pours through more paternity claims, she thinks of her mother, Grace's birthday, always a sad day around the house. The timing oddly *does* add up. Nell's mother was born February 26, 1963, though her original due date was in early March, just months after Marilyn's death in August 1962. A death, Nell is slowly learning online, in which "forensics were hopelessly flawed."

She googles Marilyn conspiracies.

"Marilyn Monroe died in 1962 at age 36 from an 'apparent' drug overdose." Nell takes notice that the word "apparent" is on everything. *Apparent* murder, *apparent* suicide, *apparent, apparent…*

In googling photos and more photos, Nell realizes she could be glued to this very desk chair until the year 2040 with so much information, until she comes across Christie's Auction House, Bonhams, and Sotheby's. Some of the items listed are almost exact duplicates or similar to items gathering dust around this very cottage.

Nell pushes back the desk chair and begins pacing again, needing time to separate the world's information from her personal knowledge. This time, Nell observes her home from a new perspective…looking for hints. It's as if she can actually *feel* her brain cells intertwining and unraveling into an overloaded circuit board of multiple thoughts. Some conscious, and some from the outer reaches of her childhood memory, but all forming an intricate path to home in on one thing. The truth. Nan *could be* Marilyn Monroe…

The oven clock reads 1:30 a.m., but Nell can't stop now.

Moving to the silence of the counter, her cats, Sylvia and Ted, asleep on the window bench, Nell pours a glass of water, then chugs it. Hard.

Setting it down on the counter she returns to the biggest question of all: *Should I just call Nan?* No, it's basically 2 a.m. Besides, what might she ask her? *"Hey Nan, it's Nellie. Sorry to wake you, but are you* really *Marilyn Monroe?"* What if she gives her grandmother a heart attack on the spot!

The light of the living room computer lures Nell back. Tom had asked her about how Nan financed their lives. Good question… *The gallery? The library? Maybe government assistance and food stamps?* Nan wasn't someone to take government assistance, and besides she'd have to have provided a Social Security number unless…well, unless someone issued her a new identity.

No, Nan was always employed and always worked while Nell was in school. Nan walked home from the village with grocery bags each night and made Nell dinner at 6 p.m. sharp. She cooked, she cleaned, she worked part time and even volunteered, but she was always there for Nell and for her Sunday "Miss Manners" lessons of how to place a fork, a butter knife, and a water glass like Eloise at the Plaza.

Yes, Nan was there for Nutcracker ballet recitals, the horseback riding lessons on Saturdays in Brewster, oyster shucking on Scudder Lane, and snail collecting at Mill Way. Nan was there to cure Nell's woes and Band-Aid her toes from the constant stubs at the beach jetty. And she loved helping her with homework.

But gosh…imagine what Marilyn went through never having a mother. If what these online historians claim is true, she had nothing but caretakers, foster homes, and orphanages. *Who was her constant?* Who said, "Good night, love you. See you in the morning." Who sang lullabies and that silly little song Nan used to sing to Nell for tickles and tuck-ins? *How did that rhyme go?*

I wanna be loved by you, just you

And nobody else but you

I wanna be loved by you aloooone...

Boop-boop-de-boop!

Nell goes to IMDb to search Marilyn's film history. All films Nell's never heard of—*Some Like It Hot, Gentlemen Prefer Blondes,* and so on—because she never watched those on the TCM channel. Her grandmother chose the films, just like Nell had told Tom. Films that obviously didn't include Marilyn Monroe.

Sliding the desk chair back with full force, Nell dashes to the shelf, fingering through the books and old videos, then tossing them manically to the floor. There's no *Some Like It Hot* or *The Misfits* or any of the others listed online, except for *Bus Stop,* tucked cautiously behind a documentary on the Impressionists. *Why hadn't they watched that one together?* She'd watch it right now, but it's a VHS and Nell only has a DVD player.

Nell falls against the shelf and begins to sob like a frightened child. It's all too much to believe, yet it's becoming truer by the moment and it's about to change Nell's entire future.

Fear creeps through Nell as she begins to question who she can and can't trust.

Nell googles Marilyn's death certificate. There are thousands of images of the coroner's report. There's a wiki page dedicated to the "Death of Marilyn Monroe," a PDF with all the documents related to her death on autopsyfiles.org, and a podcase discussing "The Death of Marilyn Monroe: Accident, Suicide, or Murder?"

The "Happy Birthday, Mr. President" video is there too.

Nell raises the volume on the computer and listens to the audience vibrating with laughter at her introduction. Marilyn tiptoes across the stage in a shimmering gown so tight, her feet like a concubine. She glitters like a goddess, her golden hair caressed by the stage lighting, as Marilyn drops her mink stole to the *ooohs* and *ahhhs* of the general public. The gown is nude. Basically bare skin. Nothing left to the imagination except the thousands of men clearly fantasizing what they'd like to do to her.

At first the spotlight is so intense that Marilyn must shade her eyes to get her bearings. Nell watches as Marilyn's hand runs the length of the microphone stand, caressing it up and down. Then, Marilyn exhales the tiniest of orgasmic breaths. As Marilyn sings, Nell recognizes Nan's voice.

Except Nan's not singing to Nell; Marilyn's singing "Happy Birthday" to President John F Kennedy. Marilyn's eyes are sealed shut as if she's imagining herself underneath him instead of singing on a stage to the masses. It's what the public clearly expects. In one article they call her "a deeply troubled woman as a dressed up little girl in a beauty pageant forced to parade her goods to the world." God, how terribly depressing and totally embarrassing!

A strange emotion overtakes Nell. She brews with anger now. One of protection and sadness. One that longs to run up on that platform and toss a blanket over her Nan…protect her from the bullies, take her backstage, and rock her to safety.

As Marilyn finishes her singing, she asks "everybody!" to join along. A massive cake is hoisted out to the stage on two limbo sticks held on the shoulders of two bakers in toques—tall white chef hats. The president finally takes the stage, saying with a cool sarcastic appreciation, "Thank you. I can now retire from politics having had happy birthday sung to me in such a sweet and wholesome way." He's making fun of Marilyn. He's not taking her seriously.

Nell falls back against the chair. The clock ticks 4 a.m. She's sickened at all the windows and tabs she has opened.

Thinking of the conspiracies, Nell is ready to collapse from realization and exhaustion. The pages go on for decades, with photos to accompany President John F. Kennedy and Bobby Kennedy. There are photos of Frank Sinatra and Sammy Davis

Jr. and weekends away at the Cal Neva Lodge in Lake Tahoe. Nell's memory banks begin to flood. Her grandmother's friends, "Bobby, Frank, and Sammy." *Could it be? The same trio of names?*

In hindsight, reading about these "rat" boys—Frank, Peter, Sammy, and Dean Martin—now, they all just look and act like a bunch of middle-aged men stuck in high school adolescence. Bullies by today's standards. Nell learns that their name the "Rat Pack" comes from a night when they arrived at Humphrey Bogart's house, where Lauren Bacall observed them after a party-all-night experience and said, "You all look like a pack of rats!"

Nell pops up from the desk chair, wondering if any of them are her biological grandfather, and goes to the hallway mirror, glancing back to their faces. She looks like none of them. She returns to the computer, closes out some screens, and goes to the more respectable Kennedy men. Then back to the mirror to see if she has big, white Kennedy teeth. Turning her profile from side to side and glancing back at a photo of the two brothers, she doesn't see it.

What she sees is her grandmother's features clear as day. What she sees is Marilyn Monroe and Marie Morton, one in the same. What she sees is the break of dawn rising over Barnstable's harbor just outside her window…the sky a soft pink on cobalt blue to signal the start of a new day. The storm is done.

Nell leans against the wall to find her center, her security. In this moment, everything is okay.

Nell heads to the staircase to bed. She remembers asking her grandmother, "What are you doing, Nan?" as she sat perfectly still with her eyes shut. Nell would ask, "What do you see in your head?" and Nan would say, "I see the difficult situations," but she never explained to Nell what those were. Nell would persist, "But where does your situation live?" Nan would open her eyes and say, "In my stomach, in my shoulders, and mostly in here," and she'd point to her heart. "But I'm just fine, pumpkin. I have you."

It was clear that her grandmother—whoever she was—is a ghost of her former self. One that stopped growing, stopped changing, but perhaps started having regrets. Or maybe she regretted nothing, having loved her life in this little place in Cape Cod Bay.

Nell tears the clothes from her body without her ritual bubble bath. Then she crawls into bed, negotiating the stages of what she's feeling—grief, denial, anger, sadness. Her nose points straight at the ceiling now. Nell knows that the newly formed tears will pool evenly in both ears…instead of just one.

CHAPTER THIRTY-FIVE

It's 9:30 a.m. the next morning, the one after the night that undoubtedly changed Tom's entire life. And most certainly Nell's too. Pacing outside the gallery and sipping coffee from a to-go cup, Tom hopes Frederick will have pity on him. Tom enters as soon as Frederick flips the sign to "Open."

"Hey Frederick, is Nell in yet?"

"We'll see..." he says, rather glum, as though he can sense the energy is off. He heads to the back room.

Nell suddenly appears, with little attempt to hide her lack of sleep, her bedhead, and an old pair of sweatpants. Yet, even with bags under her eyes and a blotchy face, she looks beautiful.

"I've been up all night worried about you," says Tom, sheepishly. "Worried how this will all change you, more than if you'll ever want me back."

"It can't *really* change me," says Nell. "I'm still Nellie from the block." She gazes beyond him. "Well...Nellie from Barnstable." She attempts to downplay the circumstances. She learned long ago that calmness is strength and self-control is mastery.

"Look, I don't know your Nan, but I know you. She did an incredible job raising you."

"Yes, she sure did!" snaps Nell with an air of dismissal towards Tom. He can only imagine processing the weight of this if the story were about his *own* grandmother. "Let's get this straight," Nell continues. "My grandmother is an incredibly accomplished woman with a generous spirit. So, the burden of proof is on you, Mr. Hogan."

"I don't want to prove anything. Not anymore," says Tom, practically a whisper.

Frederick's head goes back and forth between the two like he's watching the Wimbledon final. "Can someone tell us what's going on here?" But Tom and Nell ignore his question.

Nell lifts her chin towards Tom. "Am I talking to Tom Hogan the reporter or Tom Hogan the man?"

"Tom Hogan the man, I swear to God," he says, crossing his heart with his finger.

Nell pretends to busy herself with paperwork on the desk, fingering through some receipts.

Tom moves closer. "I should have told you I was a reporter right away. I'm sorry. It was a tough situation for me."

"Why?" demands Nell.

Frederick watches on, slowly sliding onto the counter stool. The best seat in the house.

"Stories don't always turn out the way we want them to or how we expect them to, okay?" says Tom. "Either way, I didn't want to hurt you."

"Tell me, then?" she asks. "How did somebody like you ever become a reporter?" Her tone moving to sarcastic pain.

"Whoa…that's a tough one," he says, running a hand through his hair. He knows she'll judge him on whatever answer he gives her. "How about that I always believed in the first amendment."

"Oh?" says Nell. "Is that the one that allows you to dig in other people's lives?" she asks, her fingers still on the paperwork, her face down.

"Look," he says, at the other side of the desk now. Frederick moves in closer too. "When I was a kid," says Tom, "I saw this old movie with *my* grandfather. It was *Call Northside 777.* Jimmy Stewart starred. My grandfather's hero. Anyway, Jimmy's assigned to do a story on this old woman who was washing the floors to raise money to hire an attorney to prove her son is innocent of murder. Jimmy's sure the kid is guilty. But he digs and he digs and finally he finds out that a witness in the case lied. And he does it by looking at the newspaper coverage of the trial. Somewhere, I guess I still believe there's got to be a story like that for me to cover. Somebody I can save."

"How do you know when you find someone who needs saving?" asks Nell, her voice cracking, her lip biting back tears.

"Like this. Like us," says Tom, going around to the other side of the desk now. He runs a finger over the corner of her eye to wipe it. She looks up into his eyes now. "Look Nell, I was just doing my job, but my job didn't include falling in love with you. And I just love you with the simplicity of pure love. That's the honest-to-God full story. Something I've never even known until I met you, beautiful, wonderful, *amazing* Penelope Morton."

Frederick gasps with delight, his hands cupped to his heart. Nell shoots Frederick a look that says, *Whose side are you on?* Nell regains her composure. "My Nan used to tell me men should all wear team jerseys that read 'Liar' on the front with their names on the back."

Tom says nothing now, only hanging his head in shame. Nell lowers her gaze to the floor too. Frederick is dumbfounded. Silence all around.

Tom looks up first. "Frederick, I need some time with Nell here."

"Of course," he says, standing there.

"Alone," says Tom.

Frederick backs out of the room, bowing to them.

Once he's gone, Tom asks, "Does he know?"

"No," says Nell, "Unless it's already in today's paper."

"Of *course* not," he says, taking her arms to turn her body to him. "Listen, there's a man roaming around town right now this second. A tabloid piece of shit."

"We've been through this, Tommy. I understand that you're Tom Hogan the man first and a reporter second."

Tom laughs. "I wasn't referring to me. I was referring to Sidney Spooner. An asshole colleague whose only care is about getting this story because he just wants to impress his asshole father. This is the kind of thing Spooner will *thrive* on."

Nell exhales hard. She's all but given up. "Look, I'm still trying to process this story myself. I need time and space away from it all. From you, from *it*..." She turns to go.

Tom grabs her arm. Turns her back. "Nell, I'm in love with you. Take as long as you want. I'm not going to run the story. Not now or ever." He stares deep into her eyes, studying their depth. "But *he will*. If you want me to help, I need to know what it is I'm trying to save. The truth, Nell. I need the truth about your Nan and where she is."

"She's alive," says Nell, breaking from his grasp. "But I'm not ready to tell you where."

"Okay, fair enough," he says. "But *you* are very much alive right here and right now. I just don't want Spooner to ruin your life with a page-one story."

Nell moves to the paintings on the wall, her fingers gliding across each one, as if in a trance. "Do you know what it's like being the center of your grandmother's existence?" asks Nell. "Do you *know* what it's like to know you can't go anywhere just in case somebody recognizes her? I didn't know what that was like until last night when you put all the puzzle pieces together. Do I wish she told me first? Sure."

"Nell, I—"

But Nell puts her hand up to stop him from speaking. "I once asked Nan where she grew up. Was she alone? She told me she was never alone. I asked her why? Who was she with? She didn't answer right away. But then she said her entire childhood was a scam. A disaster. She went from foster care to foster care and her mother—my *great*-grandmother—who wasn't so great, had been out of the picture all along." Nell takes a deep breath, then exhales with a shake of her head. "Of course, though Nan was technically alone, she was never alone. Not really. From what I learned last night, there was a time when my Nan was apparently surrounded by staff, by producers, by fans, and the press that hounded her day in and day out. No wonder she was always so nervous when she heard the shutter click of a camera at my ballet recital." Nell hisses under breath. "That woman—my grandmother—became so programmed. In the end, her autonomy slipped away. Until she came here. And then she was saved."

"I think she's a hero. A superstar *not* for being Marilyn, but for finding a way to be real," says Tom.

"She was a hero because she was a survivor...you were right when you said that," adds Nell, turning back to face him, wiping her tears from her eyes. "I would have liked the swinging sixties. It's why I was dressed in that costume the night I met you. Women got angry and they took action. Well, sort of. Or at least they tried to. But my nan had to take a different action that wasn't angry. It was brave. It was raw. It was risky, and damn, it was wide open to anything."

"But it worked," says Tom, hopeful and relieved that Nell's allowing him the luxury of a conversation. "Think of the 2016 election!" he says, his tone like an excited kid. "The theme was anger. Trump was angry, Sanders was angry, and Hillary got angry when Trump loomed over her in that debate. But she did nothing. Maybe she needed to *act* angry. But the thing is, even if she had, *angry* isn't as sexy on a woman as *sad* is on a woman. Do you see that? Sadness is somehow acceptable. I know because I had a mother who was sad all the time after my father died. Well, Marilyn had that sad skill. And you have that sad skill right now...how you're acting, it makes me want to protect you. And her too, if you'll let me."

"That's very sweet, Tommy, but I don't need protecting. Nan and I made it this far. But you're right. It's all some gross unfairness. I mean, to live, she had to diminish herself to nothingness. If what you say is true, then that had to be the biggest acting job in her entire acting career." Nell pauses. "To think, this stupid world thinks my grandmother's most important event was singing "Happy Birthday" to some president or signing autographs because she married some big-time home run hitter. No, Nan's greatest moments were rubbing Vicks on my back when I had bronchitis and teaching me to sing the national anthem. She's the woman who held me on the nights when I asked when we could go to heaven to visit my mother, and we'd snuggle into each other and cry. That's my Nan. And that's the woman this community loves. We stick together here...Mayor Bisbee, and Henry, and Elizabeth, who was my mom's best friend until she died. Then Elizabeth became Nan's best friend. My Auntie Beth, as I call her. They're the people that will protect us from some two-bit reporter named..."

"Sidney Spooner," whispers Tom, going over to kiss Nell's forehead, then raising her tear-stained face in his hands. "Thank you, beautiful Nellie."

"For what?"

"For telling me what we're fighting for."

CHAPTER THIRTY-SIX

Spooner tugs mercilessly at the gallery door that reads "Closed for Lunch." Frederick, on the phone, knits his brow from where he sits licking his yogurt spoon. "Don't worry, sweetie," he says into the receiver. "I can handle a dick."

Spooner continues rattling the glass, pounding with his fist, and making gestures like he's Marcel Marceau on crack.

Frederick primps himself a bit, then sashays to the door singing Connie Francis's "Where the Boys Are." "Well, hello there," says Frederick, his tone overly exaggerated. "Aren't we a feisty client *hungry* for a big, *piece* of…art."

Spooner pushes past Frederick and starts to study the paintings on the wall.

"Perhaps an abstract for the boudoir?" asks Frederick.

"This stuff sucks!" says Spooner. "Do people pay for this garbage?"

"Big bucks, big boy, believe me," says Frederick.

"Then you got a bunch of suckers living up here."

"Don't I wish."

Spooner remains at arm's length from Frederick, who's moving in like a vulture on a carcass.

"Is Grace Morton here?" asks Spooner.

"Sadly, Grace is no longer with us."

"Are you saying she was fired or she's dead?"

"Deceased," says Frederick, a look of pain crossing his face.

"What about Marie Morton, the owner?" asks Spooner.

"Alas, no. And her granddaughter, Ms. Morton, the present proprietor, is not in at the moment." Spooner's eyes light up like he's using the strategy card in blackjack. "But surely there's something we can do for you," says Frederick, extending a hand. "My name is "Fred-erick. And you would be?"

Spooner doesn't take Frederick's hand. In fact, he backs off a bit. "Look, Freddie—"

"Fred-erick. Fred, hyphen, Erick." He winks.

"Whatever. My name is Sid Spooner. I'm from Los Angeles, and I need to speak to the Morton granddaughter."

Frederick moves in towards Spooner, who backs away in equal amount of time. "I noticed you never smile…"

"Bad for my collagen," says, Spooner, imitating Frederick by waving an imaginary wand around his face.

"Very funny," says Frederick, moving in closer to Spooner.

"So, where is she?"

"She's rehearsing lines," says Frederick. "She'll be at the theatre later but *cannot* be disturbed. We, however, would be happy to give you whatever information you might need for however long it might take."

"Where's this theatre?"

"It's in Barnstable. But Ms. Morton is not to be bothered right now."

Spooner opens the door to leave. "I'm not going to bother her. I'm just going to give her a history lesson."

"Oh please," says Frederick, dashing faster than usual to the door. "Don't run off. We'd love to sit and chat." Frederick watches Spooner walk up the street before mumbling under his breath, "It's a good thing he's straight."

CHAPTER THIRTY-SEVEN

Tom stands positioning himself against the fireplace mantel with his elbow leaning on the ledge for support...mostly the emotional kind.

Nell assumes a seat on the sofa, fluffing some pillows and getting comfortable. "Well, go on," she says sarcastically. "This ought to be good." She folds her arms.

He stares at her. Mainly her hair. "I'm just fascinated by your new look," he says. Her hair is cropped in a bob with the bangs longer and angled, and it's been highlighted blonde. The granddaughter of Marilyn Monroe is now crystal clear in an image that the world might recognize.

She playfully runs her fingers through her wavy locks. "Yes, I'm embracing my inner Marilyn."

Tom lets out a huge exhale and begins. "She became Marilyn Monroe legally in 1956, though she'd been using the name all along. The name 'Marilyn' was chosen by Ben Lyon, a casting director at Fox Studios, who thought she was the most gorgeous golden-haired woman he'd ever seen. He told Marilyn that under the contract he had a right to change her name from Norma Jeane to something more movie star–sounding. He liked a Broadway star named Marilyn Miller. That's when he said to your grandmother, 'To me...you're a Marilyn!' So, she asked 'Can I use my own grandmother's name? Monroe?'" Tom now paces as he talks, but Nell is glued to his every word. "Ida Bolender was a religious foster care parent and the neighbor to Della Monroe, your *great-*

great-grandmother," explains Tom. "Della was born in Mexico, and she had a daughter named Gladys, your great-grandmother."

"Yes," says Nell. "I know those names. I've been doing my research just in case."

"By the age of twenty-four, your great-grandmother was already on her second husband, a guy named Martin Edward Mortensen but not necessarily the father of her third unborn child. When Della's daughter—your unwed great-grandmother, Gladys Baker—got pregnant the third time, Della saw her neighbor Ida as a savoir to soon-to-be born Norma Jeane. I guess she also tried to nail the pregnancy on some guy named Charles Stanley Gifford, but he knew Gladys, um, slept around…" He pauses to take in Nell's emotions. "Sorry about that," he says.

Nell shrugs. "But Norma Jeane was born the same day as my grandmother, June 1, 1926, right?"

"Correct," says Tom. "In an LA hospital. Of course, Gladys was looked down upon in a time when being a single mother was unacceptable. So, she put the name 'Edward Mortenson' on the birth certificate just to give your grandmother a legal name."

"Okay, fair enough. It was the twenties. Women did what they had to do," says Nell, clasping her knees and sinking back into the sofa.

"Except they spelled the name 'Mortensen' with an 'o' so it was 'Mortenson.' But anyway, that's when Norma Jeane was handed over to Ida Bolender, the neighbor. But it's also when a woman named Grace McKee came into Norma's life."

"She must be the woman that Nan named my mother after," affirms Nell. "I assume this original Grace must have loved little Norma Jeane?"

"Right. And she'd soon become a constant. But the shitty news was that Della and Gladys complained of the 'voices' in their heads. They felt they were being stalked. So, sadly, your family has a long history of mental illness," says Tom, his voice going softer. "Just like you told me on our stroll that day."

"So, my great-great-grandmother died in a psychiatric ward?"

"Yes, how did you know that?"

"Like I told you," Nell gulps, sitting forward. "Nan always told me mental illness ran in the family. She just never really talked about the players."

"Well, the good news was that your grandmother, Norma Jeane, was thriving as a child living with Ida and her husband, Wayne," says Tom, still pacing and trying to remain gallant. "Ida and Wayne really loved being foster parents. They even tried to adopt Norma Jeane, which would have made a world of difference to her entire life, but Gladys wouldn't allow it. And it was kind of sad because I read stuff—and I don't know how much you want me to tell you…"

"Seriously?" asks Nell. "Tell me all of it. What's to hide now?"

"Just stuff like she had a pet dog—"

"Tippy! Was it Tippy?" asks Nell, her voice like a little girl. "And she was hit by a car?"

"Yeah, and Norma came home from school to see her dead dog on the sidewalk."

"Oh, the poor thing. I mean Nan. And the dog," says Nell. "No wonder she wanted to name one of our old cats Tippy, but she thought it was bad luck, so we didn't."

"Well, getting back to Grace," says Tom, "She was Gladys's best friend, and they worked together splicing film negatives for a movie company. They were even roommates. I read that Grace wanted to be an actress."

Just then, the cats, Sylvia and Ted, jump on the sofa on cue, moving around Nell. Sylvia settles on her lap while Ted curls up on the backside of the sofa. "Go on…" says Nell, ignoring them.

"The two women—Gladys and Grace—would take Norma Jeane for visitations, but it was a disaster because Norma Jeane had begun to think of Ida and Wayne as her parents. Gladys didn't like that, so she decided to give Norma Jeane to a new foster care family, the Atkinsons. Supposedly it would only be a temporary situation. The Atkinsons dabbled in show biz, so it seemed a good fit for whatever reason."

"Good fit? It's disgusting that they uprooted my grandmother that way. That would never happen today, would it?" asks Nell. "I mean, I don't know a lot about foster care, but I can't imagine the constant movement and insecurity."

Tom sits across from Nell on a stool. "It gets kinda worse. Gladys bought a home, but she didn't want Norma living there, even though Grace kept insisting that the child needed her mother. But Gladys refused, so Grace suggested that the Atkinsons move in with them so that Norma would have the best of all worlds. Under one roof. They'd all be a family. All of them." Tom tries to sugarcoat it with a happy ending, though he knows it's only the beginning of more doom and gloom. "And Grace loved movies, so she'd take Norma Jeane to matinees. Grace was the one to convince Norma Jeane that one day she *too* could be a big star on the big screen."

"I'm glad she had Grace. No wonder she named my own mother after her," says Nell, stroking Sylvia now.

Tom pulls the stool closer to Nell as he keeps spilling. "Then Gladys went into a sanitarium, and Grace became Norma's legal guardian. But as Norma Jeane grew into an adolescent, it was clear she was special and beautiful. A star. She had the 'it' factor. It's all been written about, but the only part that doesn't make sense is that Grace dumped her into another orphanage. Historians think it's because Grace was on her third marriage, and the new guy, a *fourth* husband named Ervin-something-or-another, wouldn't want to raise someone else's child. And I guess in those days, you couldn't blame Grace."

"Okay, so did she stay in the orphanage?" asks Nell.

"No, she got out. And that's around the time that Grace and Ida, the first caretaker who *should have* been allowed to adopt her all along, got into a legal battle over custody. It's also when Norma learned she had a half-sister named Bernice. There's a lot that's not clear, but I guess she moved in with someone named Ana Lower who ended up arranging a marriage for sixteen-year-old Norma Jeane and Jim Dougherty. Your grandmother married Dougherty in 1942. I mean, marriage was probably your grandmother's best option to stay out of orphanages."

The story comes at Nell like high-beam headlights on a blackened highway. "Good God! How sad that young women didn't have choices in those days," says Nell, getting up to head to the window. "I hope those nice people—Ida and Wayne—came to Norma Jeane's wedding?"

"They did," says Tom, standing up behind Nell, and rubbing her back. "But then they got divorced. And your grandmother married Joe DiMaggio." Tom moves to the other side of the room and picks up one of the bobble heads. "This guy." Nell turns to see and nods. "You know the famous flying dress scene? Maybe you don't. But it's from the movie *The Seven Year Itch.* DiMaggio wasn't there when the public made such a fuss about seeing underneath your grandmother's dress, but he was furious and jealous, so it was the beginning of the end of their marriage."

"Sounds like a total ego maniac."

Tom exhales. "By today's standard's yeah, I'd say so. But she had other husbands—Arthur Miller, the writer. At that point, she'd become larger than life and was officially Marilyn Monroe the movie star." Tom puts his hands in his pockets. "By the way, you actually *gave* me that autographed ball from DiMaggio. I'll bring it back."

"Keep it," Nell whispers, wanting to get back to the juice of the story. "So, then she did movies that apparently I wasn't allowed to see on the old movie channel." Nell folds her arms.

"Yeah, lots of movies. She wanted to be taken seriously, not just seen as the dumb blonde. She actually turned to her good friend, Frank Sinatra, and lived with him for a while."

"As a lover?" asks Nell.

"Just a friend. He was having trouble with Ava Gardner, the love of his life. They consoled each other."

"He must be the 'Frank' she's talked about," says Nell, shaking her head and seeing how everything seems to fit. Everything including her grandmother's pain. It's as if Marilyn's life could have been elegant but instead turned out to be like sipping champagne from a straw. "I wonder what was more difficult for her," asks Nell, turning to face Tom now, "pretending to be Marilyn Monroe or pretending to be Norma Jeane?

"I think reclaiming Norma Jeane was the hardest thing of all," says Tom with a frightened shrug, worried that he'll say the wrong thing again. "I mean, I don't know the answers, but I can't imagine being up against the lot of Harvey Weinsteins of her time. Powerful and manipulative moguls."

"Did she have a support system? At all?" asks Nell.

"She longed for her Aunt Grace. And she relied on a guy named Lee Strasberg who ran the Actors Studio. His wife, Paula, became one of her best friends. Maybe because Marilyn was different. If Joan Crawford was a *real* actress, then Marilyn Monroe was just considered a bombshell."

"Beauty can only get you so far in life," says Nell, moving to the kitchen and trying to act normal. "Should I be making us lunch?"

"I'd like to finish telling you the story just now. I can't eat." Nell nods and spins back to the living room. "A lot of actors depended on drugs to enhance their careers," says Tom. "Not just women, but men too, like Marlon Brando. And, of course, your grandmother."

"And what of Arthur Miller?" she says, moving to the bookshelf, and fingering across a dusty shelf that sits in his honor of his work, beginning with a very tattered copy of *Focus, The Crucible,* and all the way through 1963's *Jane's Blanket.* Nell stops on a short story collection called *I Don't Need You Anymore*, published in 1967. "Hmmm..." smirks Nell. "Interesting. And written after Marilyn's death." Tom goes to the shelf to take a closer look. "Did you know I starred in *The Crucible* in High school?" adds Nell. "I played Abigail Williams."

"Nan must have *loved* that," he says. "It sucks it didn't work with Miller."

"Why do you suppose that was?"

"Sources say she felt intellectually inadequate next to him. And that she had a hard time living in the present when her past was so screwed up."

"I read online that she got pregnant by Miller and lost the baby and had some other miscarriages," says Nell, looking to Tom as if he has all the answers. "The web is so disgusting the things that they say about someone's personal life. I hate people who gossip when the person isn't in the room to defend themselves." Her words hang for a moment.

"Yes, it's true, Nellie, but who knows about these things? I mean, it's kind of personal for a woman to know what's real and what's not. The only thing I *do* know is that by the time she had your mother, Grace, nobody on the planet was going to take that away from her or interfere with her future." Tom goes to Nell to take her in his arms. She resists. Keeping her arms at her side. He hugs her nonetheless. "Look, she defied the odds and the rumors that she couldn't have kids. But God decided she could."

Nell pulls back. "I'm glad she had Doctor Greenson. Everything seems to point to the fact that he and his wife loved her like a daughter." Nell moves to the computer desk, leaning her hands backwards on the edge for support, but faces Tom. "What of the Kennedys? I mean, they're right here in Hyannisport. How do the rumors fit in?"

"She met President John F. Kennedy in July 1960, the night he accepted the Democratic party nomination for President, and—"

Nell's house phone rings. She debates whether to answer and then glances at the mantle to see the clock. "Shit! It can't be! I have rehearsal. It must be the director calling." Nell looks to Tom for direction as well.

"Do you want to finish this later?" he asks, his voice dipping down with disappointment.

"I think we have to," says Nell. "Or in the words of Nan, 'the show must go on.'"

They both share a look. One that says she believes she can trust Tom.

"Let me just leave you with this much…okay?" he says, going to her side and taking her elbows in both his hands. "Marilyn wanted to escape. She buried Norma Jeane so she could be Marilyn, and then the irony was that she wanted to bury Marilyn to be…what? Norma Jeane again? I don't think so. There's no going back."

"No," says Nell. "She evolved. To Marie Morton. My grandmother. My hero. My love for her won't change. But I must decide whether to tell her that I know or not."

Nell moves from Tom, going into show mode, grabbing her purse from the chair, and the script pages with her lines from the coffee table.

"After the whole Arthur Miller thing, she committed herself to a New York hospital," says Tom following her. "A fake name. Faye Miller. She knew it was time to get her life in order. But the sad thing is that her mother, Gladys, was committed to Rock Haven in California. She was finally diagnosed a paranoid schizophrenic."

"I get it. My family was nuts, but my Nan turned it around. And I can only take so much of this story. Yikes! I gotta go," says Nell, ushering him to the door with haste or is it shock? She locks it and heads up the walkway. "But it helps me to understand a lot of things right now..." Her tone suggests many meanings. That of understanding her grandmother's history but also understanding the amount of time Tom had put into nailing this story and its history. "Come by. Watch me rehearse," she calls back.

"Okay, I will," says Tom watching her go. It's clear Nell needs little rehearsing at this real-life drama.

CHAPTER THIRTY-EIGHT

Spooner stalls at the double white doors of the Playhouse because his cell phone is ringing. A call from Tony Spittone. *Shit!* He puts the phone to his ear. "Hey Tony…so listen, I've got some really bad news," says Spooner, putting on his best sympathy act. "Your daughter, Grace Morton, is a dead end." A pause. And then, "Um, she's dead." Another pause as Spooner worries whether he'll be paid or not. "But the good news is you have a granddaughter who's very much alive!" Spooner notices Tom coming towards him. "I haven't seen her yet but…Tony? Tony? You there? Sorry, I can't hear you. Huh? Service sucks here!"

~

When they hang up, Tony Spittone sits on the edge of a bedspread in the floral room of an inn, just up the street from Spooner's inn. He looks visibly shaken. He's got the Canterbury Suite at the Ashley Manor, which is ironically the same inn where Tom is staying, albeit in a much smaller room, but still lovely. Tony Spittone's hands rest on his knees like he's in prayer for the soul of his dead daughter.

~

Tom is at the door of the theatre now, facing Spooner, catching him off guard. "Spooner! I know why you're here!"

"Do you, fuckwit?" says Spooner. "I think I've got one up on you," he says as they both move to open the double doors.

"After you, asshole," says Tom, extending a hand.

Spooner enters and stares down the rows of seats to the stage, where Nell has just entered from the wings, looking for all the world like the most luscious movie star. The lighting highlights her angelic features against a white halter sundress, as if it's summertime. She's absolutely *delicious* to witness. And, judging by her iconic dress, a knock-off of the costume from Marilyn's iconic movie, you'd almost expect the subway grate to blow under its hem, except this is a much different production. This is *The Vagina Monologues*.

"Holy shit!" says Spooner, staring in awe at her. "She's hot!"

A "*Shhh!*" echoes from one of the two people in the rehearsal.

"The heart is capable of sacrifice. So is the vagina," says Nell from stage. "The heart is able to forgive and repair. It can change its shape to let us in. It can *expand* to let us out. So can the vagina. It can *ache* for us and stretch for us, *die* for us and bleed and bleed us into this difficult, wondrous world. I was there in the room. I remember."

"What the hell kind of show is this?" asks Spooner.

"*The Vagina Monologues*," hisses Tom. "Out of your league."

Nell tugs her dress down to her knees, script in hands while listening to the director give direction from the audience seats. She nods, raises her script eyelevel, and continues walking across the stage in thought. She continues, "The clitoris is pure in purpose. It is the only organ in the body designed purely for pleasure."

"No shit," says Spooner. "Now we're talkin'!"

The director says something amusing that neither Tom nor Spooner can hear as they're glued on Nell's beauty. Nell laughs. An infectious laugh. Her head thrown back, her hair glistening in the stage light, Tom is staring at her for the longest moment until he catches Spooner snapping photos with his iPhone.

"What? I can't take a photo?" says Spooner to Tom. "Do you realize she looks like Marilyn Monroe?"

"Give me that camera!" says Tom, grabbing at his phone. And the two men scuffle. Spooner knocks over a podium, which gets Nell's attention. She shields her eyes from the lights to see the ruckus.

"Excuse me, but you're not supposed to be in here," Nell says to Spooner. "Tickets don't go on sale until March."

"Great, suppose I can get house seats from the star?" he flirts.

"You'll have to check with my, um, boyfriend on that…" she giggles.

"Where is he?"

"Standing right next to you," says Nell.

Spooner dagger-eyes Tom with a look that says he can't possibly be having sex with this gorgeous creature.

"Take it from the top," says the director, whose face we still can't see in the darkened theatre.

Nell shuffles through her pages but looks confused. "Do you want me to go the beginning? Or are you asking for 'Looking at it, I started crying?'"

"Crying," calls out the director.

"Okay, sorry," Nell apologizes. "I'm just a little out of it today. Got some weird news."

"I can see that," says the director.

Nell nods and goes into the role. "Looking at it, I started crying. Maybe it was knowing that I had to give up the fantasy, the enormous life consuming fantasy, that someone or something was going to do this for me—the fantasy that someone was coming to lead my life, to choose direction, to give me orgasms."

"And, Cut!" shouts the director.

The house lights go back up, and Nell is left on the stage, ignoring the men and penciling in some changes, when Spooner approaches the stage edge.

"Hi there, I'm Sid Spooner," he says, jumping up on stage as smoothly as hopping a fence. "Why don't you show a new guy around town. Dinner?"

She gives him an exasperated glance. "Didn't I just tell you I have a boyfriend?"

He sighs. Spooner's not used to rejection.

"And besides," she adds as though dangling the carrot she *knows* he's here to chomp, "My grandmother always told me to know your worth, even if it means being without a date."

"You mean like she knew *her* worth?" he says. "Like she *ever* went dateless?"

Nell shakes her head in disgust and begins to walk backstage, but Spooner follows her. Tom is heading their way. Nell looks back and hisses, "This is a new one. Not *me* following the bad boy but the bad boy following me."

Tom grabs Spooner by the arm and turns him. Hard. "Trying to fuck her and fucking me over aren't the same thing."

"I think I'll fuck her first," says Spooner. "Then I'll fuck with your story!"

"You're so pathetic they need a new word for pathetic," says Tom, "You don't know the first thing about integrity in journalism. Leave her alone."

"C'mon, Hogan," says Spooner. "Guy to guy. Please tell me you're only protecting her because you're having a monologue with her vagina?"

"You're lucky I don't kick your ass," says Tom.

"Well, are you?"

"What's it to you?"

They're at her dressing room door now, and Spooner barges in, Tom on his heels.

"Ah, Miss Morton," asks Spooner, putting on his reporter voice. "You think your acting bug came from your DNA?"

"Excuse me?" says Nell, startled, but wiping off her lipstick and staring at him through the mirror. "My mother didn't act."

"I meant your grandmother," he says. "My bad."

"My grandmother?" asks Nell. She spins her stool so she's facing Spooner. "My grandmother's greatest performance was when she'd have to grieve in silence over my mother's grave. We always left daisies. We went there almost every day before supper even when it rained."

"That's enough, Spooner," says Tom, "I think you should leave."

"I can handle him," says Nell, putting up a hand to Tom.

"Listen, Nell," says Spooner, "I'm touched by your very sweet grave-visiting memories, but you can't tell me you don't know. I mean sure, you were just a baby when your grandmother was in her sixties, all post-menopausal looking and all, but you can't tell me you couldn't see how she *sucked* the sex out of every breath she breathed. She wasn't just a sex symbol…she was *thee* sex symbol!"

"You've got about two seconds to get out of here, Spooner," says Tom, ready to punch him.

"C'mon, you had to see it," Spooner persists.

Nell stands up and lays on an all-out Hollywood slap across Spooner's face. "Get the hell out of here. Now."

"Ooh, I love 'em feisty." Spooner says, holding his stinging cheek before turning to go. He turns back at the door. "And what about your grandfather?" Spooner's comment comes out of left field. "Don't you want to know about him?"

Nell knits her brow. "I'm certain my grandfather is dead."

"Well, then, he eats pretty good for a dead man," says Spooner, hand on the door handle. Nell and Tom glare at him. "I had dinner with him in LA just last week."

"Does this mean you've come all this way to tell me who my grandfather was?"

"Maybe, maybe not," says Spooner. "Maybe you don't really want to know."

Nell rises and stalks over to him. She runs a finger across his chest in a very Marilyn Monroe way. "Oh, I'd love to know. And maybe about my daddy too. I hate leaving a fairy tale right in the middle." Spooner tries to place an arm around her as Tom watches on, curious to see what exactly Spooner has to say. "So, Mr. Spooner, who's my daddy?"

"I'll be your daddy if you like."

Nell pushes him away and puts a hand up to Tom to stop him from interfering.

"No, really, what is it that you know?" asks Nell.

"Okay," says Spooner. "It's Angelo Spittone. The well-known Hollywood mobster. Only he goes by 'Tony Spits.' But I'm sure that as his granddaughter you can call him anything you want."

"Well, isn't this nice?" she says, containing her otherwise-shaken composure to both Tom and Spooner. "A mafioso grandpa and a movie star grandma. How all-American can you get?"

"You asked," says Spooner, his chin jutting forward in satisfaction. And having the last word, he turns to go.

Tom kicks the door shut and is left staring at Nell, who's now trembling. Tom moves cautiously to her and takes her into his arms. She holds on tightly.

"I told you he was an asshole," Tom whispers, and then pulling back to look at her. "He'll say anything. But we have to figure out how to stop him. Not from being an asshole, I mean—that'll never change—but from telling your story. And fast."

Nell moves back to her mirror with a despondent look. "I'm tired," she says. "I know you mean well, but I must ask you to leave. I want to go home and rest. I don't feel very good from all this news, and I just need to be alone...decide what's right."

"I understand," says Tom. But he doesn't, not really, because leaving her alone means she has a choice to make. And in this life, as we know, choices give us either great joy...or great regret.

He's hoping for the former. He's hoping he's her eventual choice.

CHAPTER THIRTY-NINE

Impressive, sky-reaching pine trees surround Nell as she climbs a path towards a log cabin. With hands on her hips, stopping to reclaim her breath, she watches the smoke emitting from the cabin's chimney. We don't know where she is—could be Maine, could be Vermont, could be any snowy New England place—but we see Nell moving closer to a woman whose back is to her.

The woman has golden white hair loosely pulled in a chignon. She's stretched on a chaise lounge, her face caressed by a rising sun, her nose buried in a novel. She's bundled in a big plaid blanket. The sound of approaching footsteps, the crunching of leaves, the panting of breath makes her glance up from the pages. She sees Nell coming closer.

"Nan!" calls Nell. "Nan?" But the woman doesn't turn to face her. Breathless, Nell gets closer to the woman, desperate for her to look up. "Nan!" Please!" But when the woman turns, her face morphs into that of Nell's dead mother. The face we've seen in photos at Nell's cottage. Except this face is bloodied from the moped accident.

Nell can't breathe; she's hyperventilating.

And then—

Nell bolts upright in bed, gasping for air, perspiring. She's not sure where she is until she realizes she's in her bedroom in Barnstable. It was all just a dream.

Her startled cats, Sylvia and Ted, leap down from the foot of the bed. Nell's shoulder loosens in relief as she gulps a large breath of air, glancing around her silent bedroom.

Glancing at the alarm clock, she realizes it's past midnight. She's been sleeping since five.

Nell tosses back the sheets to reveal a flimsy nightgown, and she tucks her feet into UGG slippers, grabbing her robe from the door hook.

She moves to her computer and googles her grandmother and Frank Sinatra. Moving the mouse to the store options on her playlist, she purchases Frank Sinatra's entire album of classics.

She already knows the songs well since Nan used to listen to them all the time. Imagine if Nan knew of Sirius Radio? She'd have had it tuned to "Seriously Sinatra" for every car ride!

His songs are sweet songs about a woman and a man for the most part, which is a relief to Nell that Ol' Blue Eyes was kind to her grandmother. The iconic journalist Gay Talese wrote the most famous article about Sinatra called "Frank Sinatra Has a Cold." It is considered to be the greatest piece of nonfiction ever included in *Esquire* magazine. Nell knows this because she once found the article, long turned yellow, taped inside the top of Nan's hope chest.

Her mind goes deep into her memory bank. Sinatra was that kind of Italian guy who saw women as either a "Madonna" or a "whore." It's a theory about the behavior of macho men. A Madonna is saintly—like a mom, a female neighbor, or a female colleague. The whore is the one-night stand, the good-time broad. Certainly, Nan was Sinatra's Madonna, and he was always protecting her. And Nell has just realized he didn't die until 1998. *Is it possible he ever visited them when she was a little girl? Did he know?*

Nell longs to call Nan and just ask her questions but given the current circumstances—reporters, social media, Spooner!—she doesn't want to scare her. And besides, her grandmother always taught her that when you don't know what to do, do nothing.

Nell moves to the kitchen to microwave some tomato basil soup, her mind jumping to female heroes and feminists. Poor Marilyn worked her way out of pinup-girl mentality.

As the microwave dings, Nell realizes she's begun to morph Nan into Marilyn and vice versa. One in the same.

Nell sips the soup from a mug, feeling conflicted in her emotions. How strange for Nan to be a woman of such beauty imprisoned *by* that beauty. She allowed them to create her into their pretty porcelain doll—their eternal fantasy.

Nell taps her Instagram feed. Searches for Marilyn Monroe. #MarilynMonroe, #MMonthofLove, #missyouMarilyn, and so on. Hmmm...crazy to believe, but when Marilyn died, she got what she wanted. A home. From Nell's way of seeing things, Nan, Norma Jeane, and Marilyn got to live as one in this story-book cottage and make their own happily ever after. Nan sans a man!

Nell stares at Nan's paintings with new perspective now. They come to life from the walls. The pain, the patriotism, the hidden stories.

The clock ticks 2:30 a.m. On the last search engine, Nell comes across a song called "Marilyn Monroe" by Pharrell Williams from his album *G I R L*. But Nell is instead drawn to Elton John's "Candle in the Wind."

As the lyrics "*Goodbye Norma Jeane*" come on, Nell decides to blast it.

Nell lets her robe fall to the living room floor. She's left standing in her flesh-toned nightgown in front of a mirror, admiring herself. Yes, this is who Nell is. And this the house that makes her proud to be the granddaughter of the one and only Norma Jeane Baker, Marilyn Monroe, and Marie Morton. Nell mimics with a fake microphone...proud to be here in this moment. Proud to know that Elton John celebrated her grandmother's life.

There's a part of this that feels creepy and a part that feels cool. Nell gets a bursting impulse, moving to the landline phone on the wall. There is no crossing back now.

It rings. Nell speaks into the receiver. “Hi, it’s me. I know it’s late. And I’m glad you didn’t pick up, so I’ll just leave you this message. I wondered if I could see you for breakfast in the morning. But not in town. Someplace obscure. Um, maybe down in Brewster? It’s important that we talk. Call me. Oh, and I love you.”

Finishing her call, she moves like a mouse at midnight to the window, gazing into the darkened night. You might think Nell is too young to know the lyrics to “Candle in the Wind,” but quite the contrary. Nan and she used to sing to that very song when they were doing household chores together. With little effort, the words come easy for Nell, her breath steaming up the glass as she reminisces.

CHAPTER FORTY

The diner operates like a typical breakfast haunt—the sizzling of bacon on the griddle, orders for eggs over easy being shouted to the short-order cook, and waitresses balancing dirty plates while pouring the coffee refills. Coffee is *always* a priority.

The posters on the wall attract Nell's attention as she slides into the ripped red vinyl booth. A tired collection of prints: The mustard-colored print featuring a black cat—"Tournée du Chat Noir" by Rodolphe Salis—hangs next to a faded one of Edward Hopper's "Nighthawks" above the world-famous picture of Albert Einstein sticking his tongue out. Next to that, the black-and-white poster of the little French boy running through Parisian streets with a baguette under his arm. But it's the last one that Nell turns to study. It's her Nan as a young woman, perched on white stilettos with the hem of her white ruffled dress blowing up above the subway grate, exposing her white panties. Nell's seen the picture a million times in her life, but it was a backdrop. She never studied it until today. Nell sees it in the eyes now. Marilyn really *is* Nan…

Just then, Elizabeth from The Porpoise slides into Nell's booth, sitting across from her. Their eyes meet with uncertainty. "You had me worried when you called so late," says Elizabeth.

"I know…about everything," says Nell, with a snappy assuredness to her tone. She gestures her shoulder, tipping her head towards the Marilyn poster on the wall. "Do you know?"

"Oh, dear," says Elizabeth, hanging her head in an exaggerated motion. "I need coffee."

As if on cue, the waitress is there to take their orders. "Um, scrambled eggs and tofu with a mint tea, no sugar," says Nell. "Thanks." She offers a polite smile and hands the waitress the menu but keeps her stare on Elizabeth.

"Poached eggs, side of bacon, and a coffee. Large," says Elizabeth. The waitress departs. "Well, had to happen sooner or later. Amazed she was able to conceal it this long," says Elizabeth, taking Nell's hands in hers and glancing over Nell's shoulder at the Marilyn poster. "You okay? I'm so sorry, kid."

"How long have you known?" asks Nell.

"As long as your mother knew..." says Elizabeth.

"So, she *did* know," says Nell, "Oh my God!" She drops her head into her hands and begins sobbing.

"Oh honey," says Elizabeth glancing around.

Nell raises her head and wipes her eyes. She manages a smile at Elizabeth. "I'm okay. Really. I'm relieved to know the answer about whether she knew or not." Nell exhales and takes a moment. Elizabeth reaches across the table to take her hand. Nell takes it and then says, "And I'm fascinated by all the intricacies, all the secrets. I mean, look what you had to endure as her friend all these years." Nell realizes that Elizabeth has been to her what Grace McKee must have been to Marilyn/Nan.

"Your grandmother is an incredible woman," says Elizabeth. "But Marilyn had to act and look a certain way. Just like that poster. She turned it on, especially for the many men in her life. It was survival, kiddo. But when she became a mother to *your* mother—Grace—she left that all behind, so I hope you can find it in your heart to forgive her."

"Okay, but you had to survive, Auntie Beth," says Nell as the waitress brings their coffee and tea, "so you chose a waitressing job." Nell smiles as the waitress acknowledges her comment too.

"Your grandmother chose to act. She had a calling. She was a starving actress who needed to fulfill something I never had a calling for," says Elizabeth, adding cream to her coffee. "But you know what kid? Life is all about desire and consequence. It's better to live your life with flaws than to live life as someone else in some fake and unfulfilled way. She's herself now. She's not the fake Marilyn that Hollywood created. She's paid for her consequences. That was a very long time ago."

"I know, I get it," says Nell, removing the tea bag from her mug. "But you have to understand that I go to bed one day thinking I have a sweet old granny, and the next day I wake up to learn she's America's most iconic sex symbol!"

"She's still a sweet old granny, and don't you ever forget that," says Elizabeth with the upmost respect in her tone. "Does she know that you know?"

Nell begins to tear up again and shakes her head *no*.

"Thank God," says Elizabeth, sitting back relieved. "It would kill her. I really think it would kill her."

"I think I'm beginning to understand that."

"Took your grandmother years to undo the damage and the insecurity and oh my god, the panic. She had to learn to stop trying so hard. Trying so hard only robbed her of her power. Boy, don't I remember. Course I was a little girl with Gracey, but in hindsight, and after Grace's death, I could see what your grandmother learned. Learning to relive is hard work." Elizabeth sips her coffee. "I'll be there for her forever. For you too, Nellie."

"You were a good friend to my Nan to keep it a secret."

"I was your mother's friend first. Then your Nan and I grieved together at Grace's funeral."

"I want to know more about my mother now," says Nell. "When, if ever, were you planning to tell me?"

"Your Nan didn't want you to know the details until long after she was gone."

"I see," says Nell, her eyes swelling with tears.

"Sweet pea, I didn't find out until your mom found out."

"Until *my* mother found out?"

"Yes, we found out together. Grace and I heard your Nan on the phone with someone. A man. It was late at night. We were out on the porch, but the window was open. Heard an earful. Heard her arguing with some man about her payments due her from the studio. Your mother was rubbing her belly with you when she found out. And your mother went through exactly what you're going through right now. The question was whether or not to let her mother know that she knew."

"Did she?" asks Nan, sitting upright.

"Yes," says Elizabeth, her tone suggesting it wasn't a good thing.

"And what happened?" Their breakfast orders arrive. The two women sit back to eye over their plates, but then go back to leaning forward, food untouched.

"What happened?" says Elizabeth. "I'll tell you what happened. Your mother and your Nan got into a terrible fight. She called Nan a liar and a slut." Nell is speechless. "It was different back then, Nellie. Those things were embarrassing. Getting divorced was bad enough, let alone finding out you're the pregnant daughter of the woman every man in the world wanted to have sex with." Elizabeth pauses. "You're old enough for me to say those things to now..."

Nell smirks. "Then Nan didn't want me to know because she was afraid we'd fight too, and then she might lose me. The way she did with my mother."

"Something like that."

"Do you think my mother tried to kill herself because she couldn't handle the truth?" asks Nell, casting her eyes down at her untouched eggs.

Elizabeth looks over Nell's shoulder at the poster again and thinks for a moment before answering. "No," she says...soft, but deadpan. But Nell isn't sure by Elizabeth's tone that she means it. "Nellie," says Elizabeth, buttering the toast on her breakfast plate,

"When your grandmother was pregnant with your mother, she felt that bringing a new little 'Norma Jeane' into the world would solve all her problems. And it did. Or so she told Gracey, and Gracey told me. It was so obvious your grandmother adored her daughter more than anything on the planet."

"I read someplace that she felt her daughter would be a princess in a fairy tale," says Nell.

"That's right," says Elizabeth, finishing her coffee, and motioning for a refill. "She was fixated on that baby. Always felt she could create the perfect little Marilyn through a daughter."

"God," says Nell. "It all makes me ill. And then poor Nan loses the one thing she most loved." Nell stabs at her eggs. "What a toxic journey. It's almost Shakespearean." Nell's mind drifts to the agents and the producers her Nan had to sleep with to get ahead. The entire #MeToo movement takes on new perspective when Nell realizes it's her grandmother who had to do certain things to get ahead in a time when women couldn't get equal pay, couldn't have legal abortions…

"Where'd you go, sweetheart?" says Elizabeth, taking Nell's fingers and playing with them.

"I'm not sure which life was more an illusion. The Marilyn Monroe one or the Marie Morton one?"

"The Marilyn one, for sure," says Elizabeth. "There's been so many times I've wanted her to look the world straight in the eye and have them look straight back with the truth."

"But?" asks Nell, dropping her fork to really hear her answer.

"She loved you more than she needed to be right…or to prove anything. Can you imagine what might have happened to your existence if she spilled the beans? You'd certainly never have had the life you loved here growing up peacefully." Elizabeth sips her coffee and puts it down, thinking. "Can you imagine Nan on social media? I mean, really?"

"Nan hates social media. All that 'Look at me! It's me!'" squeals Nell, imitating her grandmother.

"Honey," says Elizabeth, looking down at her egg plate. "I can't tell you what I think you should do. You have to decide. I tried giving advice once about your grandmother's past, and it backfired on me. Your mother was furious with me when I advised her to not say anything. But for lack of better judgement, she didn't take my advice and reamed into your grandmother. And for a while in the aftermath, I was in the bullet path. Gracey didn't speak to me…and that was hard. She was my best friend, the sister I never had, and in a way, my mother love, since mine died of cancer when I was a kid. It's why I always felt responsible for you, Nellie. You're like my own daughter, you know."

"Thank you, Auntie Beth, but did you see it coming? My mom's death?"

"No, honey, I didn't. None of us did. I just wish they'd find the guy whose car hit her."

Nell stares down to her teacup, staring into its water as if she can read leaves. As if the leaves might be saying, "It was a moped accident, not a suicide."

The check arrives, and Elizabeth snatches it before leaning in to squeeze Nell's wrist. "Look at me, honey," says Elizabeth. When Nell looks up, she sees true kindness in her eyes. "Life is too short not to go at *everything* from a place of love," says Elizbeth. "You know who taught me that? Your Nan. We rush about in the first half of our lives trying to put together the definition of who we are. And then in the second part, we realize we're rushing about trying to unscramble the mess from the first half."

"Your point?"

"Enjoy the first half of your life. Just take it one day at a time so it evens out, okay?" says Elizabeth. "You're still young."

"What if I inherit my Nan's craziness…her addictions?"

"What?" asks Elizabeth. "Don't be silly. Your Nan kicked it all. They were so quick to prescribe drugs—sleeping pills, pain killers—crazy Western way of problem solving. Be proud of your grandmother. She fought addiction and she sought out spirituality. And then, she instilled that into you. *You!*" Elizabeth points her finger to Nell's chest. "You're your mother and your grandmother now, sweetheart. All the good bits."

"I'm learning to face my demons—and apparently their demons—head on."

"Speaking of," says Elizabeth. "That Sidney Spooner. Bad news. But that Tommy Hogan? He's a keeper."

Nell unleashes a massive toothy smile. She tips her head to the ceiling and declares, "Someone once said something like, um, we fall in love with people who have all the characteristics we wish we had but can't access."

"Sounds like something Nan said," says Elizabeth, with a bit of sarcasm. "Honey, I don't' know about that, but what I see is two kids with good souls and good intentions. Don't' be mad at him that he first came here to chase a story. It brought him to you. He's a good egg. And I know good eggs," says Elizabeth, eyeing the last of her breakfast and leaving a few dollars in tip on the table.

"Now that I know all of this, it's like I used to live outside of a shaken snow globe looking in, but with him, we're inside of the snow globe together, whatever the shakeup ahead."

"Okay, well, that's an original way of looking at love," says Elizabeth. "But do you love him?"

She nods. "He's forcing me—not by controlling me, but just by being who he is—to change into the best me I can be. So yes, I'm falling hard for him. I guess when you know you just know."

"Boy, your mom would have been so proud of you," says Elizabeth. "When I was your age, I was worried about scoring Aerosmith concert tickets and walking three miles to buy some weed." The two giggle. "Now I just illegally grow it in my backyard."

Nell gasps. "Auntie Beth!"

Elizabeth does a *Shhhh* with her finger and a wink.

The two stand up to go, and Elizabeth takes Nell square by the shoulders. "Nan's going to love Tommy. When you're ready, I mean." Nell nods her head with satisfaction. "It will be good for her to finally see one of the Monroe/Morton girls find true love."

CHAPTER FORTY-ONE

It's lunchtime at the Old Yarmouth Inn, a centuries-old favorite for American grub in a tavern setting. Tom orders his usual clam chowder and a sandwich. Across from him, Tony Spittone orders baked littleneck clams casino and a burger. Their Arnold Palmers arrive, the two swirling their straws to mix the beverages.

"Salut!" says Tony Spittone.

"Salut!" says Tom, meeting his sad eyes. He knows Spittone's in pain because his daughter, Grace, is dead.

"How'd you know it was me behind Spooner's investigation?" asks Tony Spittone, tearing open a sugar packet to pour into his drink.

Tom's order of clam chowder is set in front of him. He tears open the little oyster crackers, plopping them into the soup, and thinks on his answer. "My editor, a guy named Glenn Ritter, was always bugging me to hang around Spooner and try to learn how to be a better reporter. But I don't like Spooner. And I don't trust him. I saw how he stole his stories, always looking at people's computer screens and going through trash bins. Not to mention sleeping around with all the office girls hoping they'd spill info."

Tony Spittone chuckles, picking up a fork to dig into his first clamshell.

"So," Tom continues, "I started doing things like my editor did instead. He's a guy who really *cared* about finding the heart of a story. I observed. I listened. Made my subject feel important. Like Lolly, the dying coroner, who had nothing to lose when he finally came clean on his story." Tom slurps his soup. Too hot. "And if I kept my enemy Spooner closer, I'd help someone worth helping. That turned out to be you." Tom attempts another small sip of his chowder, glancing up to Spits. "And there's a friend at the office. She tipped me off too."

Spits nods but says nothing. Assessing Tom Hogan.

"But, you know," Tom continues, "my uncle had a small movie-set catering service in the early seventies. Some of your people visited him one day and told him he shouldn't be working independent films anymore. There was no profit in it. And no safety. I think it took about four visits and one of his trucks being burned before he got your message and joined up."

"It was business, kid. Gotta protect our unions," says Tony Spittone. "Sorry your uncle got hurt or something."

"No, he didn't get hurt or something. He just didn't much care for your way of doing business, and frankly, neither do I."

There's a long pause as Tony Spittone scrapes the last bits of his clam shell and sizes up Tom. He thinks the kid's got balls. "What happened to your uncle?"

"Died of cancer twenty years ago."

"Sorry to hear that. The Lord takes the best of them," says Tony Spittone.

"Yeah," says Tom, knitting his brow. "Only the good die young."

"But here we are," says Tony Spittone, sitting back to allow space for the burger being placed down in front of him. "Let's say grace." Such a contradiction that Tony Spits would be stretching his hands out to Tom in prayer. Tom obliges. Spits lowers his eyes and says, "Thank you, oh Lord, for these thy bounties we are about to receive. Amen."

Tom blesses himself. "Amen."

"I know how much you care for the girl. Nell," says Tony Spittone. "I heard it in your voice when you called. And I know you don't want her life ruined. Believe me, kid, living in a fishbowl ain't no fun at all, no matter how big a fish you are...if you catch my drift."

"Why did you want to find your daughter after all these years?" asks Tom.

The look in Tony Spittone's face is one of deep regret. A man who knows the good *and* the bad in his life can't be undone now. "I wanted to find her because I wanted to know if Marilyn got away with it all. I knew by finding her kid, I'd find the truth. And she made it. The plan worked."

"Wait, *her* kid?" asks Tom. "So if it's not you, Spits, then who was Grace's father?"

Tony Spittone looks in the distance. He picks up a french fry and takes a bite almost robotically, thinking a long time as he chews on one and then another. He finally looks at Tom. "Was it me? Doubt it. My guess is she was already pregnant the night she escaped," he says, a salty french fry draped between his fingers. "Was it Jack? Could be. Bobby? I don't think so. He had his hands full with a brood of kids..." Spits shoves the fries into his mouth. "Besides," he continues, dabbing ketchup from his lips, "Ethel invited Marilyn to her house parties. I doubt there was hanky-panky. Hell, Marilyn was asked to portray Ethel in a movie version of her husband Bobby's book...ah..." A long pause.

"*The Enemy Within*?" asks Tom.

"Yeah, that one," says Tony Spittone. "And besides, Ethel wouldn't have tolerated an affair. She was old-school. She fit in with the boys. Football on the compound lawn and all that." Spits sighs and answers the question with a question. "So...who was the father to Grace? Maybe Joe Schmoe from Idaho. Who the hell knows? Maybe some big Hollywood exec."

Tom nods, but his mind spins. If Tony Spittone doesn't know Grace's birth father, that means Nell will go through life, too, not knowing who her real grandfather was, let alone her real dad. Its history repeating itself. It's like little Norma Jeane not knowing her real father when Gladys slapped the named "Mortenson" on the birth certificate.

Tony Spittone can read the anguish in Tom's face. "I know this," says Tony Spittone. "Don't let a good thing get away. I let her grandmother get away years ago. Go get your Nell. Go get the girl."

"You let her grandmother get away? What do you mean?"

"Long time ago," says Tony Spittone. "When I was doin' dirty work. Somebody said she knew too much about certain things that were none of her business. I was sent to...make sure she never told nobody."

"To kill her?"

Tony Spittone ignores the question. "After the Cal Neva bash with Sammy Giancana and the boys, she goes home. Spends a few days unmonitored. She gets money from the bank, prepares to disappear."

"Arranging the big life change? The getaway?" asks Tom.

"Yeah," says Spits. "I went to her bungalow...which is why it took so long between the time that crazy housekeeper, Eunice, found Marilyn's body and called the police. When I got there, she seduced me."

"Eunice?" says Tom, thinking it sounds rather creepy.

"No, not Eunice...Marilyn! She seduced me. It didn't take much." A sly smile of memory crosses Tony Spittone's face. "She knew why I'd been sent. And she told me she already had a plan to drop out of sight. All she needed was somebody who could help her not leave any tracks. So...I hung out, smoked a stogie or two, and waited while she packed her bags."

Tom's eyes are as wide as the Grand Canyon. "Holy Shit! You're the one who helped her get away? Before Sterling Powers drove her here? Did you pay off Noguchi? Was it Bobby who gave her a new identity? Was Hoffa involved? Did you—"

Tony Spittone waves his hand in the air. "You ask too many questions, kid. Even for a reporter. But for the sake of argument,

Hoffa was nothing but a two-bit putz. A son-of-a-bitch." He takes a seriously mean bite out of his burger. He chews like he's biting off the head of Jimmy Hoffa. Swallows. Wipes his mouth on his napkin. "Don't do what I did. Like I said, go get her. Go get the girl."

Tom smiles. "I plan on it! And maybe someday, you can see Marilyn."

"See her?" says Tony Spittone. Goosebumps spread down his arms. "She's alive?"

"You ask too many questions, kid," says Tom, imitating Spits. Tony Spittone sits back and nods his head. "You got chutzpah, kid."

"I love Nellie so much, so when she's ready, I hope she'll take me to meet her."

Tony Spittone feels Tom's sincerity. It reminds him of what he felt for Marilyn half a century ago. Marilyn was so mythologized that somehow the real woman was forgotten. Until now. Until this. Until Nell. Tony Spittone looks down to hold the table edge but blesses himself first. It's clear that he's a big softie in his old age. Tom reaches out to him, taps his hand.

"Hey, Spits, listen, I've got an idea," says Tom. "How about you be Nellie's grandfather? The one she never had."

A few moments pass, and Tony Spittone looks up with tears in his eyes, which is not something Tom expected from a mobster. "Maybe, kid. But right now…I gotta get outta here. It's like my pal Bulger said, 'Always on the move.'"

"You know Whitey?" says Tom. "Did you know he died recently?"

"Too many questions, kid. Too many questions." And then he signals for the check, which arrives moments later. Tom turns the bill to his side of the table and reaches for his wallet, but Tony Spittone puts his hand out to stop him. "Aspettare!" *Wait.* "It's on me. I insist." Tony Spittone pulls out a wad of crisp hundred-dollar bills.

He licks his finger, and peels through them to separate one of the bills. Places a hundred dollars down on the sticky table before he stands up and goes to Tom's side. Standing over Tom, he bends to take both his cheeks in his hands and squeezes. It hurts, but Tom doesn't dare to move. "Be a good boy," says Tony Spittone. "Tell the waitress keep the change. It's a rough life on tips, if you catch my drift."

CHAPTER FORTY-TWO

It's late afternoon when Tom arrives at Nell's front door, where he finds her dressed in a coat and funky woolen hat. "Can we walk and talk? Do you mind?" she asks, ushering him right out the door and closing it behind her. "I just need a break from the house. I've been *glued* to the computer."

"Of course," says Tom. "Whatever you want."

As they head up the driveway, she speaks first, "Go on, tell me more..."

"Sure," says Tom. "I'm just sorry it has to be me telling you all of this..." He looks to her profile, to her eyes, but she's looking straight ahead and dodging the sidewalk cracks. Tom does the same, explaining where he left off. "Okay, so, Greenson began upping Marilyn's doses of Nembutal," Tom explains. "You should know he wasn't a popular person in her circles to start with. Maybe to her, but not to Frank and the gang. Joe DiMaggio was coming around again then too, and I'm not sure how the two men interacted. But I think Sinatra's feelings were more protective than passionate. Besides, he liked tough dames, like Ava and his mother, Dolly. To Ol' Blue Eyes, Marilyn was weak. At least, that's what I've read."

Nell isn't looking at Tom as he speaks. She's processing what he's saying, her eyes still glued on the road ahead. They even walk like it's a business connection rather than a romantic one. Their hands firmly planted in their own pockets.

"So," he continues, "Lawford had some special party for the president, and he invited Frank, who couldn't make it because—"

"He had a cold," adds Nell.

"Okay, yes, so let me get back to Greenson, who was a control freak over Marilyn's life. Some called him the 'psychological Svengali.' He decided she was manic-depressive, which is bipolar by today's medical terms. Apparently, Greenson wanted her to get rid of her unhealthy connection to her past so she could heal. Start a new life."

"Did you know that I read someplace that Marilyn—um, Nan, never even decorated the new bungalow she bought?"

"Who needs an interior designer when you're planning to escape, right?" asks Tom. "Greenson helped her escape when the housekeeper called him that night. Well, he and another guy, a mobster named Spits. Ah, we have to talk about him. He's another story, but let's get through this one first," assures Tom. "Sinatra was really involved with Sam Giancana and the mob. He called the president 'TP' and had a helicopter landing installed in his yard and had Secret Service lines put in the house to make JFK's visits comfortable. But JFK couldn't be involved with Frank if Frank was involved with the mob, so that's when it became a soap opera. And I guess JFK upped and left. Stayed at Bill Cosby's house."

"Gross," says Nell. "That creepy actor who drugged women?"

"Yeah, but they didn't know he was creepy back then," says Tom. "Listen, it gets dark after that. I mean, your Nan started getting obsessed with the president and calling the White House and all this other not so favorable stuff."

"I read about it," says Nell, tipping her nose to the cold air, watching her breath go in and out. "We've all been desperate women doing stupid things over some guy, you know."

"There was some final weekend event at Cal Nev, Sinatra's place, and nobody knew what was going down. I mean, put a celebrity singer named Frank, a movie star named Marilyn, a president named John, and a gangster named Sam in one room and snap!"

"I read that everybody's houses were wired by the FBI, CIA, Howard Hughes…" says Nell. "Nan's house, er Marilyn's house, too."

"That's right," says Tom, skipping ahead of her, turning to face her, and walking backwards, "The irony is that not one of those tapes ever surfaced. Somebody even wrote a report. If I remember correctly, it was about Bobby—three pages—written by someone labeled 'anonymous,' and the writer called those boys by their first names: Frank, Bobby, Jack. I mean, heck, what kinda report was that!"

"God, you could never get away with stuff like they did today," says Nell.

"Over the years, more stories and articles surfaced, but from what I could detect, none of the sources were ever verified," says Tom.

There's a spooky silence to that last comment as they walk for a moment, her mind collecting the evidence that really seems to make sense, and Tom frightful he might say one wrong thing to lose her again.

"Despite all those bad boys she hung with," says Nell, "she was in good spirits the night she supposedly died."

"Yeah, on the phone with all her friends."

Nell takes another breath of fresh air, blowing it out to see small smoke rings in the cold. They're in front of the Lothrop Hill Cemetery now. "Did you ever have something you just wanted to erase?"

"Ah, sure, but not of this magnitude," he says, squeezing her hand. "I want to take away all your pain and make it my pain."

"Thank you, that's very sweet," says Nell looking deep into his eyes. "I'm not sure it's pain exactly, but I did have breakfast with Aunt Beth this morning. She said you're a good egg."

"Scrambled or over easy?" jokes Tom.

"I'd say over-easy," says Nell, leaning in to kiss him. "She doesn't think I should tell Nan just yet. I think I should go through the pain first." Nell looks up to the sky. "What is it that Rumi says? Something like 'the cure for the pain is in the pain.'"

"Or you could look at it this way..." says Tom. "It's like the Red Sox. For years, the thrill was hoping the Sox would snatch the Pennant and they didn't. Then, finally, they won. In 2000. I mean, once that happened, it was never the same. The longing, the hope, the ninety years of wishing was over."

"Does this have some sort of Joe DiMaggio connection?" jokes Nell. "I told you that you can keep the autographed ball."

"No," he chuckles, "I'm just saying justice delayed is really justice anticipated. Someday, the time will be right."

"Okay," she says. "Carpe diem."

"But, um, whatever we're doing here in this cemetery, can I ask you a question first?" Nell nods. Tom continues, "If we end up together... I mean, with enough love, we can work this out and conquer the Marilyn conspiracies. Nell," he says, putting his hand up to her chest, "maybe you'd consider living with me in the near future?"

There's a suspended silence for a moment. She's not saying yes and she's not saying no.

But she suppresses a smile, which isn't easy. "C'mon, I want you to meet someone," says Nell, taking his hand and leading him through the narrow passageway of a road into Lothrop Hill Cemetery.

CHAPTER FORTY-THREE

The 3 p.m. winter sun carves weird shadows across the gravestones, which might frighten someone not used to walking in cemeteries…like Tom. He holds onto Nell's hand tightly. Some graves date back to before the Revolutionary War, like Thomas Hinckley in 1706 and the cemetery's namesake, Lothrop himself, in 1653 with a tall monument. Hand in hand, Tom and Nell pass the various markers—Hinkley, Cobb, the Bursleys, and someone named Sturgis, for whom the local library was named.

Tromping down the narrow road covered in last fall's leaves, Tom, who isn't into cemeteries let alone old creepy ones, lightens the mood with a joke: "Know how many people are dead in this cemetery?" Nell shrugs. "All of them," he says.

"And my mother is one of them. Grace Morton. Down at the bottom of the hill. Where the gravestones are more recent."

"Oh," says Tom, feeling like an idiot for making a joke. "I'm sorry. And I'm honored to finally meet her."

They move through the markers up a particular row now. Nell begins to get anxious.

Tom stops her before they get any closer to her mother's grave. "I love you, Nell, and I want you to think on our future because I'm in it for the long haul."

"I am," she says matter-of-factly, taking his hand with a bit of force as she walks the final steps to her mother's gravestone. "My mom might be dead, and the world thought they could bury my nan, but boy, were they wrong…" Nell wipes tears of recognition. "Nan wasn't a dumb blonde. She fooled the world."

"You been talking to Lolly?"

"No," she says. "Though I wish he were still alive so I could thank him for bringing me the truth and bringing you to me." Tom moves in for a hug and they hold each other for a very long and poignant moment.

Then, Nell pulls back and casts her eyes down to Grace's grave, carved with a snowbird in its top right corner. "Mom," she says, looking down to the marker, "this is Tom Hogan."

"Hello, Grace," says Tom. "Pleased to meet you. I'm in love with your beautiful daughter."

"And I've just said yes to his idea of moving in together. I think you would have approved. I know Nan will…"

Tom lights up, taking Nell into his arms. They hug again, until Tom takes her face into his hands and begins to kiss Nell slowly at first, and then with intense passion. That is…until their romantic and sentimental moment is broken by the rustle of something coming from behind a large shrub. Tom squints his eyes to see…

"What the?" asks Tom.

"Hey, you led me to her grave," says Spooner, wiping dirt off his pants and coming towards them. "Very romantic ending, you two. I even took a photo for your future wedding album."

"Why are you still in town?" asks Nell. "How insanely invasive *are* you?"

"Insanely invasive enough to get this story so I can go off to sail some yacht around the world. *That's* how invasive," sports Spooner. "You know I've seen some pretty dumb newspapers in my time, but are you kidding that your *Cape Cod Times,* your *Barnstable Patriot,* and all the others didn't uncover this? Or was your grandmother sleeping with all those editors to keep them quiet?"

This time Tom goes full force at Spooner, knocking him hard into a gravestone and practically breaking his nose. Blood drips down his shirt, temporarily startling Spooner, but it doesn't stop him from ramming Tom. "Stupid bitch!" yells Spooner. "Where's your grandmother? Take me to her, and I'll leave you alone!"

"Why should I?" asks Nell, trying to break them apart. But Tom's knocked him to the ground again.

"Because she has no right to hide from the world like this," says Spooner, struggling to stand and holding his nose from the pain. "She took away millions of people's dreams for fifty years; to have her own private joke on all the people who gave her every bit of love they had. She owes them. And it's time she paid up."

"I beg your pardon?" says Nell, holding an arm across Tom's chest. He's ready to pulverize Spooner. Again. "Fine," says Nell, succumbing to Spooner. "You want my grandmother?"

"Yes!" says Spooner."

"Marilyn Monroe?" asks Nell.

"Hell, yes!" says Spooner, wiping his bloodied face on his coat sleeve.

"Meet me at the Millway Marina in one hour, and I'll take you to her."

"Seriously?"

"Yes!"

"Fucking ay!" says Spooner, trying to regain his composure, standing now, wiping his muddy pants off with one hand, the other securing his swollen nose.

He looks up to Tom and Nell already tromping back up the hill. They don't turn to look back.

CHAPTER FORTY-FOUR

Gray-shingled houses weave through the hills on the outskirts of the harbor. Boats are shrink-wrapped for the winter. Only a handful are tied up at the moorings as the wind whips across the frigid sea. A Toyota Tacoma pulls up in the lot. Scotty Harden drives with Charley Button sitting shotgun, dressed in full foul-weather gear. Nell and Tom's boots rattle the metal pier where they walk straight towards them, waving to the fishermen. "Over here!"

Spooner arrives too, a few feet behind them, but with a phobia of docks, planks, and anything hovering above water. He shouts from a distance, "What are we doing here?"

Nell spins on him. "You said you wanted to see my grandmother, so we're going to see her."

"On a *boat?*" asks Spooner, his tone like a frightened child who just discovered the monster under his bed.

"*My,* you *are* perceptive," says Nell.

"But I hate the water," says Spooner, his arms extended for balance. "Unless it's poolside in Beverly Hills. Or maybe a yacht in Saint-Tropez."

"Don't worry about it," says Scotty. "We do this every day of our lives."

"Yeah," says Spooner. "Then I guess that's one thing you guys are good for."

They get to the end of the pier, where a huge private yacht is just ahead. It's so large it has its own zip code. Of course, it's shrink-wrapped and up on a rack.

"Well at least we're going in style," says Spooner. "But shouldn't you boys have uncovered it before I go out there and freeze my balls off?"

"Oh, that ain't the boat, my friend," says Charley.

"Then which one is it?" asks Spooner, his face going white like a tavern ghost.

The five of them walk to the tip of the pier to a small Zodiac rubber dinghy with an outboard motor attached. It bops like a balloon in the water. It's hard to believe it hasn't frozen in the harbor, so one might suspect it's just recently been set there. On purpose.

Spooner stares at it and then stares at them. "*That?*" asks Spooner. "There's no fucking way you're getting me in there!"

"Stop being such a big baby," says Tom, loving this.

"Yeah, Tommy's right," says Scotty, jumping in the dinghy first. "Look how calm the water is today." The boat bobs furiously under his weight. Charley steps in, lending a gentle hand to help Nell before Tom sweeps his arm in front of Spooner. "Please, after you. I insist."

"C'mon," says Scotty, tossing Spooner a life vest. "Let's roll! Gonna be pitch dark in an hour."

Spooner hesitantly tries to enter the bobbing boat, but Scotty and Charley have to *hoist* him in by both arms. He plops down. No sooner than Spooner exhales, Tom calls out "Henry! You made it!" Spooner looks up to see Henry approaching, zipping up his down jacket. As he gets closer, he's already finagling which foot to put into the raft first.

"He can't get in *here*!" screams Spooner. "One more person in this dinky dinghy, and I'll need the director—what's his name?—James Cameron! From *Titanic*."

"Pipe down, Sidney," says Henry. "This ain't my first rodeo," he says, snuggling between Nell and Tom. "Come to think of it, my first rodeo was in 1959 with Sterling Powers. Well, no, maybe it was '63, I can't remember."

"You better not be fucking with me," Spooner says to Nell. Nell crosses her heart, casting her eyes up to the heavens, and makes a prayer pose against her chest.

"Fasten your seatbelts, everybody," says Charley.

And they're off! Cutting through the harbor, as slow as molasses. The waves are larger than the boat. Spooner looks ready to vomit. Nell looks at Spooner, whose head is now bowed over the side. Nell looks away, covering her hand to her mouth to stifle a laugh.

"Where the *fuck* are you taking me exactly?" asks Spooner, gasping for breath between dry heaves.

"Just over to Sandy Neck Point," says Charley. "See that lighthouse?"

"Who gives a shit?" asks Spooner.

"Well, I take offense to that," says Charley, bringing the motor up as they break from the harbor to the open sea. "I'm on the board to save our lighthouses."

"It's a very special lighthouse," says Henry to Spooner. "That lighthouse on Sandy Neck Beach is at the entrance to Barnstable Harbor. First established in 1826. The current tower was built in 1857 and strengthened in the 1880s. It was discontinued in 1931, replaced by a skeleton tower which was—"

"I don't give a flying *fuck* about your history lessons," says Spooner. "I only want to see the greatest tits and ass in history! So she better be out there in some slinky sequin gown dancing on top of that lighthouse!"

Nell narrows her eyes. "Oh, you'll see her. Don't you worry. Tits are still fairly firm."

A big wave slaps the dinghy, and Spooner vomits over the side. As he sits up, trying to get his momentum, Nell says, "Look, there she is! Out there!"

With what little strength he has, Spooner crawls closer to the front of the rubber raft. His head darting left and right. Nothing but sea water and a strip of land in the distance. "I'm not interested in seeing whales if that's what you mean."

"Not whales, you idiot," says Nell. "My grandmother, right there! See?"

Spooner narrows his squint to a mirage of a woman sitting on the edge of the shore near the lighthouse. She's wrapped in a big green woolen blanket.

"Holy shit!" says Spooner. "It's *her*! It's really her!"

"Yup. That's my grandmother," says Nell, suddenly sitting erect against the raft with absolute assurance.

Henry squints out to the horizon and then taps his knee with delight. "Well, I'll be darned."

CHAPTER FORTY-FIVE

The boat is just about to the shoreline, but Spooner pushes the group back with fury, jumping over the raft's side with a sudden restored energy. His feet splash on the freezing cold shoreline, his legs practically paralyzed to his kneecaps from the frigid temperatures, but he doesn't care. This is the most incredible experience of his entire life!

Charging toward the catatonic figure sitting in the sand and staring out to the sea, Spooner approaches the woman cautiously. He looks back at the others, but Nell, Tom, and the boys watch from a distance, having just made it to shore.

"Hel-lo?" asks Spooner gingerly, "Are you? Miss Mon—" He's so taken aback he can't even get the words out.

She finally looks up at him. Her face shows minimal wrinkles, eyes twinkling blue. "Yes, I'm her," she says in the most delicate of voices. "I've been waiting a long time for you..."

"For me?" says Spooner, stunned by the compliment. He's had a lot of women in his life, but for Marilyn Monroe to be waiting for *him* is a chart-topper.

"Yes, for you," she says, "I knew eventually one of you would find me. Over fifty years is a long time to wait though."

"Oh," says Spooner, his tone disappointed. Spooner circles her. "And I'm supposed to believe you're Marilyn Monroe, just like that."

"Oh, puh-leez," she says, playfully flitting her fingers through her hair as the breeze whips her bangs into her eyes. "Did you expect me to greet you in a white dress flying up at the hem, showing my panties? Like in *Bus Stop*?"

"You mean *Seven Year Itch*," says Spooner, knitting his brow.

"Take your pick," she exhales, ever-so-sexy even for an old dame. "It's been a lot of years. Who's remembering."

"Well Marilyn Monroe would certainly remember her movies."

She stares up at him. "She chooses to forget."

Spooner looks to the fishermen, Nell, and Tom. Henry, on the other hand, has opted to stay seated in the rubber dinghy. "Aren't you guys gonna come see this?" asks Spooner. Tom shake his head *no*. Spooner calls out to Tom, his words carried in the wind, "No wonder Ritter thinks you're such a shitty reporter!" Then, Spooner paces around her some more. Studying her form. Her face regally upturned, gazing out to the sea. A look of depth and wisdom on her features.

"I still get fan mail, you know. My agents have it sent to me."

"Really? They're still alive?"

"Men, women, even kids write."

"What do they want?"

"A little touch of fame, I suppose," says Marilyn, glancing up at him. But she can sense he's not buying it. "Here..." she says, rising up to let her green blanket fall in the sand. She's wearing the sweater Frederick wore in the gallery, the large beige wrap-around Mexican knit one previously seen in the George Barris photo, Santa Monica, 1962. "Shall I sing for you?" She blows Spooner an exaggerated kiss.

"Huh?" says Spooner, suddenly deciding this isn't very sexy coming from an old woman who's now doing a little two step barefoot in the sand.

She clears her throat. "Happy birthday to you, happy birthday to you, happy birthday—Mister—Prez-a-dent.... Happy birthday to you." She puts her hands on her hips. "There. Do you believe me now?"

Now that she's standing up, Spooner looks closer at her face. "Wait a second," says Spooner. "You're that old dame from town hall. The one called Joanie! The one with the banana in her bag."

"Is that a banana in your pocket or are you just glad to see me?" she says, trying to keep up the gig.

Spooner looks to Tom. "Fuck you!" And then to Nell, "And *fuck* you!" Spooner takes his cell phone out of his pocket and tosses it hard—temper tantrum—but this time, he's thrown it a little too far. It sails into the water. "Oh, great!" he screams. "And *fuck* that *fucking* phone too!"

Joanie tosses her head back and lets out a loud laugh as she plops back to the sand to slip her feet into her socks and rubber boots. The platinum wig on her head begins to slip, so Joanie rips it from her head, tossing it to the side. "Who else am I supposed to be? Of course, I'm Joanie. My new identity. Why not? And to my precious, Nellie, I'm her grandmother." But she knows what Spooner's thinking, so she also adds, "And for your information, I got tired of platinum. I thought strawberry blonde was more conservative. Don't you think?"

"This is so fucked up," says Spooner, pacing madly and shivering from the cold. "I thought you went by the name Marie Morton, not Joanie whatever-your-last-name-is? And besides, you don't even sound like Marilyn Monroe. She had this delicate little sexy voice."

Joanie reaches under her green blanket and pulls out a pack of cigarettes. She watches Spooner watch her as she lights up. She takes a long drag and exhales. "You'd sound like this too after years of cigarettes."

"I've had enough of this stupid farce," says Spooner to the fishermen. "Take me back."

"Look," says Joanie grabbing at his arm. "Listen, young man. Who would bother pulling off a stunt like this? I really have better things to worry about than whether or not you think I am who I *know* am."

"Well, then, I have a lot to ask you."

She looks at him a beat and laughs out loud. "I don't have to answer for anything. And you don't have the right to ask." Joanie picks up her green blanket and heads to the boat.

"Just tell me one thing?" asks Spooner. "If you're really who you say you are, what gives you the right to deny the world years of your talent with this charade?"

"The right?" says Joanie. "The right? The only thing the world has the right to is..." and then she stops. "I gave the world memories that apparently never die."

Spooner looks from her to Nell and back again. Joanie continues, "There's only one person who has a right to me, and that was my daughter, and now *her* daughter, my precious granddaughter. My everything! Do you have children, Mr. Spooner?"

"Well, no, I—"

"Then there's nothing I can possibly say to you to explain the love a parent has for a child. I'll do anything to protect my Nellie, who has grown up to be a beautiful young lady."

"That's an understatement," says Spooner, glancing over at Nell, who remains stone-faced. And then he glances out to sea. His cell phone is long gone.

"Life for me has been a form of death every day. Except there's no sympathy cards, no flowers, no rituals for the grief of what I've had to silently endure." Joanie's in his face now. "Go on and make somebody else's life miserable so there's a cover story at the checkout stand tomorrow and all over the internet. I know you don't owe me anything. But, if you have a heart, you'll leave Nell out of this. This isn't about her."

"Let's go, Charley," says Joanie. "I've said all I need to say here." The group slowly heads to the boat. The two fishermen assist Joanie into the rubber dinghy first. Henry takes her hand from the inside. Then they take Nell's hand, who reaches for Tom to hop in.

"Oh no," says Spooner. "There's no way in hell *fake* Marilyn's getting in that boat with us. Somebody has to go."

Scotty, Charley, and Tom turn to look at Spooner to suggest he's short a ride back. But Nell is looking beyond Spooner, at a man walking toward them from the backside of the lighthouse.

Spooner follows Nell's eyes to see who she's looking at.

He recognizes the man. "Spits!" shouts Spooner. "What a surprise!"

Nerves crawl up Spooner's neck as he walks towards Tony Spittone. "Spits! I found her! Just like I promised!" But Tony Spittone's expression is stone cold. This is far from a reunion. The look on his face, if one can be read, reminds us that the deal was Spooner wasn't supposed to talk to anyone. Only *find* the girl.

We see a shadow come around the other side of the lighthouse. Tony Spittone's sidekick comes forward wearing big black leather gloves and punching his left fist into his right one.

Spooner puts up a hand in defense, "Look, guys, I can explain..."

"Don't worry," Joanie calls out over the waves. "They aren't going to kill you. Just rough you up a bit."

CHAPTER FORTY-SIX

You can feel the festive, high-spirit energy at The Porpoise. At the bar, Elizabeth plops down several overflowing beer mugs for the guys and cabernet for the ladies. The gang that just came from the Sandy Neck lighthouse toast a *whoop* between them, hugging and chuckling.

"Tell me what happened?" says Elizabeth, elbows on the bar. "I'm bummed I missed the action."

"Let's wait for the mayor to get in here," says Charley as the door swings open.

"Mayor!" everyone toasts. Herman Bisbee removes his overcoat and hat to hang on the hook. He's out of breath and a bit distraught as he pulls up a bar seat. "Had the railway maintenance meeting with the Land Trust when I got a call that the roof was leaking over at the Historical Society. Never ends," he says, shaking his head. "Well…how'd it go?"

"You should have seen Joanie," says Scotty. "She was hilarious!"

"I'm so amazed you pulled this off, Mom," says Charley to Joanie.

"Mom?" asks Tom, never realizing that Joanie is Charley's mother.

"Don't be so surprised that Joanie can act," adds Henry. "I remember back in '73—or was it '75? What a performance in *Cat on a Hot Tin Roof!* Never forgot it…"

"Had to act *really* good this time," says Joanie. "Get that little skunk off the scent."

"Can't believe he actually thinks that Marilyn Monroe ever lived in our town," says Scotty. But Elizabeth and Nell share a glance that reads, *She did.*

"Who's next?" asks Charley. "Michael Jackson? Caught a glimpse of him up in Chatham."

Scotty adds, "And Amy Winehouse strolls the beach down in Brewster!"

"But what if that Spooner really writes the story?" asks Charley, shaking his head and grabbing the food menu.

"So what?" says the mayor. "What editor in his right mind would print a story that says 'I found Marilyn Monroe on a Cape Cod sand dune'?" The Mayor hugs Joanie, "You're gonna be famous now." They all chuckle as Joanie tosses her head back in an exaggerated movie star gesture.

But Nell is rather quiet from their silliness.

"There won't be a story," says Tom, eyeing Nell. "I think I know who's going to put a stop to *any* story ever surfacing in Sid Spooner's lifetime."

"Chowder for our boy Tommy here!" says the mayor, patting Tom on the back and mussing his hair. Nell barely cracks a smile now.

"You okay, babe?" Tom whispers, leaning into Nell. She shrugs. It's clear that this game has been amusing, but it doesn't change the facts that her mother's *dead* and her Nan actually *is* Marilyn Monroe and they're possibly in danger. For lack of a better word, Nell's life has been nothing short of ambiguous. Life will continue to play out like a game of *what-if?* Afterall, there might be another Spooner on her trail, and someday another, and then another.

"Can we get the chowder to go?" Nell asks Tom, like a little girl pleading for sprinkles on her ice cream. He nods.

"Make it two chowders to go, Beth," he says, kissing Nell's forehead. Elizabeth is heavy on the hand, spooning two overflowing chowders into to-go bowls with little oyster cracker packets on the side.

The group continues celebrating, comparing stories, but Nell gazes out the window to the marshes. Thinking. Her Nan's life has comprised of constantly being on the lookout, ready to make a quick escape. Like she's in a witness protection program.

CHAPTER FORTY-SEVEN

Spooner's a bit shaken up, a bit beaten up, and a lot soaking wet as he returns to his motel room. The light on the nightstand is dim, and he sits on the bed's edge, typing with one finger at his iPad previously hidden under the mattress just in case someone broke into his room.

> *Dear Editor,*
>
> *In case anything happens to me, you have to know why…*
>
> *Angelo "Tony Spits" Spittone is a liar. He's a mobster who killed me, so don't let him tell you this story is a hoax. Why? Because I discovered the biggest bombshell in your paper's history. And that's why I'm dead…*

And then Spooner stops. The word *dead* has a frightening ring to it. His.

Falling back on the bedspread, Spooner puts his arms behind his head and reminisces Tony Spittone's words in his ear from their boat ride back…

"I got keys here. To your room," said Tony Spittone, dangling a set of keys to Spooner's motel room, his luggage, and his BMW rental. Thank *God* he didn't swipe under the mattress for the iPad.

"How'd you get those keys?" Spooner dared to ask.

"This ain't no interview kid," said Spits. "Shut the fuck up."

Tony Spittone's henchman pushed Spooner along to a motorboat other side of the sandbar. Once inside, the henchman floored the motor, heading to the main shore. Back on land, he demanded Spooner exit the boat before tossing him in the backseat of a black Mercedes sedan with tinted windows. It was about as mobster cliché as it could get, but Tony Spittone hails from the '60s. It's all he knows.

When Spooner heard the pop of the trunk, he got *really* worried. *Is he going to throw my body in there?*

Tony Spittone got in the backseat. "Slide over," he told Spooner. And then, "Drive," to the brooding henchman. They pulled around to a windy road along the marshes.

"Are you gonna kill me?" asked Spooner, shaking and blubbering like a baby.

"Whadya want? Your Mommy?" asked Spits.

"No!" wallowed Spooner. "My mother could care less if I'm alive or dead. She married some drunk neighbor...doesn't even pay attention to me. It *sucks!* My parents don't even care."

"Fuckin' ay. What do I look like, Dr. Phil?" asked Spits, opening Spooner's laptop. "Turn it on." Spooner did as he was told. "Type in your password," said Spits. He did. Tony Spittone leaned in to read it. "Your password is Kardashian-three-way? What a putz."

The computer lit up to the desktop page. "Now, show me the article," demanded Spits. Spooner pressed a finger to his recent documents and opened it. "Read it to me."

Spooner gulped. Hard. Wiped the snot from his nose on his sleeve. He reads: "She is alive... Who? The most famous star in the history of the movies, that's who." Spooner sniffles harder. "She lives on Cape Cod, posing as a town clerk. In the greatest role of her life, Marilyn—"

"That sucks," said Spits, shaking his head. "That's your story?"

"And who are *you*?" asked Spooner. "James *fucking* Patterson?"

Tony Spittone said nothing, but Spooner watched the henchman's eyes meet Tony Spittone's eyes in the rearview mirror. He nodded. The brakes slammed. *Shit, this is it!* But instead, Tony Spittone grabbed the laptop, handed it to the henchman, who—with two bare hands, mind you—cracked it in half, lowered the window, and tossed it out into a silent marsh. A flock of startled geese flew upward.

Spooner squinted to see his computer sinking in the muck.

Then, Spits looked straight ahead as he spoke. "You broke our deal, kid. Where I come from, that's not good."

"So, what happens now?" asked Spooner.

"Do you know who Bugsy Siegel is?"

"The *gangster*?"

"No, the famous florist," he deadpanned. "And I don't take too kindly to that terminology."

"Gangster?" Spooner persisted. Tony Spittone shot him a look. If looks could kill… Spooner shrinks. "Are you going to kill me?" asked Spooner. "Just tell me already! I'm peeing my pants here!"

"Depends on you," said Tony Spittone. "I'm only half pissed off at you because while my precious Gracey is dead, her baby girl is alive." Tony Spittone looked out the window, gazing up at the moon and stars. "My days of killing are over. Bugsy always said *Stop before forty…*"

"The *age* of forty or forty *murders*?" asked Spooner, swallowing hard. Silence. Then...

"Only thing I gotta kill is your story. And that's me saying that, not Bugsy."

"Okay," said Spooner, sinking into the seat and feeling very small. "That'll work."

"I'm just curious," says Spits. "How much is that story worth? Whadya think they'd pay you? $1,000? $10,000?"

"If I'm lucky," says Spooner.

Tony Spittone hissed under his breath. "Turns out your integrity isn't that expensive, is it?" Spits pinned Spooner with a scathing look, then continued, "You know what modesty is? It's the opposite of 'pride,' where everybody is full of themselves. But modesty is an underrated virtue." Tony Spittone looked to Spooner as if eyeing a pathetic spoiled brat. "That's how Bugsy, Hoffa, and Sammy G…how all of us operated in the good ole days. Modesty. Take a lesson."

"Because I want to be gangster?" asked Spooner before retracting. "Sorry, I'm sorry, okay. Bad choice of a word."

"And there was none of this daddy's money shit. We came from hard knocks. Self-made."

Spooner didn't dare voice what he was thinking. *Self-made gangsters?*

Tony Spittone turned quickly and put his finger under Spooner's nose before reaching into his back pocket. *This is it! He's going to shoot him!* "Watch yourself, kid." Tony Spittone retrieved a flip phone from his pocket. Opened it. Punched in a number. Except there was no cell service. "Pull up," he said to the driver, moving his little flip phone to the left and to the right until he finally got service. The number rang. When the call was answered, Spits said, "Mr. Ritter?" A pause. "Amico! This is Tony Spittone. Fine, thank you, sir. The story we discussed…*kill it.*" Another pause. "Right. It's all bullshit." Tony Spittone shook his head while the editor responded. "Kids these days!" A chuckle was heard from the other end of the phone. "The kid's going to go work for his father in New York after he takes a long vacation, so consider this his termination notice."

Spooner grasped onto the door handle so tightly it might crack in his fingers.

Tony Spittone flipped his phone closed. "So, here's the deal, kid. You have a choice. I can kill you, or…I hear it's great this time of year in Sicily. You like Italy?" Spooner shrugged his shoulders. Tony Spittone cracked his knuckles. "How about Alaska?"

Spooner shrugged again. "You decide," said Tony Spittone. "But you don't say nothing to nobody or I'm done messing around. Because I'll be watching you. I got people in Italy..."

"Then I pick Alaska," gulped Spooner.

"I got people in Alaska too, wise guy." And with that, Tony Spittone handed him two plane tickets. "I'm giving you a choice. The deadline is midnight. Tonight."

❧

Spooner, safely back in his room, sits up from the bedspread. He deletes the letter to the editor about being dead and closes the window, turning off his iPad. Moving to his suitcase, he begins packing. He grabs some loose change from the dresser and tosses a coin.

Heads it's Italy. Tails it's Alaska.

The coin lands.

He's out of here...*Arrivederci!*

CHAPTER FORTY-EIGHT

The moonlight streams through Nell's bedroom window, where she lies safely snuggled inside Tom's arms. He kisses the top of her head before saying, "I want you to know I would have fallen in love with you even if your grandmother was Grandma Molasses."

"The lady on the jar?" asks Nell, twisting her lips.

"My mom used to call me Grandma Molasses when I was a slow poke at farm chores." Nell fluffs her pillow, and he moves over onto it, continuing, "I want to know so much. Not as Tom the reporter, because I'm certain I've lost *that* job...but as Tom the guy who loves you."

"Well firstly you *must* know that I love you too. So, what do you want to know?"

"Everything. You know when you're a little kid and you're just *exploding* with questions? It's why I became a journalist. *Why is the moon round? How does water run through a spigot?*"

"Well, if you're that interested in the world and all that turtle saving, they're looking for someone to fill a space down at the Cape Cod Commission.'"

"Really?" says Tom. "Here? That would be awesome!" Tom turns on his side, re-fluffing his pillow to accommodate. The TV plays in the background on mute, showing an ad for the upcoming Academy Awards. "Did you and Nan ever watch the Oscars together?"

"Yes, every year," says Nell, rolling her eyes with dread. "*Boring*. I usually fell asleep because I had school the next day, but we'd dress up in costumes, and she'd make me Shirley Temples. I liked that part of the show." Nell moves in to be closer to Tom's face. "Nan always got very sentimental when they did that 'In Memoriam' bit. I could see tears running down her cheek from the television light casting onto her face."

"That's amazing. I bet some of those dead movie stars were her friends," says Tom. "But it's so sad she couldn't say anything or go to their funerals."

"I don't want my grandmother to die without being recognized for how and who she was in the second half of her life."

"I agree," says Tom, running his fingers through Nell's new blonde bob-style haircut.

"Someday, at the end of that Oscar remembrance, I want them to know she lived as an icon, sure, but then she really lived as a genius in disguise. I want her to be the final tribute at the Oscars where everyone is stunned to find out the truth. It's a crazy fantasy that's been stirring in my head."

"I think it's a great idea."

"I've been thinking about this whole ordeal morning, noon, and night," says Nell. "I always knew my life was somehow different. Not special. Just *different*."

"How so?" asks Tom.

"I mean, I was reciting lines from *The Crucible* when I was like ten." They both chuckle.

"She loved *The Crucible*," says Tom. "It's in so many biographies."

"Oh, great. You're like a Nan Wikipedia."

"Ophelia too," he adds, wanting to impress her to everything he's learned.

"Oh my gosh," says Nell, sitting up. "Makes total sense. She was always running lines when we gardened. I thought she was super-salted *nuts,* but she said she had a group of lesbian friends once and they all worked on stage. I was like 'whatever…'"

"Yeah, Greta Garbo, Marlene Dietrich, and one other…"

"Someone named Katharine…I think."

"Hepburn," says Tom snapping his fingers, like he's spouted the *Jeopardy!* answer. "God, I can't wait to meet your nan, though of course I won't bring any of that up. I just want to meet her as my future nan-in-law. And maybe she can meet my grandfather. Though, that'll be a tough one not to tell the truth to. He was Marilyn's biggest fan. So maybe we best not."

"What else do you want to know?" asks Nell.

"Um, did you go to church?"

"Yup, in West Barnstable. Up the street. West Parish Congregational."

"Was Nan strict like my grandpa?" asks Tom.

"She wanted me to be raised in a world that wasn't obsessed about getting things done. No chaos. No complexities. She made life silly. You know we took baths together? She shampooed my hair and I shampooed hers. And we'd sing really loud because we sounded good vibrating our voices off the tile wall. Well, I was the little kid, but she *acted* like one."

"That's cool," he says trying to still make sense of this amazing tale himself.

"She let me have playdates that always stayed for supper," says Nell. "When we drove them home, we rolled down the car windows and sang as loud as we could with the wind whipping through our hair. It was like she was reclaiming the childhood she lost and was somehow living it through me."

"She was *spared*," says Tom. "Spared a life in Hollywood that really would have killed her." Silence for a moment. Then he says, "So finish the story for me, Nell… Will you?"

"When did she leave?" asks Nell. Tom nods. "She raised me until I was eighteen. But then she told me that she wanted to retire to the woods. Now I see it coincided with when social media began to come into existence…2009 or so. She *had to* disappear. People were really into Facebook by then. All it took was one local posting something, I guess. She put up with it until I was in college. And then she went away. I can't say where..." Nell's voice trails off, wanting to change the subject. As much as she trusts Tom—as much as he's proved himself—she can't just tell him without Nan's permission because Nan doesn't even know that *she* knows yet. "Hey, I'm wide awake!" says Nell, grabbing the TV remote. "Wanna watch an old movie?"

"Sure," he says, propping up next to her, both their heads supported by the headboard.

"She hated reality shows," says Nell scrolling through the guide. "All these people being famous for being famous. Nan said she was 'old-school.' Where it was 'hands off' the movie stars. You couldn't get near them." Nell turns to Tom. "You know what Nan says—and now it makes *total* sense—'Today's fame is instantaneous. It actually discredits the hard work of someone who's earned it.'" Nell goes quiet, reflecting on her own words before leaning into kiss Tom's forehead, then his nose, and then his lips.

"What's that for?" he asks flirtatiously, stealing the remote from her hand.

"For not making a big deal out of the stuff that I'm telling you."

Tom's hits TMC, which is showing *Singing in the Rain.* Gene Kelly's performing.

"Nan always said there was something primitive and innocent about cinema back then. Not like today's franchises with *Spiderman* and *The Hunger Games.* Course I had no idea it was Marilyn Monroe's opinions. It's all so bizarre."

A few moments of old movie nostalgia, and Tom's starting to nod off. "Hey," he slurs, "Have you decided about the local women's march?" Nell says nothing, turning on her side, the movie still playing. "C'mon," he persists. "It's practically in your backyard."

But Nell's mind wanders from the idea of the march to the fact that Nan staged her own death. And now, Nell would have to stage her own *life*. Spontaneously, Nell tosses back the covers and jumps out of bed.

"Hey, where you going?" asks Tom, suddenly alerted by her movement.

"To write down some thoughts," says Nell.

"Aw, come on. I leave tomorrow, babe. Sort out my mess of a job in LA."

But she's ignoring him now. All systems go…tearing paper from the antique roll-top desk and grabbing a pen. She pulls out a chair. "In hindsight, Nan was incredibly brave and strong," Nell calls out from the next room, her chin resting on her hand. "The more I learn, the more I admire her. Not for being Marilyn Monroe, I mean, but for being a woman who fought a devastating battle with her mind and somehow overcame it all. Mind over matter…" Nell ponders, the pen at her chin. "You know," she adds, "Nan was truly every woman's hero."

"Great," Tom calls out. "Now, come to bed."

But it's too late. The words flow like a river. Nell's penning away and crossing words out like a mad woman…

> My grandmother could never be completely mine. I mean, c'mon. Like any grandma or mother, she had secrets and a past that I knew nothing about. Add in the fact that she was Marilyn Monroe…

She gazes around the walls of the living room filled with antique paintings, ship captain tables, and the Hepplewhite sideboard. If she tells the world all that this is—all that she knows—life as they know it will change. For Nan, for her, and for her someday baby…*Should she? Tell?*

CHAPTER FORTY-NINE

Cape Cod—Summer 2020

Less than three months after the Hogan/Spooner debacle, COVID crippled America. The good news was that the virus made it a great time for anyone to mask up and disappear once and for all, even if they're *not* Marilyn Monroe.

At the Hyannis Village Green, taillights can be seen crawling for miles. *Where to park?* Buses also line the harborside. From Main Street to Sea Street to South Street; masked women of all ages stop to assist the elderly ladies who navigate directions to the bandstand. One eighty-year-old sports a tee-shirt that reads "Nasty Woman."

As Nell turns the corner, she sees hundreds of women holding up signs of solidarity. Some chanting the names of those who set examples: The Salem witches, Susan B. Anthony, Anita Hill, Gloria Steinem, and many others. But not a single mention of Marilyn Monroe—she's far from *anyone's* hero.

Nell moves closer to the front under the bandstand, her hand in Tom's. She's not sure what propels her to move to the stage, but she does and climbs up. "Hi," she says, taking the microphone, lowering her mask, and wearing a t-shirt that reads "My Body, My Rules." She smiles down at Tom, who winks at her from the lawn. The crowd is just beginning to tune into her.

"My name is Nell Morton, and I'm a feminist." A few claps from the front row. "I'm also an only child. And a *lonely* child." Not much response from the crowd yet. Nevertheless, she carries on. "My mother died when I was a baby, so my grandmother raised me. My nan. My *hero*. Coming out of the 1940s, '50s, and '60s, Nan taught me so much about the waves of feminism."

More women nod in acknowledgement as they can imagine their *own* grandmother's memories. Tom finds himself sandwiched between multiple females, the only man at this march other than a handful of male journalists.

"As a woman, you do not *need* a man," says Nell, "but you can absolutely live with a good one. I'm lucky. I found a good one." She smiles. "He's here. Supporting me. Supporting women." She points him out. Everyone claps, and Tom turns to wave to the crowd.

"My nan learned the hard way to be less sugar and more spice, but that was only after she had to compromise so much of herself…to the men in Hollywood." There's a rumble through the crowds at the surprise that her grandmother was from Hollywood.

"Back in her Hollywood days, my grandmother dealt with sexual misconduct. Her desire to *please* robbed her of her power." The women in the front few rows clap. "Yet, my grandmother isn't a victim now. She's learned from her mistakes. Nan raised me to be a strong, independent woman. And I try to be all she didn't have that opportunity to be. As a little girl, she was even tossed around from foster home to foster home.

"Yet, the biggest fight wasn't her childhood, it was fighting the establishment…the studio system...the 'old guard,' as they called it. She wasn't equipped to handle that because she also needed guidance and structure, which she never really had in the first place. So, she turned to men for all that…and because power only understands power. Nan was powerless over the big-shot boys of Hollywood. As predatory men began to define her, she needed to get out of Hollywood, where she could finally get a life. *Hers*. By eventually escaping, she could discover who she really was. The real girl was still in there…the original little girl dying to be free. Not the actress going to cattle-call auditions."

The crowd applauds. Tom turns to see more women pouring in.

"It's been suggested that we must talk to our daughters—and our sons—differently than our mothers spoke to us," says Nell. "My mother never spoke to me because she died, so my grandmother had to fill *two* generation gaps of advice."

A pause as Nell looks at her notes, her eyes watering up and blurring the words…imagining what Nan must have gone through.

Nell carries on, "Catherine Deneuve denounces the feminist movement. And no, she wasn't my Hollywood grandmother." A chuckle from the crowd. "But truth is, I kind of agree with Catherine. I like flirting. If my boyfriend didn't flirt with me, well, he may not have ended up my boyfriend." Everyone chuckles more, and Tom turns beet red. "I know my grandmother was a flirt. She still is…" says Nell, moving closer to the edge of the platform. "But my grandmother also had to abort a baby. Back in the day. Yeah. In Hollywood. And then she chose to have my mother because it was when she *knew* she could. Based on her psychological health, her career, her finances, and her desire…it was her *choice* when the timing was right to bring a child into this world. Because she wanted to be the best mother or no mother at all." A large roaring round of applause. "Healthcare for women is a human right. We shouldn't be fighting for birth control and legal abortions all over again. No," says Nell, a negative taste in her mouth, albeit gaining momentum here. The crowd's cheers grow rows and rows back.

Nell moves back to the microphone, trying to figure out where she left off on her speech. Her hands are trembling. "Some of the world's most famous women go by their first names. "Cher, Madonna, Oprah…Marilyn. We all long to be kickass

Superwoman or Katniss in *The Hunger Games*, but nobody wants to be Marilyn Monroe. Why is that? Maybe we could all stand to learn a lesson from Marilyn Monroe." Silence from the crowd. "What would Marilyn do if she were alive today?" asks Nell.

The crowd makes sounds that suggest they aren't sure Marilyn Monroe is the image they would want at their women's rally.

Nell can *feel* they don't agree with her. "The powerful Hollywood men who abused Marilyn Monroe never took accountability for their actions. Shame on them. Our world is full of so much male-dominated abuse. Men, in the aftermath of love affairs, get angry and become more ego-driven as if the woman is to blame. They think that *they* were the victims. So, rather than find forgiveness and, more importantly, kindness or friendship toward the *very* woman whose only crime was loving them, they choose to be cruel to them instead. Those women are the *Marilyns* of the world."

A group of women just beneath where Nell speaks nod their heads as if they might begin to see her point. "But male anger is just fear," says Nell. "Fear they'll be discovered for what they really are. Fear that some women might one day expose their bad behavior. Fear because they have to stick to a narrative that allows them to remain the victim. Truth is they're cowardly. Truth is Marilyn Monroe was the 'grace.' Those men were the 'disgrace.'"

A large round of applause with hands and arms now above the heads of rows of women. "Yes, we can all learn a lesson from Marilyn Monroe. Moral trauma is the worst thing," says Nell, exhaling and becoming angry at her own words. "So why hasn't much changed since the days of *Mad Men*? Sure, we've tossed aside those three-hour martini lunches…but feminism?" Nell puts her hands on her hips. "I believe we got trapped in the waves of feminism. Maybe the second wave was 1968 when women said, 'I'm not going to be subservient' to, say, JFK as Marilyn was. But then feminism stalled out at *Sex and the City*," Nell stops. She's not sure where she's headed with these words she's said before, and it's certainly not on the notes she's written. She ad-libs.

"Maybe Marilyn, like my nan, was a woman ahead of her spiritual, feminist time. From an esoteric standpoint, suffering wakes us up. I mean, if only rape victims like Connie Francis or exploited women like Marilyn Monroe had a chance, right?"

Nell looks to the audience, her eyes narrowing down to the younger women her age. "We used to sing to Katy Perry's "Roar," but long before there was a song sung by Helen Reddy called "I Am Woman." The lyrics that my Nan used to sing about women who have heard it all before, who eventually bores wisdom out of pain, or something like that..." Nell listens as sixty- and seventy-year-old activists begin shouting, "I am strong. I'm invincible, I am *woman*!"

The women clap, shout out, raise their signs again, and hug each other in solidarity.

"So much is written about pleasing men," says Nell. "Just ask the late Helen Gurley Brown. But how much is written about men pleasing women? Hmmmm." Nell looks around, the audience shrugs. "Mary Tyler Moore was one of my nan's heroes. A woman who focused on ability, not on gender, and gave that ole boss of hers, Lou Grant, a run for his money. That's what Nan used to say, 'A run for his money.' I have no idea what that means!" The audience laughs. "Mary Tyler Moore was perfect. She didn't get angry. That's the template she built. Women like Mary Tyler Moore didn't take it anymore, while women like Marilyn Monroe had to *take it* and shut up." The crowd goes pin-drop silent. Nell chokes up. "You know, I work at the suicide center as a volunteer. I know that when you bottle up your anger and your fears, it can lead to depression. Or in Marilyn's case, suicide. But..."

Nell's words drop off. She bites her lip, looks toward Tom. Their eyes meet. It's as if he's the only person out there on the village green of thousands. And he knows what she's thinking.

Knows that right now she could say, "But Marilyn didn't die. She's *alive!* And guess what? *Marilyn* is my grandmother!" Nells eyes penetrate Tom's in a staring match. Except the spell is broken. What she sees is love staring back at her. Eyes full of stability and trust. *Should she tell the world right now?* Tom slowly shakes his head *no.*

"Who's your grandmother?" asks some woman hollering through hands formed as a megaphone.

"Oh, doesn't matter. Just some B-list starlet you've never heard of," says Nell. "And like Marilyn, she had to take abuse and shut up." Nell paces closer to the edge of the stage. "But, come to think of it, Marilyn Monroe is someone we can all identify with. We all have a piece of her inside of us. The daughter. The mother. The granddaughter. The victim. The beauty queen. The friend. Even my nan. Everything we revere and despise about ourselves… turns out that Marilyn is our mirror image."

Nell goes to the last page of her notes, her hand shaking. "Marilyn managed to survive as such an iconic figure all these years. Her sex appeal was so pure and unapologetic, so her image lives on today in magazines, on posters, you name it…" Nell inhales and exhales the largest gulp of air to calm her nerves. "Listen, I'm a modern-day woman with a voice. And, as you can tell, I'm going to use it." The audience can be heard stomping and cheering across the rows.

"Let's all use our voices! Let's not *ever* give up," says Nell. "Let's believe that somewhere out there is some Marilyn Monroe who might have saved herself." The crowd cheers. Nell leans into the microphone but can barely be heard. She whispers, "Thank you." Nell nods, closing her eyes to stop more tears from forming. The activists' rumble of approval moves in waves across the green. Nell steps from the podium as a chant begins: "Long Live Marilyn! Long Live Marilyn!"

Little do they know…she does.

CHAPTER FIFTY

Epilogue—1 year later

A desk in an office we don't recognize, with a sign on a door that reads: Tom Hogan—Cape Cod Commission. Inside, the office is covered with every preservation sticker you can imagine from "Save the Whales" to "Waterkeeper Alliance."

But the most *significant* statement is the preservation of Lolly's painting. The framed canvas now hangs on the wall, restored back to where this entire story started. Tom had returned to the nursing home when he went to pack up his Los Angeles life and gathered Lolly's belongings. Lolly's painting now hangs in place of the one Tom bid on—the one Spooner cracked in half. Yes, Lolly's painting reminds Tom that somewhere, someplace, Lolly is most certainly watching over him and probably smoking a Cuban stogie.

Tom moves his computer mouse around on his desktop to the morning news where articles tell him everything from America being one of the five deadliest nations for journalists, to the latest COVID numbers.

Tom clicks away from the news and shakes his head. Now his days include hosting student field walks through the terrain down in Brewster and visiting the Cape Cod Museum of Natural History. A pair of binoculars hang on the back of Tom's door along with his Woolrich field jacket.

Rocking back in his chair, he places his hands behind his head and stretches. A grin crosses his face as he looks at the photos lining his desk. The same photo of Tom and his grandfather holding up that Atlantic cod on that motorboat, last seen on his desk at his Los Angeles office. But there's some additions: A new one with Charley, Scotty, and Tom holding up the catch of the day. And next to it, his love, Nell, at the beach, splashing waves at the lens.

But wait, there's one of an infant in Tom's arms. Nell is in a hospital bed next to him, her face rosy with damp perspiration, her hair matted back, but glowing with pride and maternal energy.

Tom exhales satisfaction. Sitting forward, he sips his detox tea and scans his computer calendar of the day's agenda: Climate resilience event at 12 p.m., Town Hall. Then a Barnstable Village improvement plan at a late lunch at The Porpoise, followed by a Zoom meeting. Perhaps at 5 p.m., Tom can squeeze in a drive over to Puritan, the clothing store, to purchase that white linen shirt just before they close. Never mind that his career seems to be priming him as the next mayor, he better be sure to make it to his own *nuptials* on Saturday…

~

A crystal-clear day on Sandy Neck Beach. Low tide. A seagull side shuffles to get closer to Tom, who stands barefoot in the sand near the shoreline. He's dressed in that white linen shirt tucked into khakis. Next to him, Mayor Bisbee in a traditional navy suit as his best man. Also barefoot.

The preacher is about to begin. The witnesses for this ceremony are Tom's mother in a simple pink summer dress and Tom's grandfather who wears a blue-and-white seersucker jacket with khaki pants. Both barefoot. In Tom's mother's arms is his newborn baby, Grace Jeane Hogan. Named in part for Nell's deceased mother and for her grandmother. The baby's face is shielded with a white parasol, and she's dressed in a white cotton frock with eyelet cotton socks.

Elizabeth from The Porpoise is one of the bridesmaids in a floral summer dress, holding a bouquet of mixed pink and blue hydrangeas. Becca from the Los Angeles office is also dressed in a similar sundress and holding a hydrangea bouquet, too.

Ten feet away from Tom, is his bride, Nell, dressed in a simple white cotton sundress and holding a bouquet of daisies. She's about to be walked down the makeshift aisle in the sand on the arm of Henry—another big event to add to his historical recollections.

But nothing tops this…

Up on the boardwalk on the hillside, appearing at the rickety stairs, amidst the beach plums and tall seagrasses, we see a woman in the haze…as only a perfectly sunny Cape Cod morning can deliver. Next to her, a distinguished older Black man in khakis and a white linen shirt takes her hand to aid her in her steps. She leans in to peck his lips in gratitude. He seems to want her to go ahead…to have the spotlight.

She does.

A few clouds deliver some shade on her face, except the tide's reflection offers enough of a peek-a-boo vision. She wears oversized black sunglasses and a white kerchief…defiant platinum bangs peep out from the front. Outfitted in a white dress, but not like the one out of the film *The Seven Year Itch,* this ensemble is more along the lines of *The Great Gatsby,* she wraps a lightweight linen shawl around her arms. Appropriate yet playful, elegant yet still sexy.

Ageless.

Timeless.

She could be that image—the brand ambassador for Estée Lauder—her lived-in face so much more beautiful than the ones out there with fillers and injected lips.

This woman is maybe part Norma Jeane. Maybe part Marilyn Monroe. But she certainly is Marie Morton.

Her hand shields her face from the sun until she spies the group below in the sand, waving in recognition. As she poses, statuesque, there's something almost patriotic about America getting their fantasy.

And there you have it. She's our grandmother, our mother, our aunt, our neighbor. The one who overcame obstacles but survived with a resilient and formidable nature.

She is the very much alive Marilyn Monroe.

The group on the beach wave back. Nell calling out, "Come down, Nan, come down here!" Nan nods, and begins to descend the steps holding the railing with one hand and waving to the group with the other.

Tom's jaw hangs. He turns to Nell and asks, "Is that?"

"Of course, it is," says Nell, blowing her Nan a kiss. "She wanted to thank you in person again for giving me the life she always dreamed of." Tom is speechless. Staring. Flabbergasted. "And besides," says Nell, leaning into Tom with a gentle whisper, "She wants to see our baby, Gracey…help with the babysitting. Afterall, now Marilyn Monroe is a great-grandmother."

The End

ACKNOWLEDGMENTS

This novel couldn't have been written without the support of my dear friend, Mark Oristano. In 1999 I brought him a "What if?" idea, and we developed and co-wrote the screenplay. *I know what you're thinking...don't you write the book first and then adapt into a film?* Well, yes...but there's quite a backstory as to why the movie never happened, and why I birthed this book (backwards) twenty-seven years later...

1999 was probably the worst year of my life. I had just buried numerous family members and close friends all within the calendar-flip of one Thanksgiving to the next. And no, it wasn't from my holiday cooking.

My mother, Marie, was the last of them to die that fateful February morning. I had been teasing her on the phone, when she reprimanded, "Stop it or you'll give me a heart attack!" True to her word, she dropped dead three minutes later. Mom was too young to leave me, a lonely, only child. She was also the much-needed grandmother to my two young daughters. On top of it, I was midway through my divorce from a not-so-supportive ex-husband who made a hobby out of hating me more than he loved our children.

My support system was dead along with family, so it was up to me to navigate the world without an emotional compass. But worst of all the guilt was on. In my grief, I had placed our script in my mother's casket and promised her that this movie *would* happen. *What was I thinking?*

The loneliness of it all prompted me to get the darn screenplay produced while juggling a full-time journalist job for the local newspaper, teaching a part time writing course at UMass Boston, while caring for my house and my little girls.

Mark, my co-writer, lived in a different state. We were on different body clocks, too. I was a morning person. So, after my girls were on the elementary school bus, I'd write from the notes Mark would send me the night before. He was a night owl.

By now I had partnered with a friend, Amy Baird (*thank you Amy, I love you*) who at the time was working for Disney in LA. She was originally from the Cape, too. We formed a production company called "Seven Year Itch Productions." We were off and running. With her talent for budgets, and my "Queen of Schmooze" ability (*a nickname from Mark*) I was out to some Hollywood friends who spent summers on Nantucket. Jerry Stiller was to be the cranky dying coroner named Lolly; his wife, Anne Meara, would be the town hall woman, Marie. I still have the letter Anne wrote to me saying how honored she'd be to step into the part my mother might have played.

There was a toss-up on who would be the reporters: Christian Slater or Donnie Wahlberg. I met Christian at his Broadway play *Side Man* through a mutual friend, Stan Rosenfeld, who was a big PR guy in Hollywood. I was introduced to Donnie via John Shea, best known back then as Lex Luthor in *Lois & Clark: The New Adventures of Superman*. John had directed *Southie* with Donnie in the lead role. We were all at the Boston premiere, and all connected in one way or another to Cape Cod, Nantucket and Beantown.

Neal McDonough was cast as the "good guy" reporter, Tom Hogan. His career has since gone on to accomplish many roles including most recently the crystal-blue-eyed cowboy in the Sylvester Stallone series *Tulsa King*. We planned to shoot in

Wellfleet and Barnstable. Neal then introduced me to Bill Dear, the director of Disney's *Angels in the Outfield.*

A budding actress, Maddie Corman, would portray Grace, Marilyn Monroe's daughter. I first set eyes on Maddie when she walked into a Nantucket church during my friend Jill Burkhart's Nantucket Film Festival. Maddie 'graced' (no pun intended) the aisle, wearing a red and white gingham sundress with daisies laced through her hair, just like the character Grace that I imagined.

But I needed financing. Amy worked her magic to tighten our budget even more. Our entertainment lawyer, Steven Beer, was the attorney for NSYNC and Brittany Spears, so he assisted with legal contracts. And, while my film project didn't impress my older daughter, she thought I was the coolest mom in the universe when I scored her front row seats and VIP backstage passes to meet Justin Timberlake. (*Thank you, Steven!)*

By then, I had attached a couple of investors from a big firm, and *The Hollywood Reporter* was scheduled to run a story on Amy and me. The filming would begin around October 15, 2001. Until…just weeks before…

9/11 happened.

As the world came to a standstill, so did mine. My investors died in the tower crash. My movie was doomed.

Besides, I had invested my own seed-money for our start-up production company. At that point, as a single-working mother with a mortgage, I couldn't risk anymore short of selling the roof over my daughters' heads, which I eventually had to do. And, from what I remember, Neal and Donnie, had to move on for reshoots and promoting in London as they were the actors for the HBO series *Band of Brothers*. So, I put the screenplay away with a broken heart and a broken promise to my dead mother.

I continued as a newspaper writer and began tapping into Hearst Magazines when Helen Gurley Brown (*thank you, Helen, R.I.P.*) stepped into my mother's shoes as a close friend and advisor. She set up a meeting to secure my first national gig with *Cosmo Girl*. The rest was up to me. I went on to be a very successful magazine writer—when we *had* women's magazines on newsstands—writing for Hearst and Conde Nast and many overseas publications where my life would end up taking me. After that, my first novel, *PLAN C: JUST IN CASE* became a #1 bestseller in the UK. But Marilyn sat solo on the shelf haunting me.

Fast forward decades later: 2019. I'm at lunch with a dear friend who happens to be the world's most successful storyteller, James Patterson. Over our hamburgers and Arnold Palmers, I spilled the Marilyn Monroe story. His impulse response, "Why didn't I think of that?" Then he took a sip of his drink and said, "This is going to be huge! You'll never have time to see me or *any* friends ever again!" (*Wrong Jim, I will always have time for you.)* He continued to speak in exclamation marks. "You have to write this!" So, I took the now yellowed old script from my office closet and drafted out the novel. He was the first to read it and give input on the updated premise.

Of course, the original story was a bit off. Now, twenty-five years later with iPhones, social media, and all sorts of challenges that didn't exist back in 1999, it was a page one rewrite. Not to mention that a new generation was emerging so by now, Marilyn would probably have a granddaughter and that would be my focus. Generation Z. But another atrocity was against me: COVID. Publishers were uncertain what was next. The world stopped again. *Was this Marilyn project doomed in any format—book or movie?*

Simultaneously I was already researching an Irish love story about Hazel Lavery, an unknown Irish Heroine married to Sir John Lavery, the portrait artist. Hazel would take on the Anglo-Irish peace treaty with her close friend, Winston Churchill, and her Irish renegade lover, the IRA leader, Michael Collins. That bio fiction novel—which I finished in late 2023—was released in January of 2025.

Around summer of 2025, I read someplace that Marilyn Monroe's 100th birthday would be June 1, 2026. Even spookier, 2026 would be the 25-year anniversary of 9/11 which had sealed the fate of my film. *I had to do this! And fast!* It was now...or never. *But with whom?* My Bloomsbury publisher and editor were now long gone from that first UK novel and by the time my agent submitted the manuscript it would never make the time frame.

It was September of 2025 when I contacted Aimee Bell, a brilliant editor friend who works magic with books, but I already knew she'd tell me there was no way Gallery could publish my novel on such a tight schedule. There's so much to ingest behind the scenes with publicity, book tour schedules, and all else. *And boy, didn't I know it.* I was in the middle of my book tour for my Irish novel *The Many Lives & Loves of Hazel Lavery.*

But then I reached out to a new friend, the publisher, Anthony Ziccardi, Post Hill Press, distributed by Simon & Schuster. In an instant and an email, he understood the urgency and my vision on a tight deadline. We put the deal together practically overnight. (*Thank you, Anthony. You are my Holy Trinity. God, Jesus, Anthony Ziccardi!)*

I first met Anthony two years prior through our mutual friend, Carisa Hays. Carisa also sits on the advisory board of my Cape Cod Book Festival. *(Thank you, brilliant Carisa!)* Carisa had previously planned publicity campaigns for Michelle Obama, Barack Obama, and George W. Bush. So she knows a thing or two about publishing.

And here we are! *Exhale.* Marilyn Monroe is finally alive in so many ways.

My managing editor, Lexi Vanatta, you have been amazing in keeping me on track and teaching me about all the Meta-data required. And you trusted me with my book jacket idea. My copyeditor, Ashlyn Inman, your notes were *extraordinary!!*

I must credit my cat Graham Greene (and no, I'm not one of these idiots who uses my pet's name for a banking password so don't even think about it). Graham sat patiently on his woolen perch of the window ledge everyday while I click-clacked away to an imaginary world that gave Marilyn a much happier ending.

And finally, like Marilyn's daughter, Grace... I may have raised my children in Barnstable, but despite some crazy suspicions, I am *not* the daughter of Marilyn Monroe. Nevertheless, I was surrounded by close friends and neighbors in an airtight community that included the families of Edward Gorey, Kurt Vonnegut, Norman Mailer, and the Kennedys of Hyannisport. Their collective influence and histories have played into the fantasy of this story and for that I am forever grateful.

ABOUT THE AUTHOR

Photo by Denise Pressman

Lois Cahall is the author of *The Many Lives and Loves of Hazel Lavery, The Court of the Myrtles,* and *Plan C: Just in Case* (Bloomsbury), a #1 bestseller in the UK remaining in the top three for fiction in 2012. Lois spent her early career writing women's, men's, food, and travel articles for Hearst and Condé Nast publications. She is the former creative director of development for James Patterson Entertainment and the founder of both the Cape Cod Book Festival (2024), www.capecodbookfestival.com, and the Palm Beach Book Festival (2015), www.palmbeachbookfestival.com. Both bring in *New York Times* bestselling authors.